Story Overview

Laird Bryce MacLeod will do anything to see Scotland's history saved. Even if it means chasing down Jessie, a twenty-first century lass who might very well be his enemy. What he discovers when he catches her, however, is someone with deep, dark secrets and unanticipated intentions. Hidden truths so remarkable a whirlwind adventure through time begins.

First, they find themselves in league with Angus Óg MacDomhnaill, Lord of the Isles, a noble Scottish captain rumored in some circles to be a pirate. Danger and intrigue abound as they help the Scots capture three English supply ships and deliver their cargo to the Scottish army. As they do and more mysteries are unveiled, attraction ignites and roars to life.

Caught in the throes of newfound passion, they finally join King Robert the Bruce and face off with the English once more at the Battle of Byland Moor. Yet there's another enemy as well. An evil whose sole purpose is meant to test their hearts in a way neither saw coming. An enemy determined to rip Jessie away from Bryce forever. Will the power of love be strong enough in the end? Or will the curse that threatens Scotland be too much to overcome? Find out in *Avenged by a Highland Laird*, the epic conclusion of The MacLomain Series: A New Beginning.

~Avenged by a Highland Laird~

Series Overview

The term *a new beginning* brings to mind many things. Hope and opportunity. A fresh start. For the MacLomains and the rest of Scotland, the year twelve ninety-six meant anything but. Instead, it marked the beginning of a new and oppressed era fraught with two long wars with England. This particular series revolves around the First War of Scottish Independence that took place from twelve ninety-six to thirteen twenty-eight.

Heroes are often lost to time and folklore, especially when magic is involved. *The MacLomain Series: A New Beginning* shares those mystical tales. Stories about Scottish lairds that came to the aid of Sir William Wallace and King Robert the Bruce. Brave warriors and their lasses who single handedly changed the face of history…or so the story goes.

Best Reading Order

Sworn to a Highland Laird- Book 1
Taken by a Highland Laird- Book 2
Promised to a Highland Laird- Book 3
Avenged by a Highland Laird- Book 4

The Seafaring Rogue- Spin off

Avenged by a Highland Laird

The MacLomain Series
A New Beginning
Book Four
By
Sky Purington

~Avenged by a Highland Laird~

Edited by *Cathy McElhaney*
Cover Art by *Tara West*

Published in the United States of America

~Avenged by a Highland Laird~

Pronunciations

By popular demand, I'll now be including a glossary of pronunciations for Scottish and Viking names and places that run a little trickier to enunciate. The following names are characters you'll run across in this particular book.

Aðísla (*ah*-ue-ee-slah)
Rona (rohn-*ah*)
Iosbail (ees-*uh*-bel)
Níðhöggr (neathe-högr or neathe-herd)

If you come across other names or places you'd like to see included when reading my books, shoot me an email because every tale's pronunciation glossary is a work in progress. I love to hear from readers and consider your feedback valuable. Thanks so much for reading!

Email me anytime at Sky@SkyPurington.com or message me on Facebook.

Introduction

While the MacLomains and their Brouns know they're facing a curse determined to end Scotland, their true enemy remains a mystery. Is it the warlocks they have been fighting all along? Or could it be Jessie, a Broun lass and supposed friend who seems to have followed them on their adventures? After all, it looks like Jessie might be in league with the very warlocks set to destroy them. What better way to find out the truth then to start back at the beginning with Jessie herself. And so the story goes…

Prologue

Northern Maine
1999

J ESSIE SHOT UP in bed the moment the first flame curled around the bottom of her grandfather's old, threadbare curtains. It was already too late. There would be no stopping the fire this time.

Her heart pounded as she stumbled out of bed. Where was Mama? Did she know?

"Jessie!" her mother gasped from down the hall. "Help!"

"Keep calm, Jessie," she whispered to herself over and over again. "Stay strong for Mama. She needs you."

She always knew this day would come. That the man she called her grandfather would pass out drunk with a cigar and destroy what little they had.

By the time she made it to her bedroom door, fire was spreading quickly, crackling and roaring as it began consuming everything. Though her throat thickened and her nostrils stung, she pushed past fear and followed the sound of her mother's wracking coughs to the kitchen.

"I've got you, Mama." She bent her knees so her mother could wrap her arm around Jessie's shoulders for support. "Just hold on and walk the best you can, okay?"

"You need to find your grandfather," Mama croaked.

Jessie couldn't help but notice that her mother had said 'find' not 'help.' No surprise really. He was awful. Evil. Rotten to the core. Nevertheless, once she got her mother to safety, she took a deep breath then headed back into the burning house.

13

Smoke stung her eyes as she made her way down the hallway past rooms already consumed in flames. As she suspected, her grandfather was passed out on his bed.

"Grandfather," she yelled, shaking his shoulders. "Wake up! The house is on fire!"

As she choked on ever thickening smoke, she kept trying and trying, but he wouldn't budge. Was his skin more ashen then usual? His lips blue? She covered her mouth with the top part of her nightshirt, took shallow breaths and pressed two shaky fingers to the pulse point on his neck.

No heartbeat.

He was already dead.

Shocked, she stared at him, bereft of emotion. Was this the fate of such a cruel man? Was this the fate of a man with dark abilities? She swallowed hard as her eyes narrowed on the small ancient looking notebook on his bed stand. There it was. The cause of many a nightmare.

That was what her mother thought needed saving.

Why, though, when nothing good ever came of it? Yet even as she recoiled, she felt compelled. As though so much depended on it. So though loathe to touch it, she scooped it up and started to race out of the room, only to stop short. Fire was everywhere. The hallway was engulfed.

There was no way out.

This was it. The end she saw coming. An endless fire that ripped everything away. Fire that had all the control. Terrified, she began screaming. For who though? Her mother certainly couldn't help her. Nobody could.

"It can't end like this," she whispered and shook her head. "I won't let it."

She had lived her entire life in fear. All ten years of it. Now she was going to give up? Give in? Let everything fade away before she had a chance to live a life without her grandfather in it? She shook her head, and narrowed her eyes, madder by the moment before she roared, "Let me live!"

Heat seemed to well not only around her but within her as her vision hazed red.

This fire had *no* control over her.

She controlled *it*.

Moments later, a strange sensation rolled through her, and a twisting tunnel began to form down the hall all the way to the front door. Free of fire, it was a path of safety created solely for her. She looked from the book to the hallway. Had she manifested it or had the book? Dare she trust this? Because it could easily be some kind of trick left behind by her grandfather.

Either way, it was her only hope, so she had no choice but to risk it.

As she raced forward, it felt as though wind whipped and propelled her out even faster. Coughing, she stumbled down the steps into her mother's waiting arms.

When she looked back, the house was completely consumed.

"Good girl," her mother murmured. "You got the book."

"I did," she said warily as she tried to hand it to her.

"No." Her mother shook her head. "You need to open it, Jessie…just in case he put anything more in there."

She swallowed and shook her head, as a whole new type of fear embraced her. "No, I don't want to. We should just throw it the fire. Let it burn."

"That's the worst thing you can do if he added to it. If he saw through his threat." Mama's eyes became very calm as they met Jessie's. "The fire would only seal it. Nothing could control or stop it after that."

A shiver raced through her as she whispered, "Well, I can't control it."

"You can. You have to. You're the only one," her mother said firmly. "Now open the book."

She had dreaded this thing her entire life. What it could do. The power it had. Yet deep down she knew she had no choice. Too much could be at stake. So, hands trembling, she opened the book, wide-eyed as she realized her mother was right. Her grandfather had seen through his threat.

"Just as I thought," her mother whispered, staring down at the open page before her damp eyes returned to Jessie's. "Now you're Scotland's only hope."

~Avenged by a Highland Laird~

Chapter One

North Salem, New Hampshire
October 2017
The Day Jessie First Arrived at the Colonial

SHE LOOKED UP at the old oak tree in front of Milly's new house and realized it might be too late for Scotland. That she had taken on a great deal more than she bargained for all those years ago.

Now here she was, ready to undertake something so much bigger than her. So much more powerful. Or was it? Could she stay one step ahead of what was about to happen to Scotland's history? Could she continue to influence dark magic with such an evil goal?

"Jessie?" came Milly's faraway voice. "Sweetheart, are you all right?"

When a hand landed on her shoulder, it ripped her out of the dreamlike place she was in. Startled, she met Milly's eyes. What was her friend doing here? Moreover, how did Jessie end up here, to begin with? The last thing she remembered she was at her cabin in Maine. In fact, the last thing she recalled, she was battling with herself. She needed to go to Winter Harbor then come here. She needed to see this tree.

After that, everything was a blank.

"I'm sorry," Milly said softly. "You were really scaring us. Are you okay?" She looked around and frowned. "How did you get here?"

Shocked to realize she had been crying, Jessie quickly resumed her usual expressionless mask, wiped her tears away and shook her head. She kept her voice soft and level. "I'm not sure." She glanced from the tree to the house before she started walking down the dirt road. "I'm sorry. I have to go home."

She didn't bother saying hello to Christina or Jim but continued down the drive in hopes of finding her car. Though she had no recollection of driving here, she must have. Thankfully, she soon spied her Volkswagen Beetle.

"Oh no you don't," Milly exclaimed and stepped in front of her. "It's almost nighttime, and it's a long drive back, honey. You're spending the night."

"I cannot do that." Jessie's eyes met hers. "You know I cannot, Milly."

Her friends knew she rarely if ever left her home. What they didn't know was why. They assumed Jessie was just anti-social and likely suffered from some sort of well-masked anxiety.

"Of course you can." Milly steered her back toward the house. "There's just the four of us here, and you know everyone."

"Not Jim." Jessie didn't look in his direction. "I don't know Jim, and that's not good."

"But you've heard lots about him so in a way you do." Milly kept steering Jessie along.

She didn't put up a fight because she knew it was pointless. Not only that but she went out of her way to avoid confrontation. As Christina hopped in Jessie's car and drove it to the house, Milly made introductions. "Jessie this is Jim." She motioned between them. "Jim, Jessie."

Jim started to hold out his hand to shake but stopped, obviously aware of Jessie's aversion to being touched. "Nice to finally meet you, Jessie. I've heard a lot of good things."

"Nice to meet you as well." Jessie met his eyes, seeing what she knew she would, before she whispered, "I thought so," then kept walking.

Jim and Milly had dated for years before they became *just* friends. Though they were apparently in agreement about it, Jessie saw that he had not wanted it to end. At least back then. Now they were both beyond it, and Jim was simply a friend to them all. Well, at least Milly, Christina, and Lindsay.

Milly, it seemed, was destined for another man altogether. Adlin MacLomain. A man intricately involved in Jessie's past though he had no idea. She suspected Adlin had already contacted Milly, who was a real estate agent, under the pretense of wanting to sell this very house.

Moments later, realizing she was right, she stopped short and turned her eyes Milly's way. "So you met him then? How did it go?"

Milly frowned. "Met who?"

Jessie was a little shocked Adlin hadn't been more forthright and couldn't stop the slight raise of her brows as she touched Milly to understand better.

"Oh, I see," Jessie said softly. "He likes to play games."

"I'm not following, sweetie." Milly shook her head. "What are you talking about?"

"You met him right here in this very spot." Jessie's eyes stayed with hers. "You've met your Scotsman, Milly."

What she would not share, was his name. That was for Milly to discover on her own.

Jessie allowed them to settle her in a chair a few minutes later and said nothing when they treated her as though she'd been traumatized. Milly made her tea then everyone continued bringing in boxes and unpacking. Though tempted to help them out and say she was okay, Jessie had worked hard to create her persona.

Withdrawn. A recluse. Someone easily shaken.

It had long been a way to keep them safe. To keep Scotland safe. Now her well-laid plans were about to be tested. Her demons were rearing their heads, ready to set things in motion. Demons she fully intended to turn the tables on.

After all, she had all but birthed these demons.

Jessie patted her pocket, relieved to find her grandfather's little book there. It would make all the difference with what she intended to do.

When Jim left, and Milly and Christina joined her, they proceeded to discuss Jessie's bold statement in the driveway. She couldn't tell Milly much other than the man in the driveway was the man she was eager to meet.

Milly's eyes narrowed on the picture on his business card then went to Jessie. "We've never meddled because we respect your privacy, but I think it might be time you share a bit more about yourself." She gave her a knowing look. "Because you clearly have…something going on."

They had no idea.

"No." Jessie nodded at the picture. "I would say *you* have something going on." Her eyes turned to the fire, and she said more than intended. "At least it's just you for now."

"What do you mean just Milly for *now*?" Christina sat in the chair opposite them and sipped wine. "Because that almost sounded like you and I might become involved in whatever this great mystery is you're keeping from us."

"You all know I'm different and have accepted me regardless, so you deserve to learn more about me." Jessie's eyes went between them. "I have certain abilities. The strongest of them is the ability to sense other people's emotions." Her gaze drifted to the fire, and her voice softened. "I suppose the technical term for it would be empath." Her eyes returned to Milly's. "I felt your Scotsman's emotions out in the driveway. How strongly he feels about you. How long he has been waiting for you."

There was more to her gift. Much more. But now wasn't the time.

"I don't understand," Milly murmured.

"Not yet but you will." Jessie's eyes roamed before she looked at Milly again. "You have no idea how different you are Milly. How, like all of us, unusual you are."

"I'm sorry." Milly frowned. "Unusual?"

"And what do you mean by all of us?" Christina kicked in.

"Don't tell me you aren't starting to catch on, Milly," Jessie said. "Don't tell me you didn't feel something the very moment the Scotsman called you and you saw this house online. I know you sense it."

As she continued discussing Milly's previous life in this very house, she contemplated how she might utilize their unique gifts. Their magic. How she could assist and manipulate things as they began their upcoming adventures. Something she had been mulling over since she first met them in an online forum years ago.

How could she make sure her friends best used their magic to protect themselves and Scotland? Milly with her ability to astral project. Christina and her godlike warrioress abilities. Then, of course, Lindsay with her ability to enchant.

Soon enough Lindsay showed up, and while Jessie would have enjoyed spending time with them all, the clock was ticking. So she feigned exhaustion and lay down on the couch. All the while, she listened to them and plotted. Once everyone had gone off to bed, she pulled out her little book, sat in a chair and began something she had hoped might never happen but deep down knew would.

She began chanting and focused on the fire. On Scotland and MacLomain wizards. More than that, Scotland and MacLomain dragons. Maybe, if she did this just right, she could save her friends and avoid her fate at the same time.

Bryce MacLeod.

As she murmured and the night wore on, she put herself into an unusual sort of trance. A state of being that allowed her physical body to remain here and functioning while her spiritual presence began an adventure alongside her friends without them ever knowing.

Though some might think she was trying to play God, in truth, she was just trying to save Scotland's history from a dark curse. One that would eventually wipe out Scotland completely if she didn't help. That meant controlling creatures set to destroy everything. So, as she had been doing for a long time, she began navigating Scottish history by creating magically induced images in her little book.

As she did, fate began to unfold over the next few days though she never left her chair.

Milly traveled back in time, fell in love with Adlin, ignited her Claddagh ring and defeated their warlock. Which, in turn, put the Battle of Stirling Bridge back on track. Next came Lindsay and Conall who defeated their enemy and corrected both the Actions at Earnside and Happrew. Bringing Christina and Graham together to see through the Battle of Bannockburn, however, took a turn she hadn't expected. One that brought Sven, a MacLomain Viking ancestor into the mix.

With Sven came the symbol of a burning dragon and a warning. Death comes to Scotland. Death comes to those who fly. While it was ominous, it also gave her control over warlocks that were starting to doubt her. She could use it to remain one step ahead of them. Because as it was, they had nearly figured out the truth.

Jessie was tricking them. She had been for eighteen years now.

She did not want Scotland ruined.

She would *not* see her grandfather's curse through.

21

Bannockburn, Scotland
1314

JESSIE MANIPULATED SCOTLAND'S fate for five long days before her physical body finally left Milly's house. On that day—after seeing through a time loop she herself helped create—she went to Christina's aid in medieval Scotland.

A move that set her on a path she had hoped to avoid.

Yet here she stood in a fourteenth century Scottish forest as one of her evil minions skidded to a halt in front of her. This was it. Her last say before all ties were irrevocably severed and her control over Scotland's fate was no more.

"Hold me in front of you," she ordered the warlock. "Now!"

Though hesitant because she had never asked one of them to touch her, he did as asked. She flinched at his dark touch but kept it from her thoughts and most certainly from her body language.

Then she began counting.

Three, two, one…

She didn't flinch when Christina flew at her and swung her sword only for Graham's blade to stop it inches from Jessie's face.

"What are you *doing*?" Christina seethed at him, wide-eyed and furious before she realized that she had almost ended Jessie instead of the warlock.

"Kill me, Christina." Jessie kept her face expression-free and her voice level as her eyes held Christina's. "Graham, step away and let Christina do what she needs to do. It's the *only* way."

"Yes, kill her," the warlock rasped, his eyes trained on Christina. "Run that sword through her, *warrioress*."

The warlock assumed Christina would never do that to her friend.

Normally, he would be right.

Moments later, Bryce and Sven skidded to a stop, their eyes taking in the tense situation. Jessie made a point of not looking at them. They were too much, and she needed to stay focused.

"Absolutely not." Christina shook her head as she lowered her blade and narrowed her eyes at the warlock. "Release my friend."

"Kill me," Jessie said calmly, her eyes steady. "Or he will kill you, Christina."

Connecting specifically with Christina's magic, she made sure everything else fell away. That she sensed the steady thrum of Jessie's heart. The utter lack of fear someone facing imminent death should feel.

She was letting her know it was okay to let go.

That this was meant to be.

Then she made sure Graham got the same message. That he and Christina were in agreement. This was the only way. They should trust in that. Trust Jessie. This was what had to be done, and she understood that. She was saying goodbye. Caught in her web, convinced she was right, they did as asked.

Christina and Graham plunged their blades into Jessie at the same time.

Or so they thought.

At the last moment, evidently sensing what they were going to do, the warlock did as Jessie hoped. He thrust her aside and took the blade for her.

Then everything happened very quickly.

The warlock shuddered, his saddened eyes firmly locked on Jessie as he wailed mournfully, decomposed rapidly then burst into a cloud of ashes. Like before when the others were destroyed, a pinching sensation squeezed her chest then she grew a little lighter.

Fully aware that she was out of time, she narrowed her eyes at Sven and Bryce who narrowed their eyes right back.

"Death comes to those who fly," she whispered, for any warlock who might be listening. "Death comes to Scotland."

Then she bolted into the woods, well aware Bryce and Sven were following.

She used her ability to manipulate the spiritual realm to throw them off her trail. Now they had to track three of her. She shot off to the right while her manifestations went straight and to the left. Knowing full well that she couldn't outrun them she skidded down an embankment and then ducked beneath a rock jutting out of the ground at an angle.

With a murmured chant, she manipulated the Earth, blended in with the rock and remained perfectly still.

Seconds later, Bryce raced past only to skid to a halt and cock his head. She should have known. His dragon senses were picking her up. She barely breathed as he turned, narrowed his eyes and scanned the area.

Just like it did before, sensual heat rolled through her as she looked at him. It was no easy thing finally being so close to him. To know he truly did exist beyond what she knew, beyond the feelings she had been fighting for years.

He was more handsome than most with his chiseled features and deep-set brow. Tattoos covered his arms and shoulders, only adding to his intensity as his pale golden eyes slowly came to a stop on hers. Thickly lashed, startling eyes she didn't expect to home in on her so quickly.

She stopped breathing as his dragon surfaced and fire flared in those eyes.

"Help!" she mouthed, manipulating the air to make her words sound like a call on the wind from the opposite direction. That *should* compel him to run that way.

Yet it did not.

Instead, his fiery eyes remained narrowed as he unsheathed his dagger and slowly headed toward her. She tried to pull her gaze away, but couldn't. So she tried to control the fire in his eyes. What he saw in front of him.

Big mistake.

His muscles tensed and the fire only flared brighter as he said, "I know you're there. Show yourself, lass."

How could he possibly know she was there? Unless…she clenched her teeth as she realized what had happened. The warlocks had totally pulled away. That meant she no longer had their protection. Strange, until that moment with how exposed she felt, she had no idea how much a part of her they had become. Or the other way around. She couldn't be sure.

What she *could* be sure of was that Bryce knew she was there. As it turned out, not just him but Sven too. Seconds later, the Viking dropped down from the ledge and turned her way, his eyes just as fiery as Bryce's. Just as searing as they locked on hers.

"Show yourself, lass," Bryce repeated softly. "I willnae ask again."

Sven fell in beside him as they shifted closer. They were moving in pack formation. Or dragon pride formation, if you wanted to get technical. That meant there would be no escaping. At least not right away. Especially considering they had no idea if she was friend or foe. Not based on the things they might have heard about her.

"Put your weapons down, and I'll show myself," she replied, using the air to make sure her voice echoed from every direction.

No doubt utilizing their dragon senses to narrow down her precise location, their eyes remained trained on where she was.

"As far as we know, you're in league with the warlocks," Bryce replied. "So we willnae discard our weapons."

"I just helped destroy one," she reminded. "I would think that should make things clear as to where my loyalties lie."

"All it made clear is that you're highly unpredictable," Sven said. "Show yourself, woman. Stop playing games. Our dragons are not fooled."

The last thing she expected when she began controlling her grandfather's curse all those years ago was for Vikings to become involved. Yet it was Sven's Aunt Aðísla who had apparently caught wind of the curse and informed Grant Hamilton who, in turn, created Claddagh rings with Adlin.

That's when she realized her life wasn't going to be so simple. She would not spend it alone in the woods trying to control warlocks and keep Scotland safe. Instead, the creation of the rings had started something much more complicated.

True love connections between modern-day Brouns and medieval MacLomains.

Jessie glanced at her finger and frowned. All this time she had been able to hide the ring not only from her friends but from the warlocks. Because had they discovered it, things might have already gone terribly wrong.

"Jessie," Bryce prompted, his voice deep and distracting.

The truth was she could disarm Bryce and Sven with magic if she had to. It was their dragons she could not so easily outmaneuver. So she supposed it made sense to show herself and gain their trust so that their dragons trusted her as well.

That in mind, she murmured a chant and stepped forward.

Both broad shouldered and over six-foot-seven, neither man should feel threatened by her petite frame. Even so, she kept defiance from her gaze and did her best to look doe-eyed and innocent. No easy feat on either count seeing how she had trained herself long ago to remain expressionless. Emotions had needed to remain deeply buried which meant embracing a rather low-key, drab existence.

"Hello," she murmured. Though she typically kept her voice level and monotone, she felt it wouldn't be best under the current circumstances, so she added a smidge of fluster to her greeting. "My apologies for hiding. This is all…" Scary? Confusing? What would make sense? "Alarming."

"Alarming?" Bryce's brows shot up. "I dinnae think that was the word you were looking for, lass."

As if he knew she was debating which word to use, to begin with.

"Let's just say," it was no use playing dumb, "that I have some explaining to do."

"Aye," Bryce grumbled, his weapon still drawn as he eyed her. "At the verra least."

"For starters," Sven continued, eying her with equal uncertainty. "Why do you keep saying death to Scotland and death to those who fly?"

"For two reasons," she replied honestly, her eyes steady on Sven. "When the symbol of the dragon in flames began to appear, my warlocks took notice. I saw that as the perfect opportunity to connect it with Scotland's ruin. Something they would welcome." She kept her eyes off of Bryce. "As to death coming to those who fly? I figured it would be a good way to ensure that they believed Bryce being meant for me was no longer a possibility."

"Because you wear a ring," Bryce stated bluntly, his expression disgruntled.

"Yes," she replied. "Something they didn't know, but I feared they would eventually find out." She cleared her throat. "Considering I had every intention of helping my friends from the beginning. Helping all of you."

"So you say." Sven and Bryce didn't budge an inch as Sven prompted her to continue. "Tell us everything. Then we will decide how noble your intentions really were…*are*."

Jessie nodded, thirsty but determined not to say so. Doing what she had, being in a state of limbo for five days, was tiring. Though she didn't smell like most would after so long without a shower, she still desperately wanted to bathe, eat, drink then sleep.

"I'll tell you everything," she assured. "But first we should leave this era and seek shelter in anything surrounded by stone and close to fire. It will be harder for a warlock to get to me there." She met Bryce's eyes and said the last thing he would want to hear. "Preferably your castle because they tend to be more wary of dragons."

"Do they?" He frowned. "Because they havenae seemed all that wary of me up to this point." He shook his head. "So nay, I willnae bring you anywhere near my castle and kin. Not until you've shared far more."

"The moment I allowed a warlock to die for me, they knew I deceived them," she said firmly. "Soon enough, if not already as Christina and Graham find their way out of their time loop, the warlocks will come after me, and they will do so with a vengeance."

"Because you wear the last ring," Sven said softly.

"Yes," she replied. "And because I'm the only one who knows what's left of them and if even possible, how to stop them." Her eyes went to Bryce again. "Staying here risks everything because if I'm killed, I can promise you that there is no hope for your country." She shook her head. "The last battle that we must keep on track, the Battle of Byland Moor, *will* be changed and with it, the fate of Scotland."

"Byland Moor," he murmured, his eyes narrowed on her. "No one knows what battles we'll be fighting before Grant and Adlin."

"Except me," she said. "And the monsters I've kept under my thumb for a very long time."

His hand clenched a little tighter around the hilt of his dagger. "Monsters you controlled."

"Yes," she said softly. "Just like I've helped control my friends on their adventures through time."

"How could you control such things?" He shook his head. "When their love was fated."

"Because I was there when the rings were made." Though she didn't want to say it, the time for denying it was long past. "And I knew I was meant for a beast nearly as terrifying as the very monsters I already controlled."

~Avenged by a Highland Laird~

Chapter Two

HAD JESSIE JUST compared him to a warlock?

Bryce continued eying her with distrust. While he had heard she was small and delicate, he had not expected her to be so beautiful. With luminous hair and large, almond-shaped eyes that appeared as black as her hair, she was almost otherworldly. Her eyelashes were long and thick and her skin tone warm.

Yet he got the feeling despite her slight frame and less-than-confrontational disposition that she could take down an army with one fell swoop if she were so inclined. That what lay at the heart of her was far bigger than what he could see with his physical eye. Or even with his dragon eyes.

"I assume then that I am the terrifying beast," he said dryly. "And that you think yourself fated for me."

"I stopped assuming things a long time ago." Her tone remained soft as her eyes stayed on his. "And I will say nothing further until we leave this place."

"Which we willnae be doing until you are far more forthright with me, lass."

Sven nodded in agreement before he sensed something at the same moment as Bryce. A shift in the air. A miniscule temperature drop.

"One of them is coming." Jessie's calm disposition faltered as she shifted closer. Based on how she turned her back and scanned the forest, she was set to defend them against the warlock. "We need to leave *now*."

He and Sven glanced at each other again as they spoke within the mind. Something they could do because they were dragon kin. "*I dinnae trust her.*"

"*Nor I,*" Sven responded. "*But my dragon senses something coming that is far more untrustworthy.*"

"*Aye.*" Bryce frowned. "*But how are we to leave here without Grant or Adlin's help?*"

"*With my help.*" Jessie surprised them when she spoke into their minds as her eyes met Bryce's over her shoulder. "*I can create tunnels within fire. Preferably fires ignited by others.*"

He ignored how arousing the sound of her voice was in his mind and shook his head. "*What good will a tunnel do us?*"

"*A tunnel that can go anywhere,*" she provided. "*Even through time.*"

How powerful *was* this lass? And if what she said were true, where should they go? Because he certainly wouldn't subject his people to her without knowing far more.

"*We must go to your castle, Bryce,*" she replied. "*It's the safest place in Scotland right now.*"

He shook his head. "*Nay.*"

"*We must,*" she insisted as her eyes whipped forward again.

That's when he saw it. A shadow shifting through the trees and closing the distance quickly.

"*Sven, Bryce, either one of you,*" she said through clenched teeth as she held up her hands and began chanting. "*I need your fire, or we will die here and now.*"

A heavy frown settled on Sven's face as he shook his head. Bryce wore a frown to match. How else were they supposed to respond when Jessie was likely behind so much? From his Uncle Darach getting caught in another dimension for years to his cousin Fraser dying. She might say she was preserving Scotland's future but based on what her warlock's had done, all proof said otherwise.

"*We cannae provide you fire, lass,*" Bryce replied, weapon at the ready as the warlock shifted closer. "*We willnae.*"

"Your sister would be disappointed," she whispered before she suddenly walked forward and her chanting increased.

His sister? Ainsley? Though his twin had died in infancy, Christina claimed to have dreamt about her. That she was fully grown and standing beside Jessie and her warlocks. That she was watching out for Bryce from the afterlife.

"What do you know of my sister?" he said aloud, following her as his inner dragon grew more upset. Had Jessie somehow trapped Ainsley's spirit? Was she controlling her like she apparently controlled these warlocks? "What did you do to her?"

"What she deserved." Jessie stopped short and swung on him. "What she had coming."

Suddenly infuriated, his vision hazed with the red of the dragon. Before he could get another word out, however, he realized he had walked right into a trap. A powerful one at that.

Spying the fire in his eyes, Jessie raised her arms and resumed chanting.

What happened after that truly blew his mind.

As her magic mixed with his dragon magic, a tunnel of fire and wind formed in front of them. An unavoidable tunnel that whipped them forward. The next thing he knew, they were standing in a cave near a crackling fire.

"Bloody hell," he roared, his sword aimed at her before the last embers of time-travel died away. "Dinnae *ever* use my dragon magic against my will again!"

"I'm sorry," she said softly as she lowered her arms. "I had no choice but to take matters into my own hands."

"Och," was all he managed to mutter. Stunned by what she had done, he was at a complete loss. For the life of him, he couldn't think of anything else to say. Even his inner dragon grappled with it. This half pint of a lass had just ensorcelled every part of him *without* his permission.

Though momentarily speechless, he found his tongue soon enough as fresh anger bubbled up. "And what of my sister? Have you truly been in contact with her?"

"No," she whispered. "I said that to goad you into creating fire."

He glared at her. "I dinnae believe you."

Their eyes held as she remained silent and said nothing further.

"Where are we?" Sven said, equally disgruntled as he eyed Jessie. "And how did you manipulate Bryce's dragon fire like that?"

"We're near MacLeod Castle," she murmured, her eyes never leaving Bryce's as he held his blade at the ready. "You asked that I did not bring you there, so I didn't."

His wary eyes never left hers as Bryce allowed his dragon senses to confirm that they were, indeed, in a cave system he had often played in as a youth. Damn her for bringing them so close to his castle. He might not have been overly specific but a lass as intelligent as she clearly was, knew she was in the wrong right now. Because one way or another, she had blatantly disregarded his wishes.

"How did you know about this location?" he asked, adding to Sven's previous questions. "I suggest you begin explaining yourself because I am moments away from putting this blade to use."

He set aside the fact she likely had the power to stop him before he did.

A wizard had to have some pride after all. As did his inner dragon.

Jessie slowly sank onto a nearby rock. Though it could be a show, this was the first time he noticed how tired she seemed. "I'm sorry. I know it's past time I talk." Her eyes met Sven's, her exhaustion suddenly very obvious. "If I could just get a drink of water, I'll tell you everything. All of it."

Though hesitant at first, it was clear Sven saw the same fatigue in her eyes because he handed over his skin of water.

"Thank you," she whispered before she took several deep but somehow dainty gulps before she closed her eyes in what appeared to be bliss. When she opened them again, she started talking.

"When I was very young, around five, I knew I was different," she said softly. "I could make Mama's water boil for her tea in seconds and warm the air in the house when Grandfather put our money toward booze rather than bills. I could light the fireplace with a thought and grow vegetables in the garden just by touching the dirt." Her eyes met theirs. "At ten, Grandfather burned down our house and died but not before I saved his magical book. That's when I learned I could control the spiritual realm as well."

"I wasn't only an empath," she continued. "But an elemental witch able to manipulate not just four elements but the less talked about fifth element as well. Water, air, fire, earth, *and* spirit."

Quickly suppressed pain flashed in her eyes before she continued. "You see, Grandfather was like me only more powerful and far darker." Her eyes landed on Bryce's. "More than that, he possessed an unexplainable hatred toward Scotland. Mama always said it was because my grandmother, who died in childbirth, was from Scotland. After she passed away, he simply couldn't bear anything Scottish because it reminded him too much of her." She shook her head. "But I always thought it went deeper."

"Why?" Sven asked.

"I don't know." She frowned. "My great grandfather was from England and raised his son with a very narrow viewpoint of anyone not English. My mother thought in part that might have had something to do with his vengeance at the end…the picture he drew in his book."

"What picture?" Bryce said.

"A picture that started me on the path that led me to this very moment." She pulled a worn ancient looking book out of her pocket and handed it over. "A picture finally visible to others as Christina and Graham's time loop closed." Her eyes went between them. "A time loop I partly controlled in order to bring them together…them and their child."

Bryce's brows flew up in surprise. "Christina's pregnant?"

A soft smile came to Jessie's lips. "She is."

Bryce couldn't help a grin as he finally lowered his blade. Graham deserved as much, and he couldn't be happier.

Yet as he opened the book and started leafing through, his grin dropped. If he wasn't mistaken, these were expertly drawn images of his cousins and their lasses' adventures. It was the last picture, however, that gave him pause.

"Scotland is gone on this map," he murmured. "'Tis but England."

"That's right," she said softly. "Just as Grandfather drew it all those years ago before he passed out drunk in bed and burned our house down. An image that always reappears no matter how many times I rip it out and try to dispose of it." Her voice dropped another octave. "It was his last wish. A curse laid upon your country."

"I dinnae ken." His eyes rose to hers. "How do you know that? How are you part of it?"

"Standing outside my burning house, I opened the book and saw that picture," she replied. "Moments later, with Grandfather dead, the curse began to manifest." A haunted look lit her eyes. "When it did, the terrifying fire I had survived moments before seemed like a walk in the park." Her eyes fell to the flames between them. "At the tender age of ten, I became master to every child's worst nightmare. Creatures created out of pure hatred."

"Master." Sven's eyes narrowed on her. "Do you mean to tell us you have been controlling these warlocks since you were a *child*?" His hand drifted to the hilt of the dagger at his waist. "And yet somehow, you have not become like them?"

"I have been doing my very best not to." She clenched her jaw and swallowed hard. "By doing so, I had to become a recluse if for no other reason than to keep them close and away from others as I formulated a plan. When most girls struggled with puberty and boys, I learned to repress fluctuating emotions and kept boys far, far away for their own safety."

"These warlocks were determined to destroy everything around them then?" Bryce asked.

By this time, both he and Sven were sitting.

"No, as long as I kept firm control, the warlocks preferred to stay near me." Again, fear flashed in her eyes, but she blinked it away. "I knew if anyone came near, the warlocks would lash out. A teenage boy would get far more than he bargained for if he so much as glanced at me."

As she spoke and her life story became clearer, Bryce couldn't help but feel sad for her. Having a mother from the twenty-first century, he knew what to ask. "What about school? Did you attend?"

"No," she whispered and shook her head. "Mama home-schooled me, and we made money off the land. Magic or not, I know herbs and home-remedies, so we started selling my stuff online and made enough money to make ends meet."

"I'm surprised a man as powerful as your grandfather, drunk or not, allowed his home to burn down," Sven commented.

"He might have been powerful but rarely used his magic," she replied. "As far as I could tell, he preferred only two pastimes. Drinking and cruelty." She shrugged. "Based on his level of arrogance, I honestly don't think he thought he could die in such a simple way."

Bryce might not trust her, but it was troubling to think of any child living such a life.

"What about your living arrangements after that?" Bryce asked. "Did you have enough money saved to rebuild?"

Or did she just use magic? He decided not to ask that though, curious to see how much she would actually reveal on her own. So far she was surprising him with her forthrightness. Assuming, of course, that what she said was true. For all he knew she could simply be spinning a tale to gain their trust and sympathy.

"Mama had enough in the bank to have some men come out and clear away the wreckage," she said. "Then we started over."

Based on the way she said it, he knew times had been especially difficult.

"What of the warlocks as you started over and grew older?" Bryce asked. "They must have been alarmed when you became friends with Milly, Lindsay, and Christina, aye?"

"No," she murmured. "Not when I was the one that made sure we met...not when they thought I was just making sure everything went as planned."

"Why would the warlocks not kill your friends immediately?" Sven countered. "Would that not have fulfilled the curse right away? Because how could Scotland's history be saved without the connections they made with the MacLomains?"

"It could not have, and that's why we should all be very grateful that Grant and Adlin created the rings," she replied. "Creating the rings helped control this curse from the very beginning. Flat out killing my friends at the start was not an option. Even without the gem igniting, the rings were powerful. MacLomain, Broun connections were once again a possibility. Then, as you know, it was a matter of each couple finding true love and harnessing the power of their ring."

"How many warlocks were there?" Bryce asked.

"Six, some more powerful than others," she replied. "To go up against four men of MacLomain blood." Her eyes went between them. "In the end, though you don't know it yet, Christina and Graham battled two warlocks. That leaves just two more." She inhaled deeply. "Neither of which will be easy to destroy."

Before Bryce could say more, she continued answering his questions. "As I said, opening that book unleashed a curse. One that gave me control over my grandfather's minions but only to a degree. They were still able to influence the creation of the rings and put all of this in motion. All I could do was try to stay one step ahead." She took another sip of water. "That meant casting a spell that made sure

I met Milly, Lindsay, and Christina." She pressed her lips together. "That meant starting the most important friendships of my life on a complete lie."

"Did you force them to like you then?" Bryce murmured before he could stop himself. "Were they under the influence of magic as you became friends?"

"No, magic just nudged them in the right direction," she said. "One step closer to creatures that wanted to destroy them and their one true love."

"You say you were there when the rings were made," Sven said. "And that you knew you were meant for…Bryce?"

"I was there through my connection to my…*the* warlocks," Jessie said, white-knuckling the skin as her voice grew even softer. "Based on my connection to fire above all else, I knew the strongest possibility lay with a dragon."

He noticed that she seemed a little less disgusted by the notion of a dragon now and surmised she must have been on the defense before. He scowled when he felt pleased by her change of attitude. But then what dragon wanted to be so disliked?

"So you never knew for sure if you were meant for me," Bryce said, not sure if he was relieved or not. Why wouldn't he be? The lass could be lying through her teeth. But something about her, mayhap the vulnerable look in her eyes when they met his, told him otherwise.

Could it be she was telling the truth? That she had seen such horrors and lived such an unfortunate life because of one man's dark nature? More than that, was she so courageous that she forfeited her life to fix his mistake no matter how terrifying it had to have been?

"No, I never knew for sure if we were meant to be together." Her eyes flickered over the ring and landed on the fire. "But as I got to know my friends then felt the essence of your cousins, I had less and less doubt."

"The *essence* of my cousins?"

She nodded. "Even before they were born their spirits had an essence." Her eyes returned to his. "That, without Grant and Adlin knowing it, was part of what poured into the creation of the rings." Her eyes dropped to her ring again. "The other part was ours. We Brouns."

"How could the warlocks even be there when Grant and Adlin did such a thing?" Bryce asked, still trying to comprehend it. "It seems far-fetched even by wizardly MacLomain standards."

"Because my grandfather created the curse that birthed them. The very curse that prompted Adlin and Grant to do what they did," she said. "That's all it took." She shook her head. "After that, it gave them access to everything interconnected."

"Including you," Sven said, clearly putting all the pieces together. "But it didn't matter because you had already seized control. You were already plotting with them so that they would not plot alone."

Jessie nodded and looked at Sven. "That's right." Then her eyes met Bryce's. "I'm sorry I couldn't warn you and your family...that I couldn't warn anyone. They would've known..."

"That you were never on their side," Bryce finished her sentence when she trailed off. "That you were always opposed to both your grandfather and his curse."

She nodded but said nothing.

Bryce handed her his skin of water as well then resumed flipping through the little book. What would it have been like to be ruled by this? Better yet, so connected to the creatures that came from it? "It had to have been hard..." his eyes rose to hers, "not just controlling them but not becoming connected to them after so many years. Your childhood, adolescence then adulthood."

"I *did* become connected to them," she said more bluntly than he anticipated. "I still am in a way that's hard to understand let alone explain."

When her eyes fell to the fire again, he realized that was the only way she knew how to express herself. Actual expressions relaying how she felt were foreign. So she hid her gaze in the flames rather than embrace something she had been living without for so long. Something she had long repressed.

Simple emotions.

"But as each warlock perishes," she continued, "I feel different. Lighter." Her eyes met his again. "And I find hope in that...hope that it's not too late for me."

While he appreciated her honesty and felt a protective response to her he had not anticipated, he still found himself unable to trust her. "These warlocks have been trying to kill me and mine." He cocked his head. "And they have claimed to do so on your orders. That is, assuming, you're the wee witch Conall and Lindsay's warlock talked about then Christina and Graham's as well."

"I am," she said softly. "And he, the first warlock, was obeying my orders. The second one as well...somewhat."

"*He*," Sven murmured. "As though the warlock was worthy of being called a man."

Bryce didn't miss Jessie's slight flinch though her expression smoothed almost immediately.

"When you spend nearly two thirds of your life with manifestations that are masculine," she murmured, "you tend to forget that they should be referred to as *it*."

He nearly narrowed his eyes but stopped himself. Had he detected a slight bite to her voice?

"Tell us more about these final warlocks," he said. "Why will they be more difficult than the others to destroy?"

"Both are strong but one, upon its birth, captured something the other lacked," she murmured. "The power of my grandfather's essence."

He frowned. "That doesnae sound good."

"It's not," she replied. "Actually, nothing could be worse."

"Because he was so powerful?" Sven supplied.

"Yes." Her eyes flickered between them again. "Not only that but he's more connected to me because of it. Connected as only kin can be to kin."

Bryce considered that. "What does that mean exactly?"

"It means there's a tether between us that goes beyond what I shared with the other five," she explained. "He can sense me easier. Especially if I'm not surrounded by rock and near fire."

"Why rock and fire?" Sven asked.

"Because fire is my most powerful element," she replied. "And stone is of the Earth which is difficult for the spirit realm to see through...or sense through in this case."

"So these warlocks are more spirit than mortal?" Bryce asked.

"Yes, but only because they're part of a curse."

Neither of them missed how she trembled slightly and how pale she had become.

"Your magic has drained you, yes?" Sven asked.

"It has," she murmured, her eyes still on the fire. "Very much so."

When Sven glanced at him in question, Bryce nodded. His new friend was wondering if they trusted her enough now for Sven to leave.

"I will go hunt so you can eat." Sven stood. "Then you will rest and tell us more, yes?"

"Yes, thank you," she said softly.

After Sven left, silence settled between them as he continued to eye her.

"Christina mentioned that before she traveled back in time, you said something curious about dragons," he remarked. "You asked if another was coming that would destroy all hope of Scotland's history. More so, destroy all hope of any of us surviving. Shortly after that, Sven arrived at MacLomain Castle. By the sounds of it, you knew he was coming." He tilted his head in question. "How?" He frowned. "And why say such an ominous thing about my ancestor?"

"I believe I sensed he was coming through you." Her eyes rose to his. "Because of your dragon connection." She shrugged. "And I said it because I could never be certain when my...the warlocks were listening in. Saying such a thing seemed logical and made Sven less of a threat to them."

He supposed that made sense, but it still didn't sit all that well. Any more than most of what she said. It was an awful lot to believe considering up until mere hours ago, it very much seemed like she might be the enemy.

"You're having trouble believing all this," she whispered as her eyes returned to the flames. "And I don't blame you."

"I am," he conceded as he watched her. "Though I'll admit I hope 'tis true you're on our side. For your friends' sake if nothing else."

His eyes went to the clear gem in her ring. A gem that might very well end up matching his eyes. He frowned and glanced away. Ring or no ring, he had made an obligation to his family, and it was past time he honored it.

He was meant to marry another.

Yet despite his noble intentions, his gaze returned to Jessie's lovely face with its even features, finely arched brows and lips made for pure sin. She really was stunning with her fine-boned beauty. He scowled and eyed the fire instead. If he had figured out nothing else about her, it was that she was a virgin. Whether her story about her upbringing with the warlocks was true or not, he knew these things about lasses.

When she shifted and cleared her throat as if uncomfortable his eyes returned to her. If he wasn't mistaken, based on the pink staining her cheeks, she had caught his thoughts.

"Are you reading my mind, lass?" he asked.

"Not on purpose," she murmured. "But yes, it seems certain thoughts come through clearer than others."

He nodded, unsure whether or not he should apologize. Mainly because he still had no idea what to make of her. In the end, though, he felt remiss saying nothing at all. "My apologies then."

What he didn't add was that he wasn't all that sorry really. Not for his thoughts about her chastity anyway. While he typically preferred his lasses experienced, something about knowing the bonny little lass across from him was innocent and untouched by another man appealed to his inner dragon.

Sven returned in short time, and they set to skinning and cooking his game. Meanwhile, though she tried to hold her own, it became more and more obvious that Jessie needed rest.

Bryce might not entirely trust her, but he refused to see her uncomfortable. So he removed his fur cloak and wrapped it around her shoulders. "'Twill not only warm you but offer comfort when you rest."

"Thank you," she whispered, her eyes glassy with exhaustion by the time Sven handed her the meat. Little was said as they ate, then soon after she curled onto her side, wrapped his fur tighter around her and continued staring at the fire.

Sven, a man of little words, pulled a small piece of wood from his pocket and began whittling. Bryce sensed heavy thoughts weighed on his mind that had nothing to do with their current adventure.

"Are you carving that for her then?" Jessie whispered.

Sven's hands froze on the wood as his eyes narrowed slightly on her. "Who?"

She blinked. "I don't know." Then she frowned. "Or do I?..."

40

Before Sven could question her further, her eyelids fluttered then slid shut, and her breathing evened.

When Sven went to speak to her again, Bryce shook his head, far more aware of the lass than he should be. "Dinnae bother. She is well and truly asleep." His eyes went to the Viking. "Is it true? Are ye carving that for a lass?"

Sven offered no response but went back to whittling. Bryce knew better than to continue the conversation. When Sven was done talking, that was it. He resumed thinking deep thoughts that remained a mystery.

Bryce sighed, finished his food then lay down as well.

Though he didn't expect it considering his current company, he slept so well he never sensed anyone approach first thing in the morning. Unfortunately, that made for a very rude awakening when he opened his eyes to a sizzling, impregnable wall of fire between him and Jessie.

~Avenged by a Highland Laird~

Chapter Three

WHEN JESSIE AWOKE to two strangers with flaming eyes staring down at her, she instinctively threw up a wall of fire.

Fire, as it turned out, that no dragon could infiltrate.

"'Tis all right," Bryce exclaimed as he leapt to his feet. "They are my parents."

But of course they were, and she could see that now that her haze of slumber had cleared. Though younger, Bryce was the spitting image of his father.

Embarrassed by her instinctual and revealing response, she dropped the firewall instantly and managed a weak explanation. "I'm so sorry. I'm afraid you startled me."

The man's eyes narrowed on her as he rumbled, "What kind of magic *was* that, lass?"

"'Tis her kind and I will better explain it in a moment." Bryce made introductions. "Ma, Da, this is Jessie." He glanced at her then his parents. "Jessie, meet my parents, Rònan and Erin MacLeod."

With dark, curly hair and intelligent eyes, Erin was a truly lovely woman. Only a few inches taller than Jessie, she had the presence of someone much taller. As though she allowed no one to look down at her, despite her small stature.

"Nice to meet you," Jessie murmured, not quite able to meet their eyes.

They nodded at her in return, clearly wary, and she didn't blame them. It wasn't every day a dragon came across fire that they couldn't penetrate.

"Where have you been, Son?" Though Erin's frown seemed more directed at Jessie, she spoke to Bryce. "You've been gone over two months!"

"Two *months*?" Bryce met her frown then looked at Jessie. "How is that possible?"

"I'm sorry." She shook her head. "It likely happened because of my connection to Graham and Christina's time loop." Her eyes went to Erin. "I take it they returned home to MacLomain Castle recently?"

"They did." Erin's eyes narrowed. "How do you know that?"

"Have you spoken to Adlin or Grant?" Bryce interrupted as he embraced his parents. "Have they caught you up on everything that's been happening?"

"We have," came Grant's voice as he and Adlin entered the cave, their eyes never leaving Jessie. She couldn't blame them for their distrust either. Not based on what they knew of her.

Thankfully, Bryce wasted no time on introductions but instead proceeded to tell them everything she had shared with him thus far. Meanwhile, Jessie did her best to remain composed and unaffected. Strong. Unafraid. Because after a good night's sleep, she was more aware than ever of her disconnection from the warlocks. A weakening she knew was coming but still wasn't prepared for.

By the time Bryce was finished, Grant and Adlin's expressions were a bit less distrustful and a little more speculative.

"So all this," Adlin said. "The reason we created the rings and are now trying to keep Scotland's battles on track is because of an old man's curse in the twenty-first century?"

Jessie nodded. "Yes…a very powerful old man."

"Aye," Grant murmured, considering her. "So you, an elemental witch, descend from him. Given that, what would you have called him considering his type of magic, lass?"

She had pondered that often and only ever came to one conclusion. "I suppose, considering we shared the same gifts but his intentions were dark that he was, like his creations, a warlock…perhaps an elemental warlock?"

"That is a sound assumption," Grant agreed. "I have never come across such a creature." He cocked his head. "But then I've never met an elemental witch the likes of you either." His eyes went to

Bryce as he extended his elbow to her. "Might I escort Jessie back to your castle?"

While Jessie thought for sure Bryce would look to his parents or even Sven for their backing, or approval, he did not. Instead, his eyes met hers and held as he considered Grant's request.

She was caught unaware by the way his look stirred her blood. Though not a sensual connection, it invoked a lustful response. Something, quite frankly, she was surprised she was capable of at the moment. But she was and based on the way his brows lowered sharply, and his lips turned down ever-so-slightly, he felt it too.

"Aye, you can bring her to the castle," Bryce murmured. "But only if she remains under the watchful eye of a dragon at all times."

"Good then." Grant prompted her to take his elbow, and they started on their way. Fully aware that she wished to remain surrounded by rock, Grant chanted, and moments later they were in MacLeod Castle's courtyard.

She stared up at the rugged, sea-worn yet beautiful castle perched above the North Sea. Battered by generations of wind and salt, it was striking in an indefinable way. Fierce and unforgiving yet sturdy and dependable. It would never give up or stop protecting its people.

It suited Bryce, and she almost said as much but held back.

He intimidated her in a way that most people did not. She wasn't quite sure why because he didn't seem to have an overbearing personality. But then maybe it had nothing to do with personality and everything to do with the way he was eying her the night before. Better yet, the thoughts he had been having about her sexual prowess...or lack thereof.

Or perhaps it was because of one of the few things she had yet to share. Something he would eventually need to know. Something that, in some ways, could make the less talked about sixth warlock more of a threat than anything.

She continued to eye her surroundings. At this point, she was fairly used to being in the medieval period. As it was, her spiritual self had been in this era plenty lately.

As she and Grant started up the castle stairs, he continued talking. "We still have much to discuss, but I remain curious about one thing above all else." Despite his age, his eyes were exceptionally sharp as they met hers. "As I'm sure you know, my kin and I lost a lad named Fraser a few years back. Only recently we've heard he might be alive somewhere. Is that true?" His tone darkened so slightly she almost didn't catch it. "Did one of your warlocks do something to him?"

"I don't know...not yet," she replied, as respectful as possible. "Though, based on some of the comments one of them made, I think it's likely."

Grant's eyes narrowed. "What comments?" His eyes narrowed further. "And what warlock?"

"One of the only two left. The one that does not carry the essence of my grandfather," she murmured. "Please keep in mind that though I've done my best to control them over the years, evil is not so easily tamed." She didn't shy away from his steadfast gaze. "They did things without me knowing. Things they felt would dishearten the MacLomains. Things they hoped would cause unrest in your clan and weaken your kin, even your people."

"Such as trapping Darach in another dimension for several years," he replied.

"Yes," she said. "Things like that." She shook her head. "And I'm so sorry...not only for the pain it put you all through but for the time lost." She bit back a sigh. "If I could have come to you or Adlin before all this, I would have, but it was too risky. The warlocks would have followed." She kept her eyes with his so he could see how truthful she was being. "If I could have somehow helped you before all this happened, I would have without hesitation."

Grant considered her as they reached the top of the stairs. "I believe you mean that, lass."

"Good because I do," she said softly. "More than you know."

Their eyes held for a long moment before he nodded. "You said you don't know about Fraser *yet*." He frowned. "What did you mean by that? When *will* you know?"

"Likely when the warlock that cursed him is defeated," she said. "Once he's gone, and the curse is lifted, I should see anything they may have hidden from me more clearly."

"You've carried a great weight," Grant murmured as they entered the castle. "More than any wee lass should have to."

Her breath caught at the rugged, almost masculine beauty of the great hall with its massive tapestries full of angry oceanscapes and sweeping dragons roaring fire. It was perfect in a way she couldn't explain. For some reason, it felt more welcoming and safer than anywhere she had ever been.

"Welcome to MacLeod Castle, lass," Grant said softly. "And thank you for healing me at the Action of Happrew."

She was about to deny it, but when her eyes met his again, she knew it was pointless. So she simply nodded. Though he had only taken an arrow to the shoulder, he had lost a great deal of blood and was close to death. Based on the grateful look in his eyes, he knew it.

"Did you provide the clothing for my kin at Happrew's tavern as well?" he asked. "And are you responsible for the seasonal words your friends have been saying in Gaelic along their adventures?"

"I *did* provide the clothing at both the tavern and for Christina and Graham when they were yanked forward in time after the Battle of Bannockburn," she confessed. "Everyone needed clothing, and it was the least I could do." Then she shook her head. "As to the seasonal words, no, that wasn't me or my...*the* warlocks." Her eyes met Grant's. "But I sensed another presence along the way. A woman. I believe you may have seen or sensed her yourself."

"Iosbail," Grant whispered.

Jessie nodded. She might not have made direct contact with Adlin's foster sister from a previous life, but she was fairly certain that's exactly who it was.

Grant eyed her for a moment, his words kinder than she anticipated considering the content of his next question. "No matter how hard you tried to do otherwise, you grew verra attached to these warlocks of yours, aye?"

Though Bryce and Sven had asked nearly the same question, she found herself being far more honest with Grant. "In some ways yes, very much so. In other ways, no."

He nodded thanks to a servant when she handed him and Jessie mugs of whisky.

"Tell me more, lass," he murmured.

"It's hard to explain." She frowned. "I suppose the best way to put it is that there's a balance to be found in everything. Light always possesses some darkness and darkness, light. Because I had been there at their conception, I was able to see what little good the warlocks had and focused on that over the long years. It was what got me by."

"And what good did you discover?" he said softly, watching her closely.

"It was the small things they didn't do when they could have." She remained vague for now because she just wasn't ready to share that one warlock rose above the rest in this regard. "They could have created far more havoc in my life." She shook her head. "They could have hurt the few people I allowed around me."

"Your mother," he murmured.

"Yes, Mama." She went to that nameless place in her mind she used to squelch emotions before they surfaced. "For the most part, they didn't hurt anyone close to me. They were often silent sentinels." Her voice dropped to a whisper. "Always watching me. Waiting...anticipating..."

"For the day to come when the curse began to unravel," he said, filling in the blanks when she trailed off.

"Yes." A shiver went through her as she again felt the remnants of her separation from them. "Their whole existence and a great deal of my existence has been in wait for this." Her eyes swept over the great hall before they landed on Bryce by the fire and she whispered, "Him."

She felt Grant's frown without looking at him.

"What do you mean? Is Bryce in imminent danger?"

She blinked several times, snapping out of her reverie. "No, of course not." She shook her head, embarrassed she had lost herself for a moment. "All I'm saying I suppose is that I recognize the allure of darkness but have always focused on the light within."

"'Tis good because you're right," Grant replied, his astute eyes still watching her. "There is always a bit of light in darkness and vice versa."

Jessie nodded, took a tiny sip of whisky and flinched.

"'Tis not to your liking then, lass?" Bryce asked, suddenly there when moments before he had been a distance away. While she could liken it to dragon magic, she had a feeling it had more to do with her weakening powers and his influence over her in general.

"The whisky's fine," she murmured. She kept her eyes trained on the fire rather than look at him. "It's just the first time I've ever tasted it. Any alcohol for that matter."

"*Truly?*"

"Truly. I never dared imbibe." Her eyes drifted to him despite herself. She might be well trained to remain non-responsive to most things, but she wasn't overly fond of his incredulous, disbelieving tone. "Like I told you, I had to remain in control at all times." She shook her head. "That meant alcohol was too much of a risk."

As just a few small sips of whisky spread through her veins, she realized she had been wiser than ever not to imbibe sooner. Now, however, it didn't much matter. Or at least at this moment.

Bryce's eyes narrowed slightly at what she thought was her tone. "You should eat, lass. Come, we will get you some food..."

The moment his hand touched her back to usher her along, she froze. There was a reason she didn't like to be touched. Why, like most things, she tried to avoid it. Her empathic abilities could run rampant.

Just like they were right now.

She could feel Bryce's every emotion from his concern for his clan and country to his need to see through his family obligations. More so, she could sense his draw to her. His need to remain close at all times. To understand and reveal her every last secret.

Then she felt more, and it was all physical. His attraction to her was far stronger than he wanted it to be. She knew it last night with his thoughts but now, standing in his castle, it was a hundred times stronger.

He was aroused.

He desired her.

"No," she gasped and stepped away, more an automatic reaction than anything else.

"I'm sorry, lass," he replied. "I only meant to escort you to where you could sit and eat. 'Tis unwise to drink whisky on an empty stomach."

Again she kept her eyes glued to the fire rather than look at him. "Actually, I'm not really hungry though I could use a bath and fresh clothing."

"It's all ready to go," Erin said as she joined them. Her eyes went to Bryce, and she spoke within his mind likely so Jessie couldn't hear it. *"Don't worry, I know you want a dragon with her at all times so I'll keep a close eye on her."*

Before he had a chance to respond, Jessie spoke. "I would prefer to be honest from the start." Her eyes flickered from Erin's to

Bryce's before returning to the fire. "Though it doesn't happen all the time, more often than not I can hear when Bryce has a telepathic conversation. Your best hope of privacy with your son would be found standing near water. It's my least powerful element." She shook her head. "Hopefully, as I adjust to the connection I share with Bryce, I'll be able to better control our telepathic bond."

Grant looked at her in amazement. "You were able to reach out to Graham via water like you did and it's your *least* powerful element?"

Jessie only nodded.

Of course, they had figured out she was the one in the forest on Graham and Christina's adventure. She still had a sore abdomen to prove it. Though the dagger he had whipped only hit her spirit self, it left an imprint on her physical body. It was almost like losing a limb but still feeling it afterward. The mind was, without a doubt, far more powerful than people realized.

"I think mayhap you are more than a mere elemental witch, lass," Grant said softly. "I believe strongly you might verra well be an arch-wizard."

Bryce's and Erin's brows shot up in surprise.

"Aye, I think yer right," came a deep voice as a man around Grant's age appeared out of the crowd. Despite his years and white hair, there was no missing his strength or the family resemblance to Bryce. He nodded at her. "Welcome to Castle MacLeod, lass. My name is Colin MacLeod, and I'm Bryce's grandfather."

"Hello," she murmured, able to meet his eyes far easier than anyone else's. Not a shock really considering she had been in such close contact with his granddaughter in the spirit realm. "It's nice to meet you as well, Colin."

Grant looked from Colin to Jessie, clearly aware of her comfort with him.

"Ye remind me a great deal of my late wife, Torra," Colin said. "As does the amount of power ye possess." His eyes went to Grant. "Surely ye sense it, Cousin."

"Aye," Grant murmured. "'Tis similar yet repressed. Likely because of the warlocks' influence."

Jessie knew a great deal about Torra thanks to Ainsley. Actually, she knew a great deal about all of those with MacLomain blood because of Bryce's sister.

It seemed, based on the way Colin was eying her, he sensed her intricate connection with his immediate family, deceased or otherwise. "I look forward to speaking with you more later, lass."

She nodded, in complete agreement.

Though Grant and Torra had been very close and fellow arch-wizards, she wasn't overly surprised that Colin was picking up Jessie's connection to Torra's kin better. He and his wife had not only been deeply in love, but she was dragon, so the bond went a little deeper. Or should she say the residual magic they shared together never truly went away.

Her eyes swept over Bryce but didn't linger. If they shared a true love MacLomain, Broun connection, it would be just as strong. She swallowed. Not *if* but more likely *when*. Because without the warlocks she had grown weaker which meant she needed something else to help her grow stronger again. Her eyes dropped to her ring. Nothing would be more powerful than igniting this.

"Come along then, Jessie," Erin said as she ushered Jessie up the stairs. "Thank you for being honest back there."

Jessie nodded, well aware she was talking about being able to overhear Bryce speak telepathically.

"I'd also like to be honest," Erin continued once they reached the top of the stairs. "As I'm sure you understand, I'm very uncomfortable with you being meant for my son." She stopped and met Jessie's eyes. "Not only are you able to create fire that our dragons can't penetrate but you *were* in league with the warlocks no matter how good your intentions." She frowned. "That means all of us are putting an awful lot of faith in you right now."

"I understand your reservations," Jessie said. She kept her head held high and her eyes firmly locked with Erin's no matter how uncomfortable. Bryce's mother would appreciate it. "I hope by the time all is said and done that I'm able to win your trust."

Erin searched her eyes for a long moment before she nodded and murmured, "Me too, Jessie."

What she didn't expect though she should have anticipated was to find Milly and Christina waiting for her when Erin opened the door to a chamber. Instead of smiling both stood from the small table they were sitting at and looked at her with uncertainty.

She had been dreading this moment.

The disappointment in their eyes when they saw her again.

For the first time since this all began, she had to bite back emotions so strong she might have even cried. In fact, much to her shock, her eyes grew moist.

Surprisingly, their eyes grew moist too.

"It's okay, darlin'," Christina murmured and closed the distance faster than Milly. "We're all caught up thanks to our telepathic connection with Grant." She shook her head, and though it was clear she wanted to touch Jessie, she didn't. "We know you've been trying to help all along."

"And we know how much you've sacrificed," Milly added, compassionate. "Sorry if you saw something else in our eyes at first." She shook her head. "We're still processing everything."

"You are?" Jessie whispered, unsure. "I mean you're not upset..."

"No," they both said at once and shook their heads before Milly continued. "We just wish you didn't have to go through so much alone. That you could have shared with us so we could've helped carry your burden."

Both relieved but frightened they might not be completely truthful, Jessie shocked them when she pulled them into a group hug. Bombarded by a rush of mixed emotions, she held on tight as they embraced her.

As to be expected there were trace amounts of doubt, but the vast majority of what they felt was love and concern for her. For the most part, they trusted every word of explanation she had given and stood by her. They didn't want to lose her and intended to do everything in their power to help her fight every last demon that had kept her repressed for so long.

"Thank you," she whispered, unable to stop the stubborn tear that slipped free. "Thank you so much."

There wasn't a dry eye as they pulled back.

"Just look at that," Christina murmured as she brushed Jessie's tear away. "I knew you had it in you, honey." She shook her head. "I'm just so sorry you've had to learn to suppress your emotions like you have. But now all that's over with." She squeezed her hand. "You can feel to your heart's content, sugar."

"I'll try," Jessie whispered trying out of instinct to get her emotions under control.

"Come sit down, sweetie." Milly led her to a chair. "Eat and take a bath then we'll get you into some fresh clothes."

Jessie nodded and took another small sip of whisky before she set it aside and nibbled on some bannock. Erin didn't go far but sat on the edge of the bed.

"I'm afraid I can't leave the room while you're bathing," Erin said. "But I will keep my eyes averted."

"You don't have to stay," Christina replied. "We're going to be staying with her."

"No, she has to," Jessie said softly. "That's Bryce's wish, and I well understand."

Milly and Christina frowned but said nothing more about it. They understood too. So they caught up while Jessie ate. She tried to fill in the blanks the best she could about everything that had happened to them up until now.

"That's crazy about Graham's knife not actually hitting you." Christina shook her head. "He's glad to hear it though." She made a circle with her finger. "And that time loop was something else." Her eyes narrowed. "I can't believe you were sitting in the chair…but not. Though I started to figure it out in the end." She cocked her head at Jessie. "So my driving need to keep the fire burning in the living room…that was you, wasn't it?"

Obviously, they were telepathically connected with their MacLomains. All of which she was sure Grant had been in touch with by now.

"Yes, I compelled you to keep the fire going," Jessie replied. "It magnified my magic and helped me time-travel."

Christina nodded and grinned. "Well, I'm just glad I could be there for you."

Jessie nodded, still amazed by how wonderful they were being.

"I'm sorry that I've been dishonest with both of you all this time." Jessie's eyes went to the fire on the hearth. "That our entire friendship has been based on a lie."

"No, it hasn't, Jessie." Milly shook her head. "Now that we know your reasons, we completely understand why you had to do what you did." She reached across the table and took her hand, squeezing it until Jessie met her eyes. "We love you for all the moments in between. The fun times we've had."

"That's right," Christina agreed. "And don't you forget it."

Jessie could only manage a small nod as another rush of emotion overwhelmed her. She swallowed hard before she finally murmured, "And Lindsay?"

"She feels the same way as us," Milly assured. "She would've been here if she could have but don't worry, you'll see her soon enough."

"Good," she whispered, more relieved than she let on that they all still seemed to care so much. It was more than she had hoped for.

"Naturally, we have more questions but now's not the time," Milly said. "I know you've been here for a while in spirit form, but still, this has got to be a lot."

"It is," Jessie murmured as she nibbled. "But know that I'll answer any questions you have whenever you like." Her eyes flickered from Christina to Milly. "If nothing else, I owe it to you."

"I don't know, honey," Christina replied. "The way I see it you've been protecting not only us but the whole country of Scotland for a long time so I'd say we owe it to you to give you a little breathing room."

Again overwhelmed by their response, all she could do was nod once more as her eyes went to the water. "I'd love to bathe if it's all right with you."

"Sure," Christina exclaimed. "Would you like us to stay or wait outside?"

Jessie glanced from Erin back to them. What she would prefer was to bathe in private. Even so. "Maybe just a few minutes alone…well, with Erin here of course."

They nodded and headed for the door before Milly stopped in passing, put a hand on her shoulder and met her eyes. "If you need us, just holler. We'll be waiting outside the door."

"Thank you." She put her hand over Milly's. "I'll be okay."

After they left, Erin stuck her hand in the tub of water and chanted. "There we go. All warmed up." Her eyes met Jessie's as she gestured at a small table beside the tub. "Everything you need is right there. Soap and a towel as well as shampoo and a concoction to condition your hair with that I whipped up. A change of clothes is on the bed."

"Thank you. I appreciate it." As soon as Erin turned away and looked out the window, Jessie stripped down and slipped into the blissfully warm water. Though it felt wonderful and she was tempted to linger, she was uncomfortably aware of Bryce's mother.

"You seem to have had a nice reunion with your friends," Erin said softly, likely trying to ease the awkward situation. Because truthfully, they both knew that if Jessie could stop a dragon with fire than having a dragon keep an eye on her was sort of pointless. "I'm glad. Friends and family are very important."

"Yes, they are," Jessie responded.

Silence stretched before Erin finally said what was really weighing on her mind. "Bryce *is* meant for you, isn't he? And you've known it for a long time."

Jessie swallowed hard, unsure if she should answer this or not. So she remained as truthful as she was capable of at the moment. "Yes, there is a very good chance, and I *have* known it for a long time."

Silence settled again as Erin likely contemplated that before she finally said, "Are you aware he's promised to marry another?"

"I am," Jessie murmured.

"And your thoughts on that?" Erin prompted.

Her thoughts were varied and complicated, but she certainly had no intention of sharing that just yet. "My thoughts don't go much beyond ensuring Scotland's survival." She made her voice firm and was absolutely honest with Erin. "That means I intend to make sure the magic of my ring is ignited, no matter what it takes."

If Erin was taken aback by Jessie's straightforward response, she didn't let on. "True love can't be forced."

"I wouldn't know," Jessie replied. "Nor do I have any idea how to force love." She kept her voice firm though she would much rather get to know Erin better and perhaps bond. Nonetheless, she had been in control of all this for far too long and showing weakness now, especially to a woman like Erin, wasn't wise. "What I do know is that the MacLomain, Broun connection exists and that it's powerful. More than that, I have faith in it to find me when the time is right."

Erin remained silent after that. Jessie didn't blame her. Not only had a woman come along that probably struck her as powerful as Grant and Adlin but pretty much declared she would have her son if it meant saving Scotland.

Yet she got the feeling Erin had been testing her. Not only that but she suspected Erin sensed Jessie's connection with her daughter. How could she not? Dragons were known for the deep bond they made with their offspring no matter how short their lives might have been.

After she toweled off, Jessie put on a lovely crème colored dress with flecks of moss that made her darker skin tone grow more luminous. It was fitted closer to her body than anything she had ever worn. She peered down at her cleavage, unsure, as she murmured a chant to manipulate air and cinched up the back. Oh, goodness, that did nothing but plump her breasts up even more.

"You look beautiful," Erin said softly, having finally turned Jessie's way.

"Thanks," she whispered, not at all comfortable in something so revealing. She touched her hair, manipulated the air and dried it instantly.

"You don't worry about using your magic then?" Erin asked as she eyed Jessie over, making adjustments here and there. "The warlocks you were so close to for so long can't sense it?"

"No, not here," Jessie replied. "When I am no longer surrounded by stone or fire, they likely will though." She didn't avert her eyes when Erin's returned to hers but remained forthright because she felt Bryce's mother deserved as much. "Once we travel beyond these castle walls, I will become the number one target of my...the warlocks even before the fate of Scotland." And though she hated to be so blunt, she knew Erin would prefer it. After all, once upon a time in the twenty-first century, Erin had been military. "Not only that but I will be more weakened and vulnerable than ever now that I no longer have the warlocks' protection...or connection so to speak."

Erin didn't bat a lash or lose eye contact with Jessie but notched her chin in defiance. "You might be weakened in some regards but based on what I see in your eyes, not in the ways that will matter most." Her eyes narrowed slightly. "Because you're not afraid of them, right? You're not afraid of these last two warlocks you face." Before Jessie could respond, she continued firmly. "Because if you are, getting over that is the first thing you need to do or all else is lost."

"I know." Jessie nodded, glad however odd the conversation may be that someone saw what she had to do. "It won't be easy, though."

"Nothing so important ever is." Erin surprised her when she held Jessie's hands between hers as their eyes remained locked. "But you *will* do it. And you will do it with every last bit of strength you have."

"Absolutely," she began but trailed off when something unexpected started to happen.

In a split second, Bryce's life flashed before her eyes. Him as a baby, a child then all the years between then and now. When he walked, then embraced his dragon for the first time. Enthralled and bewitched by everything being shown to her, she almost didn't catch what was going on. Regrettably, by the time she did, it was already too late.

A purple dragon stared back at her in her mind's eye.

The moment their eyes connected, the situation was taken out of her hands entirely as the dragon roared then flew straight into her.

Jessie broke contact with Erin and staggered back.

"What did you *do*?" Jessie whispered as she felt a whole new type of power fill her.

Moments later the door flew open and not only Erin's husband Rònan stood there but Bryce.

"What did you do to me?" Jessie whispered again as red flickered in her vision.

"You'll never fly alongside me again, my love," Rònan said hoarsely as his eyes met Erin's. "You'll never shift."

"No, but at least our son stands more of a fighting chance now," Erin managed to say before she fell only to be caught by Rònan just before she hit the floor.

Jessie shook her head in denial as Bryce's eyes met hers and he confirmed the worst.

"Ma just gave ye all her magic," he said softly, pain in his voice. "Ye now possess the essence of the dragon."

Chapter Four

B RYCE STOOD IN front of the fire in the great hall and tried not to brood. Why the bloody hell had he ever let Jessie into his castle and near his family? Now his mother was out cold in bed, having forfeited her magic to a complete stranger. Worse than that, it was all he could do to keep his eyes off the lass who had put her there.

While he knew Jessie had a unique, untouchable beauty before, now, dressed as she was, she appeared exceptional. Exquisite. She had dainty curves he hadn't realized were there, hair that shined as if caught in the moonlight, and skin so soft and touchable he swore he could feel it clear across the room. He sensed her Scottish and English bloodlines, but it was her gypsy heritage that shone through in her skin tone and looks. Maybe even in her magic.

"This was not the wee lass's fault," his grandfather murmured as he joined him and handed him a mug of whisky. "We both know yer ma would not give up her magic if she didnae see great hope in Jessie."

"I didnae think such a thing was even possible." Bryce shook his head. "What if Jessie took it from her somehow?" he growled, tearing his gaze from Jessie at long last to meet his grandfather's eyes. "What if she's fooling us all and is still working with the warlocks?"

"Does your ma strike you as the type of lass to be so easily fooled?" Grandda perked his snowy white brows. "Moreover, do ye truly believe she'd forfeit her magic if she didnae believe in Jessie with all her heart…with all her dragon's heart?"

"She barely knows the lass," Bryce exclaimed. "So nay, I dinnae see much logic in her actions."

"Because ye havenae had a wee one of yer own yet, lad." Grandda rested his hand on Bryce's shoulder. "What yer ma did, what her dragon did, was verra telling." His eyes never wavered. "Bryce, no matter how short the time they spent together in that chamber, yer ma saw something admirable enough in Jessie to give up her greatest gift. Her ability to embrace her other half." He shook his head. "Erin would never do such a thing on a whim. She would only ever do it if she truly believed and had absolute faith that her actions would see a favorable outcome." His voice softened. "And there is nothing she wouldnae do for ye, lad. Nothing at all."

As their eyes held, Bryce saw the conviction in his grandfather's gaze. Truth told though it was hard to grasp everything that had just happened, he knew he was right. Ma would have never done the unthinkable and give her magic to another unless she had absolute faith in them.

"Why though?" Bryce murmured before he could stop himself. "What did Ma see that I dinnae? What certainty does she have in Jessie?"

His grandfather's eyes drifted to Jessie and held for a moment before returning to Bryce. "Yer ma sees what I see, Grandson." He nodded, his eyes prideful and even a little moist. "Hope."

"Hope?" Bryce said, baffled.

"Aye." Grandda notched his chin. "Hope for all of us. Scotland. And ye...always ye."

"But I'm to be with another," he reminded. "Grandma said it herself. 'Twas her and Ainsley's vision."

"Aye, 'twas and I felt the truth of it in my bones," Grandda said softly. "A vision that only ever had yer best interest in mind. That only ever saw a hopeful future for Scotland."

Bryce sighed, shook his head and took another swig of whisky. He wished he could see what they saw in Jessie but unfortunately, logic seemed to flee him every time he looked her way. Instead, he became enraptured by her in another way altogether. One far too lustful for a chieftain that should be focused on his kin and country above all else. But then, he reasoned, was not focusing on a lass who might threaten both doing just that? So it really was best to keep an eye on her. There was little he could do about the fact she was so beautiful and distracting. To that end, some might say no enemy could be better armed.

"Even if ye arenae meant for one another," his grandda continued softly, "'tis not so bad that ye can only focus on one thing when ye look at her. She's a truly lovely lass."

Bryce tore his gaze from Jessie, eyed his grandfather and shook his head. "So do ye want me to ignore my obligations to our clan or not? This other lass I'm meant to marry? Because it sounds like ye want me to pursue Jessie."

"I want ye to follow yer heart, lad. Just as I followed mine with yer grandma so long ago." He clasped Bryce's shoulder and held his eyes. "Follow yer heart no matter where that takes ye, aye?"

Bryce narrowed his eyes as something rather daunting occurred to him. "Is Ma inside her somehow? Because that might prove awkward."

Colin chuckled. "'Tis good yer keeping yer humor." He shook his head. "Nay, yer ma only shared the essence of her dragon, nothing more. She isnae inside the lass."

Their shared moment of levity vanished as his da joined them. "Yer ma's awake and asking for ye, Bryce."

"Aye, then." He started to head that way before his father caught his arm and met his eyes. "She's asking for Jessie too."

Bryce frowned. "Aye?"

"Aye," Da confirmed. "So ye best bring the wee lassie along."

Bryce grumbled under his breath but did as asked and headed her way. Naturally, the closer he got the more tempting her allure. It didn't surprise him in the least that Milly and Christina were a solid wall of protection between her and several of his clansmen. Yet he knew her beauty and frailty were only an illusion. With a wiggle of her little finger and a nonchalant chant, she could easily protect herself from their advances.

Likely anticipating why he was heading her way, Jessie murmured something to her friends then headed in his direction. Though men swarmed in, they backed off quickly when they saw the look on their laird's face. A look, Bryce realized with frustration, that might very well appear possessive.

"My mother would like to see you," he announced as he steered Jessie toward the stairs.

She nodded. "I know."

"Doesn't Jessie look beautiful, Bryce?" Christina piped up as she trailed them up the stairs.

Bryce stopped and frowned at her. "Why are you following us, lass?"

"Because Jessie's my friend and it's damn well time someone look after her rather than her looking after everyone else." She patted the hilt of the blade at her side and grinned. "And who better than a demi-god warrioress?"

"You're a witch with godly powers, not a demi-god," he reminded.

"Tomato, tamahto." She shrugged, gave him a pointed look and returned to her previous assessment. "*I* think Jessie looks absolutely stunning."

So did he but he wasn't quite ready to pay her compliments yet.

"Come, then," he grumbled and kept walking. "But you'll wait outside Ma's door, Christina."

"Yeah, yeah."

He reminded her again before he and Jessie entered his parent's chambers and he closed the door, leaving Christina in the hallway.

Not surprisingly, his mother wasn't in bed where she belonged but sitting at a small table.

"Ah, there you are." She gestured at a chair beside her. "Jessie please sit because Bryce won't."

Jessie nodded and thanked her before she sat. Where some lasses might be inclined to thank someone when they gave them their dragon magic, she remained silent.

He, however, did no such thing.

"Why did you do it, Ma?" He frowned and shook his head, trying to keep his anger under wrap. "How could you do such a thing to Da? He's your dragon mate!"

"Watch your tone, Son." She gestured at the other chair. "You know what, why don't you sit down after all." Her eyes narrowed when he hesitated. "*Now.*"

She might be half his size and without dragon magic but when his mother issued an order, he listened. Silence settled as she eyed the two of them before finally speaking. "I did what I did for the greater good of Scotland and do not regret my actions." Her eyes leveled on Jessie. "While yes, you are one of the strongest women I've ever met, you're also one of the most repressed. It's that, what you keep buried so deep inside, that my dragon magic will coax to the surface." She shook her head. "You won't shift into a dragon. It's not like that."

Jessie nodded that she understood before Erin continued. "My magic is no longer part of me but very much a part of you. We are not connected in any way. Do you understand?"

"Yes," Jessie replied. "I can feel it…" She nodded again. "It's very strong, and I'm thankful."

"I didnae know a dragon could give up their magic," Bryce began, but Ma put up a hand, shook her head and silenced him as she continued speaking with Jessie.

"Embrace the magic I've given you and trust it." His mother took Jessie's hand and held her eyes. "Make it yours and allow it to offer you new light, guidance, and strength. Allow it to bring you joy where there has never been any." She cocked her head. "Can you do that? *Will* you?"

Jessie nodded again and if he wasn't mistaken, blinked away a glimmer of moisture.

"And you, my son." His mother's eyes swung his way. "You will not harbor anger at Jessie for my choices. She didn't ask me to do this. I did it because her journey back from where she's been is far more difficult than you can imagine." She clenched her jaw. "And if this country is to have any hope at all, she needs help. Not just from me but from all of us."

Bryce kept frowning. "How do you know she needs help?"

"I think what you meant to ask is 'how can I help'?" She met his frown. "Your father and I are well aware that you've been trying to dodge your prearranged marriage so now you have a chance to redeem yourself."

He arched his brows. "Redeem myself? You're asking me to break my pledge to our clan now that I've finally realized the error of my ways!"

"I never said break your pledge," she replied, a flicker of unexpected challenge in her eyes. "Unless, of course, you intend to try to ignite the power of Jessie's ring with her." She shrugged. "That, I suppose, might mean breaking your pledge."

Bryce crossed his arms over his chest and narrowed his eyes. "You're playing games with me."

"No," Ma said bluntly, her eyes unwavering as they stayed with his. "I'm focusing on what I feel is more important right now." Her eyes went from Jessie back to him. "And that's you being the admirable man I know you are. That means you'll stand by Jessie's side and protect her while you two at long last free both her and Scotland from this God-forsaken curse." She reached across and took his hand, never letting go of Jessie's. The look in her eyes was both emotional and strong. "Will you do that for me, Son? Will you help Jessie save our country?"

"There isnae anything I wouldnae do for ye, Ma," he grumbled, his brogue thickening as he did his best to keep emotion at bay. "Ye know that."

"Good." His mother squeezed his hand and was about to pull away, but he stopped her by placing his free hand over hers.

"Will ye be all right, Ma?" Eyes firmly locked with hers, he embraced his dragon and let his vision haze red so he could see any truth she might be hiding. "Or will losing yer dragon end up harming ye in some way?"

"I'll be just fine," she assured and pulled away. "So put your dragon eyes away, Son."

She was hiding something but what? If it was illness, his dragon should have sensed it.

"I've said everything I intend to say," his mother announced as she poured ale into two mugs. "Now I'm going to spend time with my husband so I can put his mind at ease." She slid the mugs in front of Bryce and Jessie. "Meanwhile, you two will take this time to talk." Her eyes landed squarely on Jessie. "And you will explain what Colin already knows. You will tell my son exactly how you are connected to his twin sister and you won't spare a detail. Do you understand?"

Bryce's eyes shot to Jessie as her eyes drifted to the fire and she murmured, "Of course."

"Oh, no. Enough with hiding your gaze in the flames." Ma gently tipped Jessie's chin until she turned her head and met Bryce's eyes. "Time to face things."

"Okay," Jessie whispered as his mother left.

She cleared her throat, rallied her courage and started talking. "I first came in contact with your sister Ainsley during the creation of the rings...well her essence anyway." Though he sensed she wanted to look at the fire again, she sat up taller and continued. "In a strange way, we grew up together." She blinked several times as though stopping moisture before it had a chance to form. "She grew in the afterlife as she would have here…and she was my only friend for a very long time."

He tried to respond but couldn't he was so caught off guard by her revelation.

"She's been trying to protect you all this time," she said softly. "That's why not just Milly but especially Christina's gem shone the color of your eyes. She was desperate to connect you with a Broun so that you would be protected by the power of the MacLomain, Broun connection." She shook her head. "Lindsay's ring was the only one she couldn't manipulate because she and Conall had connected for the first time via the oak outside MacLomain Castle."

A deafening silence fell as he processed what she had said. He wasn't sure what troubled him more. That his deceased sister hadn't passed on to somewhere peaceful or that Jessie's existence really was so remote that she had counted a ghost as her closest friend.

Finally, still coming to grips with the enormity of what she had shared, he took a deep swig of ale then asked about yet another thing that worried him. "The warlocks know about Ainsley then?"

"Yes," she confirmed. "But they think she's my sister, not yours."

He frowned, not expecting that answer. "Why?"

"It explained why she would have been there at the creation of the rings," she said. "And it kept them from going after her."

His heart leapt into his throat. "Will they now that they know you betrayed them?"

"No," she whispered and swallowed hard. Though she remained stiff and her face expressionless, a single tear rolled down her cheek. "She's free of all this now and moved into the light. They can't touch her there." Her eyes stayed with his. "I'm so sorry, Bryce."

Overwhelmed, he set his drink down and stared at her. He didn't realize until this moment how hopeful he had been that Ainsley was still out there somewhere. In all honesty, until this moment he didn't realize that he had hoped by some miracle that she might reappear like Uncle Darach had.

Evidently sensing he was having trouble with her information, she said, "When and if you're ready, I'll continue."

All he could manage was a single nod.

"Like Kenna, Ainsley also sacrificed for the good of Scotland on Christina and Graham's adventure," she said softly. "By creating the magic that you and Christina harnessed on the first day of The Battle of Bannockburn, she helped see history through." She clenched her jaw as another tear slid free. "As such, she and her inner dragon became part of their time loop. When it closed, she was set free from the place in between and moved on to what many would call Heaven." Her voice dropped to a whisper. "Her every thought was of protecting you and your kin at all cost...especially you, Bryce...her twin brother."

He shook his head in denial even though he felt the truth of it in her words. He could see it in her eyes. Ainsley was really and truly gone.

"I wish it could have been different," she whispered. "I wish she hadn't become part of all this, to begin with." She finally brushed away her tears but did as his mother asked, and kept her eyes with his. "Even so, I feel privileged to have known her and hope, as time goes by, you'll allow me to share my memories of her with you."

If nothing else was clear, it was that Jessie had loved Ainsley. They had shared an important bond. He nodded, still mute with disbelief and sadness. It was no easy thing to know one's sister hadn't crossed over when she died in infancy but grew up in some strange dimension in between. That she had chosen to be caught in a curse so she could protect her kin and country. So that she could protect him.

It seemed that nod was all she needed because Jessie's eyes drifted back to the safety of the fire. She left her drink untouched as her sad gaze seemed to reflect his every emotion. He knew he should thank her. That she had done a lot for him. Yet all he could do was watch her stare at the fire. More so, observe the way the flames danced in the rich darkness of her eyes.

In fact, he became mesmerized by it.

"Och, nay, not yet," he began but knew it was already too late as the air thinned and the ground dropped out from beneath them.

Like it or not, they were traveling through time and most likely beginning their adventure.

Chapter Five

Western Isles, Scotland
6 August 1322

JESSIE GASPED AS she was whipped through time against her will for the first time ever. Her chair vanished, and she thumped back against cold hard stone. By instinct, she murmured a chant, and a fire flared to life.

"Bloody hell," Bryce muttered from somewhere beyond the cave she found herself in. "Why does this sort of thing keep happening to me lately?"

Her eyes swept around the small space and found Sven. Then her eyes locked on Christina and Graham.

All she got out was, "We need to save him," before she raced in the direction of Bryce's voice. She followed a narrow stone hallway until it opened up to a raging waterfall. He was hanging, white-knuckled, on a cliff right beside it.

"Don't embrace your dragon, Bryce," she yelled. "The waterfall will rip you apart if you do."

When his eyes met hers, she sensed he knew the truth of it.

Yet that same waterfall was kicking off enough water pressure to put him under a great deal of strain. Though well-muscled and fueled with the aid of dragon magic, it was already testing his strength.

The other three skidded to a halt beside her, their eyes wide as they took in Bryce's precarious situation. When they started in his direction, determined to cross the thirty feet of sheer, bottomless space between them, she spun and roared, "Stop!"

She chanted, and another fire sprang to life nearby. Not only did she manifest it for extra cloaking from a possible warlock but because it gave her strength when facing so much water.

Her eyes went to Sven's. "I need your strength and the magic of your dragon to throw me his way." She shook her head. "But don't shift." Her eyes went to Graham. "I need your magic to make sure the waterfall gets me to him." Her eyes went to Christina's. "I need you to stand guard in case anyone sneaks up on us."

"My blade's yours," Christina assured.

"*Should* I use my magic?" Graham asked. "Willnae the warlocks sense it?"

"It's unlikely," she replied. "Between my fire and the rock surrounding us, it should be fine."

"Then mayhap I can just manipulate the water to get Bryce to safety," he pointed out. "Though in his current state of agitation his fire might evaporate it beforehand."

"He is very close to embracing his dragon." Sven leant credence to Graham's concern. "So using water alone to aid him would not be the wisest move right now."

"I need to get over there." Jessie's eyes shot to Bryce again as one hand slipped and he swung. Despite how hard she tried to fight it, fear for him tightened her chest. "Everyone please just do as I ask."

Sven nodded, meticulously decisive as he swung her up into his arms, spun hard and tossed her. Meanwhile, Graham began chanting and manipulated the water molecules coming off the waterfall to carry her the rest of the way. She landed on the small ledge above Bryce and got her bearings. The rock was slick and the area remarkably dangerous.

Because of her disconnection from the warlocks and the fact she was facing so many previously repressed emotions, terror nearly froze her in place. Yet as her eyes fell to Bryce and she saw how close he was to death, that inner calm she had become so good at rose up. She could do this. She *would* do this. Determined, pulling forth her magic, she crouched and wrapped her hand around his wrist.

"Trust me," she said softly as she met his eyes. He wasn't panicking, so that was helpful. Rather, he simply seemed frustrated. "When I say 'let go,' let go."

"Och," he muttered, his brogue thick. "Ye ask a lot, lass." He clenched his jaw, remembering what his mother had said. Something Jessie knew because she caught his thoughts. "But aye, I'll trust ye…I havenae much choice."

"Not good enough." She narrowed her eyes on his. "The only way I can save you is if you trust me…if you believe it."

He clutched the cliff and frowned, his eyes never leaving hers as he sensed the gravity of the situation. "How am I supposed to do that?"

"As a whole, it'll take some time," she conceded. "But for now, look inside yourself and know I possess the power to save you." Then she added for good measure though she wasn't necessarily sure it was true. "Your mother's magic possesses the power."

His eyes held hers for a moment longer before he nodded. Thankfully, he meant it. Enough so that when she chanted, and he was forced to let go, she drew on the earth, air, and water to swing him up beside her. Both fell back against the rock wall, breathing heavily. Him because of the strength he had exerted, her because of the magic.

"Bloody hell," he muttered and looked at her, clearly shaken. "Thank you."

"And thank you for not embracing your dragon," she replied. "I don't think I could've helped you if you had."

He nodded as he eyed their surroundings. "So what are we to do now, lass? We're trapped, are we not?"

She frowned. "Yes."

His brows shot up as his eyes whipped back to her. "Yes? That's it? Have you not a plan beyond this?"

"No." She shrugged. "I only thought to save you."

And that was the truth. She had been so terrified for him that she had formulated a plan to save him and that was it. She blinked several times at the enormity of that. Not once since the tender age of ten had she done *anything* unless it was well thought out from start to finish.

Now here she stood, with a mere two feet between her and a sheer drop and had no clue what to do next.

"How can we help?" Sven called out, clearly catching on that she hadn't thought this all the way through. "How do we get you back?"

Bryce perked a brow at her. "I dinnae see any way out of this without Sven or I embracing our dragon."

"No." She shook her head. "It's too dangerous. Not only because of the waterfall but because I'm not sure how well the rock will mask you from the warlocks if you embrace your dragons fully."

"Aye, then," he murmured, eying her with a look she couldn't quite pinpoint.

"I'm sorry," she said out of instinct. "I should have thought this through better."

"Nay," he replied. "Had you, I might've given up on you being a mere mortal."

Surprised by his response, she realized what it was she couldn't pinpoint about his look.

It was a flicker of humor.

"You find this amusing, then?" she asked, truly curious. "Us moments away from death because I didn't think things through?"

"Aye, I guess I do find it a wee bit amusing." His eyes never left hers as they balanced precariously. His next words were unexpected and made her heart skip a few beats. "But know this, if you lost your balance at this point, I *would* embrace my dragon, and I *would* save you."

Their eyes held as that sunk in.

"Because you know I can save Scotland," she finally said.

"Aye," he replied, a strange new appreciation in his eyes. "At the verra least."

"Jessie," Christina yelled over the waterfall, breaking into the strange yet intimate connection they had just made. "Are you listening to me, Jessica?"

Startled by the use of her full name and the urgency in her friend's voice, her eyes returned to Christina, Graham, and Sven.

"*People are coming, Cousin,*" Graham said into Bryce's mind, but she caught it. "*We're going to hide until we know if they're friend or foe. If you can, do the same.*"

"Bloody hell," Bryce muttered as he looked left then right.

"I heard what Graham said." Jessie gazed around as well. "I think if we can sidle behind the waterfall, we might be able to hide as well. I sense there's some extra space back there."

He eyed the roaring wall of water beside him dubiously then looked at her again. "And how do you intend we do that, lass?"

"Let me around you," she replied. "I can get us through the water."

"How do you know that's not a warlock heading our way and won't sense your magic?"

Though they seemed to have crossed several barriers in the last few minutes, she knew her next words would wipe all that away. "Because I know these warlocks." She kept her eyes on his just as Erin had asked her to. His mother might not be here, but she would show the strength Erin hoped to see in her. "I know *my* warlocks, Bryce."

She didn't miss the flash of disappointment in his eyes before he managed a small nod and held out his hand. "Aye then, lass, step around me…Ma would want me to work with you for the sake of our country."

Jessie clenched her teeth, disappointed that the small bridge they had built was so swiftly knocked down. That he was so quick to dislike her again. But that wasn't to be worried about right now.

Well aware time was running out, she carefully turned, so she was facing the wall, took his hand, and began moving. Step by step, she made her way along the ledge to the point where they would have to share a space.

She met his pale golden eyes and tried to ignore the flustered way they made her feel. "Are you ready for me to pass?"

"I am," he lied.

She could tell by his guarded expression he was nowhere near ready. Not because he was a coward but because he was aware of his effect on her. More so, how much he liked it. His wariness had nothing to do with plummeting to their death but allowing her close enough that she could pass. Close enough that he would feel the heat of her skin.

So a bridge might have been knocked down, but something else was taking its place. She worked to steady her breathing at the quickly escalating attraction between them. Now was most certainly not the time.

Yet she had known this would likely happen, didn't she? That it would be unavoidable. At least for her. How else could it be considering the secrets she still kept? Secrets she was foolish enough to have thought she could keep from him for his own safety. But then she had very little real-life practice when it came to attraction. Especially the sort she felt being so close to Bryce. He was the real thing and far more then she anticipated.

However, now definitely wasn't the time for a chat about deep dark secrets that would only upset him further.

They needed to keep moving.

Though tempted to close her eyes so she didn't drown in those piercing golden orbs of his again, she kept them open and made her move. With her hand braced on the left side of his waist, she began moving along the front of him. She was halfway across and directly in front of him when he touched the side of her waist, lowered his lips close to her ear and whispered, "Dinnae move, lass."

His words floated through her mind. *"There is a stranger standing across the way."*

"I feel him," she responded as her eyes rose to his. *"He doesn't see us yet."*

Though she thought it was her breath that caught when they're eyes met, it might have been his. Alarmed by the impact of being this close, she nearly teetered back, but his arm slipped around and pulled her even closer.

Unable to breathe at all now, she didn't look away. She couldn't if she wanted to. *"Let me go, and I'll hide us without him knowing."*

Unmistakable heat gathered in his eyes. Heat and lust he warred to contain, but she saw it...then she felt it as his arm tightened. The pale gold flecks in his thickly lashed eyes only grew brighter with curiosity. While she could tell herself that he simply wondered how she would get them out of this, she knew better. His curiosity was entirely focused on the strong chemistry between them.

Despite the waterfall's intense spray and the fact an enemy could very well be staring at them right now, she was human enough to get caught up in what was happening between them. How erotic it felt to finally be pressed against his long, hard body.

To finally lay her hands on the physical form of someone she had known for so long.

"No," she whispered, suddenly frightened as heat swept through her and pooled below. "Not now. Not yet." She swallowed hard and shook her head, suddenly lost in memories. No matter how real this might be, she had long trained herself that she couldn't trust lustful feelings when it came to him. That she should not indulge in them. "Let me go. Please."

Though her response could simply be that of a woman choosing to reject what flared between them, he seemed to sense there was more to it. His arousal turned to protectiveness as his brow furrowed in determination and his grip tightened ever-so-slightly. She couldn't help but wonder if he was inherently responding to her past. To those moments he was so much a part of without ever knowing.

"Just tell me what to do to get us out of sight," he whispered.

Grateful he was focused on anything but her now, she whispered, "Fling me toward the waterfall and don't let go."

His turbulent eyes held hers, well aware that it sounded like she was asking him to fling her to her death. Yet that couldn't be the case because she had already proven she would do whatever it took to protect him.

And if she went down, so did he.

He clenched his jaw and held her eyes a moment longer before he nodded and did as asked. Murmuring a chant, she fueled them with a combination of his dragon magic, the power of the waterfall and the wind it created.

Seconds later, though there was a moment of discomfort as the water crashed over them, they were on the other side in an area no bigger than a small bedroom. If that wasn't daunting enough, the temperature was frigid with an icy wall of roaring water on one side and cold rock on the other. Though she murmured a chant to dry them, it did little to help.

"*I shouldn't light a fire*," she said into his mind, rubbing her hands together. "*It might be detected.*"

"Aye," he agreed.

"You're hurt," she murmured, shivering as she inspected the wound on his elbow caused by the jagged rock he had been hanging from.

"'Tis but a scratch that will heal with my dragon's magic," he muttered, watching her closely. Either because of what happened moments before between them or perhaps due to her severe shivering.

"Yet you can't embrace your dragon magic yet," she reminded through chattering teeth. "And scratches can get infected."

"Och, enough, lass," he finally murmured before he pulled her into his arms, and protected her from the waterfall, his words a deep rumble, "'Tis foolish not to warm each other with body heat."

That was debatable considering how quickly they aroused one another, but she was too cold to argue so she gave in and rested her cheek against his chest. While she knew his intentions were honorable, she tensed a little in his arms. Though safer than she had been moments before, she'd never felt more vulnerable. He dwarfed her in size and strength and for the first time since she opened her grandfather's book, she felt powerless.

Could she strike him with magic if she had to? Yes. Could kill him in under a minute? Yes. Would she after all Erin had done for her? Unlikely. She squeezed her eyes shut at her own thoughts. Not *unlikely* but *no*. She wouldn't hurt him. She couldn't. Not ever.

Yet she remained on edge and cautious. She was in brand new territory and out of control. Two things she had never experienced before. While some of what she felt was still related to being separated from the warlocks, the rest had more to do with Bryce. While she thought she knew him and was fully prepared for this adventure, she was wrong. She thought she would be able to manage her reaction to him, but that wasn't the case in the least.

As a matter of fact, she couldn't seem to manage any of this

There was no sense of direction here. No planning, plotting or strategizing. And that suddenly terrified her. Spontaneity was not her strong point and was that not the very definition of an adventure? That, it seemed, might be at the root of why she felt so vulnerable with Bryce. He was part of this unknown reality she had just entered. This free fall of unstable, heart pounding moments.

"*I willnae hurt ye*," he murmured into her mind, his brogue especially thick. "*Ye have my word, lass.*"

No, she thought, he would not hurt her. She knew that. But she would hurt him, and that bothered her greatly. She supposed she had never worried about it because she was determined things wouldn't get this far. That she would be able to avoid him and keep him out of all the darkness that had been her world. Yet deep down she had always wanted this for selfish reasons, hadn't she?

"*I know you won't hurt me*," she finally responded, and left it at that. Soon they would have to talk more. She would have to tell him things. But not quite yet. Not here like this.

Neither said a word for several minutes as he held her. Meanwhile, she tried to sense what was happening beyond the waterfall but had no luck. Her focus was too skewed. Her ability to concentrate non-existent. She could only see, smell and feel him. His spicy scent and warm protective body. The way he seemed to only pull her closer and engulf her in an unexplainable way. A comforting way that was completely foreign to her.

There was something else too. A difference in him.

As Bryce had said before they crossed under the waterfall, he would risk his life for her now. Because that's precisely what he would have done if she fell. He would have embraced his dragon and likely faced death for the sole purpose of breaking her fall.

So something had changed. Perhaps his mother's words, or perhaps something more. Whatever it was, he was with her now in a way he wasn't before. Not in a sense that could ignite the ring but one step closer.

She ground her jaw and fought emotion. What would it be like to simply fall in love with a man without fear? To desire him without constantly worrying about what that might mean? She had no idea because she had never been allowed to. Nothing had been allowed but the very opposite of what she felt now.

Detachment. Control. Power.

That had been her life up until this point…until this very moment.

She trembled against him, her heart pounding before she closed her eyes and breathed deeply. So deeply that all her worries and fears faded away. For a moment in time, she felt normal. How she imagined a woman was supposed to feel when she was in the arms of a man she had been pining for the majority of her life. Like a woman at the beginning of a romance that had been just out of reach for so long. Or was it in some strange way the epic conclusion of a romance? She just didn't know anymore.

"*'Twill be all right, lass,*" he murmured into her mind, likely mistaking her response as fear. "*We havenae come this far to meet our end behind a waterfall.*"

Though she knew he spoke of the defeated warlocks, she liked to think he was referring to them. What might exist if they found the sort of connection her friends had with their MacLomains. If that is, she would be allowed to in the end.

More so, if she would be strong enough.

"*'Tis all right.*" Graham's words floated through their minds. "*'Twas friend not foe. We are coming for you.*"

"*Coming how?*" Bryce asked.

"*Ye might be surprised,*" Graham responded moments before the rock shifted behind them.

A bearded stranger stuck his head through and waved them along. "I come on behalf of King Robert the Bruce. Follow me."

When they hesitated, Graham spoke into their minds. "*You can trust him, Cousin. They've been expecting us.*"

"He's right," she murmured, stemming out her magic. "He's on our side."

His eyes met hers. "Aye?"

"Yes."

Their eyes held for another moment before he nodded. "All right. Come on then, lass."

He gripped his dagger firmly as he took her hand and led the way. They ducked into a narrow torch lit tunnel that ran along the back of the ledge they were just standing on. The way was jagged and tight, and the stagnant air smelled of smoke, brine and sea salt. Fortunately, they didn't have to walk all that far before slightly less repressive air breezed through, and it opened up.

The man they followed said nothing but waved them along through a cavern that only got bigger before they finally exited into the cool night. Wind gusted, and white-tipped waves etched the moonlit sea in the distance.

"*'Tis one of the western isles,*" Graham informed. "*Two months before the Battle of Byland Moor.*"

Jessie knew her Scottish history far better than most so she understood why they might be here. Or at least she knew how this location intertwined with the upcoming battle. Better yet how the people who lived here were involved.

"Do we know what day it is?" she asked.

When Graham told her, she nodded, curious what the warlocks might be up to that would affect this particular time in history. After all, they had arrived on the very day Angus Óg MacDomhnaill, or MacDonald, Lord of the Isles, and his firstborn son, John of Islay, had received word from King Robert the Bruce. They were to sail around the north of Scotland and stop English ships from carrying cargo to their depleted army.

Soon enough, they joined Graham, Christina and Sven then continued following several men through the forest toward the ocean. As they walked, she kept an eye out for a particular plant, not so sure she would find it in this location. Luckily she did and snatched a handful in passing before she shoved it in her pocket.

"What is that, lass?" Bryce asked, not missing a thing.

"Something that will help you," she replied, leaving it at that as they came upon a vast torch-lit oceanside village. Plenty of Birlinns—or galley ships—were in port. Finely made, they were wooden vessels propelled by oars with square sails, their design most certainly influenced by the Norse. As it was, many in these parts still owed their allegiance to the King of Norway.

That, as it turned out, made Sven with his obvious Viking looks a little less daunting. Though some people still cast them curious glances, most kept to themselves as they traveled on.

It wasn't long before they entered a surprisingly modest lodging considering it contained not only Angus himself but his son John. Both were rugged, bearded and sea worn but had the sort of broad-shouldered builds and daring eyes she figured drew plenty of women.

Angus greeted them first, not bothering with the formalities that befit such a powerful chieftain. Instead, he offered a hearty smile as he shook the men's hands and kissed the back of her and Christina's hands. Mischievousness lit his eyes as they went from his son to Jessie. She didn't realize why until she saw the appreciative lookover he gave her. If she were to guess, he had a thing for short, petite women with darker looks.

"Nice to meet ye all," John said, his voice an octave less booming than his father's as his eyes lingered on Jessie. "We've heard tale of yer possible arrival and cannae imagine as to what we owe the pleasure."

She didn't miss Bryce's possessive touch on her back as he kept a cordial enough expression and introduced them all.

"Laird of the MacLeod's ye say?" Angus eyed him over. "A good strong lot by the looks of it."

"Aye." Bryce nodded, clearly impressed by their current company. "Though not as mighty a clan as yer MacDonald's."

"Aye." Angus kept grinning as he urged them to sit around a fire and called out to a man at the entrance to bring drinks. "Sit. Rest yer weary bones, and we'll figure out why after all these years Robert's time-travelers ended up on my doorstep." His eyes went to Sven. "And why ye've a Viking the likes of him along with ye." He shrugged. "Though I'm sure he'll come in handy considering our recent orders."

Ah, so there stood a good chance they would be sailing with them.

Jessie could tell by the flicker of surprise in Graham's and Bryce's eyes that they hadn't anticipated Robert sharing that they were time-travelers.

"With all due respect," Bryce said. "Mayhap 'twould be best if ye told us more about King Robert's orders, such as they are."

"Such as they are? Ye mean how *revealing*, aye?" John answered for his father, grinning. It was obvious the two of them were good friends. "King Robert has eagerly awaited the return of his MacLomains for eight long years now and has sent word to every commander of every important battle that his friends might happen along." His eyes swept over the lot of them. "And when they did, they were to be welcomed because they were there with good reason."

Had he said all that then? Interesting that tidbit wasn't recorded in history. But then in retrospect, once the curse lifted history would go back to the way it was supposed to be. And naturally, that did not include time-travelers.

She found it amusing though that King Robert didn't seem too worried about what his commanders might think of him claiming such a nonsensical thing. Then again, he was leading his country to freedom, and as proven time and time again, was an astounding military commander, so she supposed they took him at his word. But then just look at the MacDonald's. They didn't seem the least bit fazed.

"Aye, so we welcome you as our King requested," Angus continued as they were all given mugs of ale. "And with any luck, we've a battle on the horizon." One bushy eyebrow crawled upward slowly, that same glint of mischievousness in his twinkling eyes. "So I'll be curious to see what yer part is supposed to be." He eyed them with amusement. "Because outside of yer Viking ye dinnae strike me the sort who's used to battling upon the sea."

Bryce shook his head and focused on what he had said before. "So ye know we arenae from this time? That we're from yer past?" It seemed he shared Jessie's curiosity. "And ye believe it?"

"Aye," John readily replied. He took a hearty swig of ale, wiped his mouth with the back of his hand and nodded, eagerness in his eyes. "'Tis not overly shocking to us as magic always abounds in these parts." His gaze grew more zealous as he planted his fist on his knee and eyed them all. "Yet like Da said, why here? Why now?" His eyes went to his father. "And 'twould probably be prudent of us to get some kind of proof they are who they say they are, aye?"

Sven's and Bryce's eyes narrowed as Angus replied, "It cannae hurt."

Jessie tensed as Sven's hand shifted closer to the hilt of his blade. Had they walked into a trap? Had it been that easy for their captors to take them? She had sensed nothing but curiosity and even excitement when she touched both Angus and John.

"What kind of proof are you boys lookin' for?" Christina kicked in, a deceptively pleasant smile on her face. "And why wait till now to ask for it?"

Angus chuckled, his eyes less mischievous and more direct as they swept over them again. "Well, what sort of sense would it have made to do that beyond my well-defended encampment where I wasnae surrounded by my warriors?"

Silence settled as they all eyed each other. Graham's, Bryce's and Sven's hands locked firmly around the hilt of their blades ready for a possible confrontation.

"But consider this," John continued, a little less jovial though not necessarily upset. His gaze might be calm and steady, but his words made clear he knew they were braced to fight. "Had we seen ye as a true threat those weapons of yers wouldnae have made it past our village walls and certainly not into this cottage."

"Aye," Angus agreed, taking another swig of ale. "We arenae a threat to ye just desire a wee bit o' proof is all." He made a sweeping gesture with his hand. "We're of the isles and the sea and as such have seen our fair share of mysticism. Show us a wee bit o' what only a MacLomain can do, and we'll know without a shadow of a doubt ye are who ye say ye are."

Bryce's brows bunched in question. "And what is this MacLomain proof ye seek?"

Angus' eyes went to Jessie's ring. "The Bruce says the MacLomain gem has an untouchable power about it and will shine the likes I've never seen when its magic is ignited."

Jessie kept her eyes dead ahead as Bryce spoke to her telepathically. "*Say nothing, lass. This could be a trick. These men are known for their pirating ways.*"

"*Okay,*" she replied but was sure to share with him what she had felt when she touched them. "*My empathic abilities are rarely if ever wrong.*"

"*Aye, then,*" he said. " *'Tis good to know.*"

"*I got this,*" Christina said into their minds. "*Just hang on.*"

Jessie glanced at her friend, not overly surprised they were all connecting telepathically at this point and could hear one another.

"If you want to see proof, I've got it." Christina offered a charming grin as she looked from John to Angus. "You've gotta promise though that you won't overreact but sit back and let things play out. Trust that my friends and I mean you no harm. Trust that we're your allies." Her eyes narrowed a fraction. "Can y'all do that? Can you let things play out because I promise it'll be damn fast." She snapped her fingers. "Blink of an eye."

They considered her, hesitant at first but seemingly too curious to say no as they nodded.

"Well, all right then." She held up her ring finger. "Just keep an eye on this Claddagh ring, okay?"

"Aye," they barely got out before Graham whipped his blade at the man guarding the entrance. Fast, in the blink of an eye, Christina stood beside the guardsman and grabbed the dagger moments before it met its target.

Wide-eyed, Angus and John stood, blinking in amazement as they witnessed not just Christina's supernatural speed, but her godly glow and most importantly the bright magical shine of the gem in her ring.

"Och!" Angus shook his head. "'Tis bloody true, then!"

"Aye," John whispered, amazed as a slow grin curled his lips, and he nodded at his father. "We've got the Bruce's lot with us through and through."

"Be off with ye then," Angus said to the man Graham had nearly taken out. "Let the others know we've truly friends not foes amongst us and see that proper lodgings are made up."

Even more wide-eyed than his superiors, the man nodded then left as another came in with a platter of food and set it on a table beside them. Naturally, Christina dug right in without further prompting, needing to satisfy the use of her magic, or what she called her *lightn'*.

"'Tis bloody impressive," Angus continued, eying Christina and Graham before his eyes went to Jessie and Bryce. "Ye two can do the same then?" His eyes dropped to her ring. "Make it shine like that and move so fast?"

"Aye," Bryce said before Jessie had a chance to respond. He shifted his chair closer and pulled her hand onto his lap as he smiled warmly at her. "But 'tis something we cannae do on request like Graham and Christina. Not yet."

A shiver rippled through her at the unexpected promise in his eyes. While she knew he was doing it for show, it felt so real. "Here, lass," Bryce said softly as he put some food on a plate for her. "You should eat."

She nodded and offered a small smile to Angus and John as they watched her closely, waiting to see if she would elaborate on what Bryce said about their developing connection.

"Thank you for the food and drink." She steered clear of deeper conversation. "Your hospitality is much appreciated."

"Aye," John responded. "'Tis our pleasure." His eyes never strayed from her face. "Do ye mind if I ask ye one more thing then, lass?"

"Not at all," she replied, sensing something bigger coming before he even said it.

"Good." He cocked his head. "Would ye mind telling me why there's a Norsewoman here named Aðísla claiming to be with ye?" His eyebrows perked. "Moreover, why she says yer arrival here might verra well mean our end?"

Chapter Six

B RYCE SHOOK HIS head and narrowed his eyes at Sven later that evening. "Why would she do this? Why would your Aunt Aðísla create havoc here before we even arrived?"

"I don't know." Sven frowned and shook his head. "And I'll have no further answers until she joins us."

"And when will that be?" he asked as his eyes drifted to Jessie. They had been given a small cottage of their own shortly after John's question. They weren't sent off because they couldn't provide a sufficient answer but because rumor had it a strong storm was brewing up north. So Angus and John wanted to see that the ships were well prepared.

Fortunately, the MacDonald men had more trust in the Bruce's faith in them versus the ominous words of a Viking woman. Yet Bryce got the feeling this wasn't the end of it. That they would want answers eventually.

In the meantime, Jessie was listening quietly as she made a poultice out of the flowering plant she had picked earlier. Of the Figwort variety, it was known for its healing properties, and she was determined to treat Bryce's scratch.

"I have been searching out my aunt since I first traveled to Scotland," Sven continued, a frustrated growl in his voice as he spoke stronger words than he likely intended. "Yet she remains a hidden coward."

"Is that right?" came a soft voice before none other than Aðísla entered, her sharp eyes going to Sven as he stood. "Sit, Nephew. *Now*. Then I will explain myself."

"I will not," he replied, irritation obvious in his eyes.

"You will," she shot back, her eyes narrowed. "And you'll do so out of respect not only to an elder but because you're wise enough to know that too much emotion will never get you the answers you seek in life." She cocked her head. "And without the answers you seek, how do you ever intend to keep your people safe?"

Though Sven frowned, Bryce didn't miss the flash of fear in his eyes. "What has happened back home? Do you know something?"

"I know here and now is all that matters." She urged them to join her by the fire. Though her eyes lingered on Jessie, she said nothing. Yet Bryce got the feeling she wanted to. That so much more was going on here. "I know that secrets are still kept and need to be revealed."

"What secrets?" Sven shook his head, troubled. "Tell me…tell us."

"A storm brews," Aðísla said softly. "One that could very well throw history off track." Her eyes went to Bryce. "They're sailing into dangerous weather that will likely shipwreck the lot of them." She scowled. "As I'm sure you all know, John is supposed to deliver news to Robert on the tenth that his father, Angus' fleet, is in the Tay. Not only that but he has already sent scouting ships down to the Farne islands, and the Bass Rock and sent more galleys down to blockade Humber, Bridlington, Whitby, Hartlepool, and Tynemouth." She shook her head. "If they do not arrive safely and on time, history will very likely be changed."

"And all because of weather that shouldn't exist," Jessie murmured. "A storm that never actually happened."

"That's right." Aðísla's eyes went to hers. "You know how to see them through this, yes? Because they fully intend to obey the king's request no matter the peril." Her approval was obvious. "We can only be thankful they are as eager to face danger on the high seas as we Vikings would be." She shook her head. "These men are no cowards."

Jessie clenched her jaw and held Aðísla's eyes before she looked at the fire again and murmured, "There's little I can do about what my…the warlock is doing right now unless I'm with the ships traveling through the weather itself."

"So that is what you need to do," Aðísla said. "Be with those ships." She looked from Bryce to Jessie. "Both of you." Her tone grew ominous. "If this does not happen, all will be lost." Her pained eyes went to Sven. "Which means our descendants will be lost as will their country."

Sven inhaled deeply, clearly disgruntled. "What of the burning dragon symbol that brought me here, to begin with? Does that have to do with why you're here? What will be happening to our people? The prophecy?"

"The prophecy is here and now, Nephew," she stated bluntly as her eyes again drifted to Jessie's face. "As to the dragon on fire, that is not to be worried about." Her eyes met Sven's again. "All that matters is protecting your descendants and seeing them through this curse." Her voice dropped an octave. "All that matters is that you are the man your father and Uncle Heidrek know you to be."

As their eyes held and he offered no response, her voice remained low but intensified. "*Two* kings have sent you here and ask that you protect what matters most. Do you understand, Sven?" Her eyes narrowed. "Do you *truly* understand?"

Though Bryce barely caught it, startled distress flashed in Sven's eyes before he clenched his jaw and nodded once. "I understand."

"Bloody cryptic," Bryce muttered. "All of this."

"Just as cryptic for Sven," Jessie said softly, her eyes still on the fire.

Though frustrated that she defended the Viking, he could admit to being pleased she was kind enough to come to his defense. Sven had done nothing but help him and was a good, albeit quiet friend. In truth, he couldn't be more grateful for his presence these last few weeks. A presence that rarely left Bryce's side.

"We will talk more alone, Nephew," Aðísla said as she stood and gestured at Sven. "So that our friends can rest and be up early, yes?"

He nodded and stood, bidding them goodnight before they departed. Not much in the mood to imbibe any more than Jessie seemed to be, their drinks sat untouched on the table. Though two cots had been provided in their single-room cottage, he sensed her discomfort.

"I'll find another place to," he began before she cut him off.

"No," she murmured and shook her head as her eyes flickered between him and the fire before finally settling on him. "I don't want to be alone…please."

He nodded, as she began applying the poultice. Though it had a rather pungent smell, he could only focus on her delicate scent. It reminded him of wildflowers and evergreen blowing on a springtime wind. Fresh and enticing yet earthy and sweet.

Then, as she continued to touch his skin gently, his dragon picked up another scent entirely. Arousal. In direct response, his own intense need roared to the surface. She was too close and far too tempting. Knowing full well this wasn't the time for such things, he said through clenched teeth, "'Tis all set. Thank ye, lass."

When her eyes whipped to his, it was clear she understood why he needed her to be finished. Thankfully, she nodded, then proceeded to wash her hands in a small bowl before she sat beside him and stared at the fire again.

Though she had done as he asked, Bryce was still overly aware of her. How quickly she was affecting him in general. Those moments at the waterfall had been profound. While yes, he was very impressed by how she saved him, his sole focus at the moment was how her small body had felt against his.

As he rubbed his fingers together, he could still feel the warmth of her in his hands. The firmness yet frailty of her body. Then there was the strength of her mind. The great kindness within her. A beauty that was hard to describe. He had never felt another mind the way he did hers. Not only was it arousing but comforting in a way he couldn't explain. Yet in some small way, it made him wary too.

Mainly because it was a connection he should not enjoy so immensely.

"Ye know I'm promised to marry another," he suddenly blurted softly, his brogue far thicker than intended. He frowned and kept his eyes locked on the fire.

"Yes, I know," she replied just as softly. "And I respect that."

His scowl only deepened as a part of him wanted her to show more emotion. To get a wee bit riled that he might not be available. Though he meant to remain quiet, he kept on talking. "If you respect it, then am I to assume that you dinnae intend to ignite the power of the ring with me?"

Her brows perked slightly as her eyes went to his and she reiterated, "I respect that you're promised to another."

"Yet you're here with me now." He might be many things, but foolish wasn't one of them. "And my ma gave you her magic which means she had faith in…"

He trailed off as it suddenly occurred to him that he was mayhap more foolish than he thought. Had he nearly just used his mother to convince her that she should be with him after he himself said it wasn't possible because of another lass?

"We should rest," she said.

"You should eat," he countered, well aware she had barely touched a bite in Angus' cottage. "You need food, lass."

"Sometimes," she agreed. "But in small portions at times such as these."

He tilted his head in question. "Times such as these?"

"Yes." Her eyes flickered to the fire again before landing squarely on his. "As a rule, if I feel I might need to use my magic in excess, I'm the opposite of Christina. Nourishment is not necessary. If anything, it drains my spiritual self because it pulls me back into my physical body." Her voice dropped to a whisper. "Oftentimes, I'm sort of like a monk fasting to reach a part of himself that might otherwise be unattainable."

Just when he thought Jessie couldn't surprise him any more, she did.

"Aye," was all he could manage as he mulled that over. He knew nothing of her magic or the strength of her powers. Which reminded him how much he wished Adlin and Grant were here. They could mayhap understand it better.

"I ate enough already," she assured, her eyes still on his. "I'm all right, Bryce. Really."

He almost shook his head. She was the furthest thing from all right, and he could feel it in all the little things she did without realizing. By how her forefinger slid back and forth slowly along her right thumb. By the way she swallowed a tad bit too often because her throat had gone dry. More than anything though, he sensed it in the erratic beat of her heart. It went too fast when it should go slow and too slow when it should go fast.

That's when he realized how much she tried to keep herself under control. How much she had trained herself to keep the warlocks from knowing her true reactions.

Though tempted to ask more about his sister, he wanted to understand Jessie better first. "Tell me what happened after you opened your grandfather's book." His eyes went to the pocket in her dress where he knew it lay. "Tell me about what happened in those first few years after your house burned and you became master to…" How to phrase this? "Things so powerful."

Jessie eyed him, clearly hesitant before she finally spoke. "At first, it was a living nightmare for both my mother and me." Though she wrapped her fingers together on her lap as though at ease, he caught their slight tremble as she remembered. "Though Mama hired men to remove the debris from the fire, the warlocks would not allow anyone else to rebuild. Rather, they used their magic alongside mine to reconstruct a small log cabin." She swallowed hard. "It allowed them to keep better tabs on us."

Bryce couldn't imagine what that must have been like. "I dinnae mean to sound insensitive, but I find it curious they allowed your mother to live at all."

"Only because I convinced them that I needed her as I came into my magic," she replied. "That I was far too young to be without a parent. Not to mention without a parent or legal guardian, I would be placed in another home." Her voice grew soft. "But then eventually, of course, it didn't matter."

When he frowned in question, she said, "The only reason I kept my sanity around them was because of my magic." She clenched her jaw as emotion flickered in her eyes. "Someone with no magic will end up turning very bad themselves, or eventually lose their mind." She released a choppy breath. "I'm afraid Mama fell into the latter category. Though she held on for longer than I would've expected, she was pretty much insane by the time I turned eighteen."

"Och," he whispered. "I'm so sorry, lass."

"It's okay," she murmured. "Her death was swift in the end. Once the warlocks realized how far gone she really was, they ended her life before she could possibly harm me." She trembled again. "At least the warlock who did it was mercifully fast about it."

How bloody terrible. Did Jessie's nightmares never end? He clenched his teeth in anger, more than eager to finish off these warlocks if for no other reason than to avenge her.

Determined to offer her some level of comfort, he rested his hand over hers. Though she jerked slightly at his touch, she didn't pull away as she continued talking.

"There's little to tell about the in-between years except that I was always watched closely," she said. "As I got older my friendship with Milly, Lindsay and Christina was only allowed because they served a purpose. They were part of the plan."

"For the most part, your upbringing and time since must have been verra lonesome," he said. "Did you spend a lot of time speaking with these warlocks? 'Tis hard to imagine you didnae."

"I did here and there," she conceded. "Mostly to the one tasked with spending more time with me as I grew. The same one who ended my mother. I spoke with him at length when he...*it* was around. Or should I say, when it made itself known. Because one way or another they were always watching me."

"It sounds like you were almost fond of that one," he remarked. "Shocking, considering it killed your mother."

"Yes, but like I said, it was mercifully quick." She shook her head. "The others would have drawn it out and made it excruciating to feed their own dark desires. Especially the one with my grandfather's essence."

"Is that the one affecting the weather now?"

She nodded. "Yes."

"'Tis surprising he fights us first considering how powerful he is." Something occurred to him as newfound distress flashed in her eyes. "Unless, though not necessarily more powerful, the last warlock is far more difficult for you to destroy." He narrowed his eyes. "The last one is the merciful warlock, isn't it?"

"Yes," she whispered.

"Then you must let me take control when 'tis time to face him," he said. "You must let me end him for you."

Jessie offered a single small nod, her eyes trained on the fire once more. "The only way that will be possible is by igniting the power of this ring."

"Aye." He squeezed her hand gently. "Then we will do that, lass."

"How though?" Her eyes returned to his. "When you're promised to another?"

True and it was something he'd been giving a great deal of thought to since his grandfather had said not to fight an attraction to Jessie. More so, since he witnessed what his mother was willing to do for her.

"You say you were close to Ainsley." He watched her intently. "So it stands to reason you might know more about the prophetic vision my sister shared with my dying grandmother. The one about who I'm to marry."

"I know little more than you," she murmured as she pulled her hand from his. "What I do know is that there were only four MacLomain men meant for my friends and me." Her eyes leveled with his. "And you are, without a doubt, one of them."

"So then we've a riddle to solve." He finally took a swig of ale. "Because if what you say is true than you're the lass Ainsley was talking about. It can be no other way." He cast her a curious sidelong glance. "That means she could verra well have been sending a cryptic warning, aye? Preparing me for what I might face with you?"

She frowned. "I don't understand what you're getting at."

He had to give her credit. She was very good at lying. But he saw a little something there in her guarded expression. She was keeping something from him. Something very important.

"I think you do know what I'm getting at," he said softly, his eyes never wavering from hers as he became more confident about his speculations. "Ainsley said I was destined to marry an unnamed lass who will always love another. She never said it wasnae a Broun lass. So it could verra well be you." He tilted his head and narrowed his eyes as he became more sure of himself. As the most likely possibility became clear. "So keeping in mind that *you* are my destined wife, I can only wonder…who do you love, lass? Who is it you will always love?"

Thick tension fell as their gazes held and her eyes grew moist.

While he figured for sure she would continue lying or fabricate some wild tale to defend herself, she instead shocked him when she whispered the last thing he expected.

"You."

Chapter Seven

THOUGH IT MIGHT not be the best move considering her current circumstances, Jessie took a few sips of ale before she finally came clean with Bryce. Because the truth, no matter how uncomfortable it made her, needed to be shared sooner rather than later if they hoped to save Scotland.

"When I told you that I figured I was meant to be with you because you're a dragon and my strongest element is fire, that wasn't the whole truth." She shook her head. "Not by a long shot." She took another sip of ale before she rallied her courage and met his eyes again. "As you know, one of the last two warlocks possesses a part of my grandfather's essence." Her voice softened as her eyes stayed with his. "The other warlock possesses yours, Bryce."

Renewed shock settled on his face. "That's impossible."

"No it's not," she murmured. "The warlock was at the conception of the rings as was your essence." She flinched. "The truth is, making you part of him was rather brilliant." She took another few sips and ignored the warmth spreading through her. "What better way to fight me in the end if need be?"

"'Tis truly unsettling." Bryce crossed his arms over his chest. "How did it know to steal some of my essence when my cousins' essences were part of the process as well?"

"Simple really." Jessie did her best to hold his gaze. "It took the essence of the soul most compatible with mine." She swallowed hard again. "Dark magic is capable of many things but above all recognizing good souls and bad. Even good ones that can be turned bad or vice versa. Along those same lines, it can see compatible souls lining up almost like DNA markers of close family members." She shrugged. "So yes, while there was the slightest possibility the warlock could've been wrong when he picked yours, it turned out he wasn't."

"Och," Bryce muttered as he downed half his mug then eyed her again. "So am I to understand I'm missing part of my soul?"

"Yes and no," she said. "What he took from you was more cloned than anything…sort of…it's very hard to explain."

"Well, try." A heavy frown settled on his face. "Please."

"While what he took from you doesn't affect the man you've become or the soul growth you've experienced in this life, you're bound to feel complete in an unexplainable way once he's gone," she said. "Yet, as you've grown so has he. In fact, it was the part of you in him that kept me strong all these years. The only real light that existed for me."

He downed the rest of his ale, his eyes never leaving hers as his brogue grew so thick she barely understood him. "So I'm to ken ye fell in love with this warlock version of me then, aye?" His brows snapped together. "So I'm in competition with…myself." He managed to pour more ale without ever taking his eyes off of her. "And ye'll always be in love with him according to Ainsley." He shook his head. "How do we ignite yer ring then?" His brows shot up. "More than that, how do we, *I*, really trust ye through all this when ye love the bloody enemy?"

"It's not him I love," she whispered. "It's you." She shook her head, frustrated. "What Ainsley shared with your grandmother was the only way to prepare you for me without flat out saying it. As it was, the warlocks could sometimes track her too. If they did, they would think, based on her words, that I remain devoted to them…him. That I was very much on their side." She kept shaking her head. "But as I've already said, I'm not." She clenched her jaw. "I never was."

"But how do I know that with any certainty?" he said. "Unlike you, I dinnae have the benefit of knowing you better, or at least parts of you, as you did with me."

"Not yet," she murmured. "But I strongly suspect you will as our journey continues." Her eyes never left his. "As we grow closer, I believe you will start to recall his memories of me. Your memories so to speak. Once he's gone, and you get your essence back, you should remember everything."

"But they *arenae* my memories," he argued, a flash of aggravation in his eyes. "They are his...*its*."

"But they *will* be yours in the end." She dropped her eyes to the fire again, not sure what else she could say to convince him.

"I dinnae ken why Ainsley would bother preparing me for you," he muttered, "when you yourself said she was desperate to connect me with a Broun lass so I would be protected by the MacLomain, Broun connection."

"You can't fault the impulsive act of someone that loves you so much and is determined to protect you," she said softly. "Ainsley knew full well what the warlocks were capable of and while yes, she knew you and I were destined for one another she was terrified for you." She shook her head. "She never should have contacted your grandmother, but I think in some ways it was impossible for her to stay away. You were her family though she had very little time with you."

She cleared her throat, uncomfortable continuing though she did regardless. "Your sister very much wanted us to be together and got that message across to you and your family the only way she knew how."

Silence fell for a stretch as his eyes settled on the fire and he digested what she had shared. Every second felt like an eternity. How did he truly feel about being meant for her? Did he believe what she had said about Ainsley? While tempted to follow his thoughts, she did her best to keep her mind respectfully disconnected from his. This was a lot of troubling information for anyone, and he deserved his privacy while he came to terms with it.

After what seemed like centuries, he murmured, "We will rest for the eve then on the morrow you will begin telling me about some of these memories you and the warlock shared. 'Tis important that I get a better idea of what I'm up against...how close you truly got to him..."

The suspicious way he said it made her eyes go to his. What she saw there, however, was not what she expected. While yes, there was some doubt, there was also jealousy. Though a strange little bolt of pleasure went through her at that, she focused on what he was really getting at.

"I shared no intimacies with him," she said, being honest. "That's not to say he didn't want as much."

Bryce's eyes narrowed a fraction. "Did you as well?"

"I'd be lying if I said that on occasion I wasn't curious. He was the closest I've ever come to love or being desired by a man." She shook her head. "Yet I always knew his touch would be no different than the others. Very, very unpleasant. Contact with something born of evil is indescribable." She took a deep breath and pushed memories of her mother down. "That's why I was so grateful Mama's death was swift."

Bryce nodded but said nothing more as they went to bed. No matter how much she tried to give him privacy, his troubling thoughts still came through here and there. How sad he was about her life. How frustrated he was that a warlock had stolen a small piece of him before he was even conceived. Angry that his sister had somehow gotten wrapped up in all this.

She was a little surprised by what was most prevalent in his mind though. That a warlock had so many memories with her when he did not. That the warlock was there to offer her some small measure of peace where Bryce was not.

Yet who he was at heart *was* there with her all along. Because what the warlock stole from him was a mere piece of a whole that was good. That was Bryce. A man who would do anything to protect those he cared about. Moreover, a man who would always protect someone in danger.

Though she thought she would have trouble sleeping alone in the same room with him, the opposite proved true, and she drifted off to sleep quickly. When she woke, it was daylight, and he was roasting rabbit on a small spit over the fire.

As if he knew she was waking up, his eyes went to hers, and he nodded. "Good morn, lass."

"Good morning," she murmured, relieved that he didn't seem upset anymore.

"I hunted." He gestured at the table. "And brought in some fresh water." His eyes went to a satchel. "Christina made sure you had a change of clothes too."

She nodded, thankful, as she joined him and took a few sips of water. "I appreciate all this."

He nodded and said nothing more at first. When he did finally speak, his words were measured. "While I didn't go into much detail, you should know that for their own safety, I warned Graham,

Christina, Sven, and Aðísla about how verra dangerous the last warlock really is." His eyes turned to hers. "And that it might have a hold over you that we all need to prepare for."

She nodded, understanding his need to share with them. Because if things took an unfortunate turn and she wasn't strong enough in the end, it would be necessary for them to treat her like the enemy.

"Furthermore," he continued as he removed the cooked rabbit and began slicing off several pieces. "I've decided that though I'm eager to learn more about the connection you shared with the last warlock, you've been through a lot and dinnae need to be pestered straightaway."

His eyes returned to hers as he handed her a plate of meat. "I also wanted to thank you for being so honest with me last night. You've dealt with far more than most and need good people around you now." He shook his head. "Sharing such things could have verra well put you at risk if we chose not to believe you."

Would it ever have.

"But we *do* believe you, Jessie," he went on. "*I* believe you." He poured her some more water. "So now we will move forward with trust between us rather than doubt. Because as far as I can see, there is no other way. Not if we hope to ignite the power of your ring."

She didn't realize how truly concerned she had been until he said those words. Until he gave her such sound reassurance. She blinked several times as an unexpected wave of emotion rolled over her.

"Thank you," she whispered. "You don't know how grateful I am to hear you say that."

"Aye, then," he murmured. He cleared his throat before his eyes met hers and he made a declaration she didn't see coming. "I intend to move forward with the certain knowledge that you are without a doubt the lass I'm meant to marry. Therefore, I will pursue you with that in mind." He shook his head and took her hand. "That means I will make sure you have no further designs on a simple piece of me when you can have the whole of me."

Her cheeks warmed beneath the determination in his eyes, the flicker of fire. She saw not just his but his dragon's intent. Before all was said and done, he meant to seduce her. Which made perfect sense and was truly the only way to ignite the ring. Still, she suddenly felt like a novice. She had no experience. Nothing to offer him.

"Dinnae worry, lass," he said softly, obviously catching those thoughts. "I have enough experience for us both." Her heart skipped a beat as he brushed his finger over the tender flesh of her inner wrist. "When the time comes, the last thing that will be on your mind will be pleasing me." The devil lit his eyes and the corner of his lips curled up. "In truth, ye'll be unable to focus on anything but how I make ye feel."

Now her cheeks were flat out burning. While some women might be put off by his forthright arrogance, she wasn't. Mainly because she knew it was the truth and in some small way appreciated his confidence. After all, a part of her had wanted this for a very long time. Him. The chance to be together when she had begun to give up hope.

As they ate, they chatted about less serious things. Normal stuff like the types of food they liked and enjoyable pastimes. She shared her love for herbs and skills at healing. He shared his various responsibilities as laird that, naturally, made up a big part of his life.

"The poultice soothed my wound greatly," he said. "Thank you, lass."

"Of course," she replied, glad to hear it.

"Though I thought to wait, I find myself eager to know more about my sister," he finally said, his eyes both sad and curious as they met hers. "Might you share a wee bit about the time you spent with Ainsley? What she was like?"

While some might speculate he was testing her to see how well she really knew his sister, she sensed that wasn't his intention at all. He had already made the decision to pursue Jessie with or without this information. He simply wanted to know the sister he never got a chance to meet.

"It would be my pleasure." Jessie offered a soft smile as she remembered her friend. "In some ways, she was a lot like you. Protective, brave," she shook her head, "a little stubborn." Then she smiled. "Definitely playful. She loved embracing her dragon and flying all over New England." She chuckled. "I think she gave conspiracy theorists more to talk about than Area 51."

A small smile ghosted his face. "What is Area 51?"

"A highly classified Air Force facility in Nevada," she informed. "Long speculated to be a place where the government hides anything related to extra-terrestrials." She gave him a pointed look and even a wink. "So basically, like Ainsley's dragon, not all that believable."

"So she could shift even in spirit form," he mused. "I would not have thought it."

"She could, and she was beautiful." Jessie had been so impressed. "She was black as night and huge...and of course mischievous." She looked up at the ceiling and smiled as though it were the night sky in Maine. "She picked evenings bright with moonlight so that those who were more susceptible to seeing spirits wouldn't miss her."

"Her dragon looks like mine then," he said softly. "I always wondered when I imagined what it would've been like to fly alongside her." He shook his head. "I suppose it makes sense she would look like me considering we were twins."

Though he clearly warred with a variety of emotions, the look in his eyes was only thankful as they met hers and she continued sharing stories. While most memories of Ainsley were very good and Jessie's only salvation, her friend had a more secretive side too.

"But she was also mysterious."

"How so," he asked.

"I just always got the feeling she kept something from me," she said. "And that whatever it was bothered her greatly."

They didn't talk much more about it because there wasn't much to say. Jessie had no idea then and certainly no clue now as to what her friend might have been hiding from her. She supposed at this point it didn't matter because Ainsley was gone. Or at least it had felt that way until sharing childhood memories with Bryce. Reminiscing with her brother kept Ainsley alive in some small way, and Jessie was grateful for it.

"So did the warlocks worry that you might be a dragon too?" Bryce asked. "Considering they thought you two were sisters."

"No, they knew everything I was." She shook her head. "So I was no threat."

"Yet as it turned out, you verra much were," he murmured, clearly impressed by her as they continued talking. Unfortunately, however, considering how much she enjoyed chatting with him, they eventually had to get going.

By the time she changed—during which he waited outside—he seemed much more at ease with her than before. She, in turn, felt the same. It was one thing to know him in a sense through the warlock and another to get to know the man himself. As far as she could tell, he was as noble and kind as she always knew he would be. Unlike the warlock, however, he had a sense of humor and was quick to smile.

"So has Angus or John confirmed that history has unfolded as it should have up to this point?" she asked as she joined him and they started toward the ships where everyone else was supposed to meet them. The day was cloudy and somewhat windy. Not too bad a day for sailing.

"Aye, all seems to have gone as history tells it, and it has been an eventful year for King Edward II." He grinned as they reflected on everything that had happened leading up to Robert the Bruce requesting Angus' aid. "As told, it started badly with a continuing revolt by Edward's cousin, the Earl of Lancaster and Humphrey de Bohun, Earl of Hereford after Edward reneged on undertakings made at a parliament in 1321 to limit him and his favorites abuses of power." He shook his head. "And as reported, Edward was further enraged by the judicial murder of Piers Gaveston whose head was presented to the Earl of Lancaster."

Edward and Piers had shared a very close relationship. Though some accounts said they were merely dear friends, most claimed they were lovers.

"As we know, Piers' murder angered him enough that Edward enlisted the aid of Sir Andrew Harclay," she said, "and defeated Lancaster and Hereford at the battle of Boroughbridge in March."

"Aye." Bryce scowled. "Encouraged by his success in downing two of his most dangerous enemies, the bloody bastard decided to invade Scotland. Accompanied by his wife Queen Isabella, he marched to Edinburgh with an army estimated to be no more than sixty thousand strong."

Jessie nodded as she reflected on what had been happening in this country since Graham and Christina's adventure in thirteen fourteen. The series of events that led to Edward's recent invasion.

King Robert the Bruce had sought a peace treaty so that the war ravaged realm of Scotland could recover. Of course, this treaty would also recognize Scotland as an independent kingdom with himself as its rightful king.

Unfortunately, Edward agreed to no such thing.

So, each year Robert instigated forays into Northern England to extract tribute and gather booty to help rebuild the bankrupt Scottish economy. Accordingly, he sent Sir James Douglas and Sir Thomas Randolph in a series of wide ranging raids into Northumberland, Cumberland, Lancashire, Durham and Yorkshire to accomplish his goals. The hope was that by doing so, it would put enough pressure on the English barons to persuade Edward to agree to the treaty after all.

Each year Scotland's coffers were slowly replenished, and the process of rebuilding started. Despite the serious ebbing of a high percentage of the English economy to Scotland, Edward still refused to negotiate. That meant a good number of his lords were in revolt and his position was becoming untenable.

As it turned out, it was two of those lords, both dangerous enemies, that Edward defeated at Boroughbridge, so it was no wonder he felt emboldened enough to strike Scotland once again.

"You know a great deal about my country's history," Bryce remarked, clearly impressed as he followed her thoughts.

"More then you can imagine," she said, remembering all too well the endless research. "I had to in order to be ready. I had much to anticipate."

"'Tis hard to imagine," he said softly, taking her hand as the crowd thickened, "that you could have kept track of everything."

"It came easier than it would for most," she explained, "because I was part of the curse and so closely affiliated with the warlocks." She shook her head. "Destroying Scotland was the sole purpose of their existence which meant they were very thorough about its history…as was I through them."

Bryce nodded, as they chatted about and continued reflecting on the years that led up to now.

Naturally, angered by Edward's invasion, Robert the Bruce reacted with savage energy and resolve. Giving citizens fair warning in advance to evacuate, he instituted a 'Scorched earth' policy in the Merse and Lothians. All the livestock were driven to safe places.

Granaries were emptied and what could not be transported away was set on fire. The roofs of houses were torn off and burnt, and any growing crops were trampled to deny them to the English.

Bridges were destroyed, wells befouled with manure and carcasses and streams were dammed causing morasses and floods. He sent James Douglas and four thousand moss-troopers—marauders who operated in the mosses or bogs—with two thousand highland clansmen to harry the English army in Durham as they marched north. There they burned all before them including food, forage, and shelter that might be of use to the English.

"King Robert himself led an expedition of eight thousand light cavalry and highland clansmen," Bryce remarked as he gestured at the ships ahead, "supported by the galleys of Angus in a long range sweeping raid into the northwest of England, sacking Preston and pillaging scores of other towns."

By doing this, King Robert hoped that Edward would turn back to defend his northern shires, but instead, Edward fell out with Sir Andrew Harclay on policy and ordered him to confine Bruce to Northern England while Edward ravaged Scotland.

"Sir Andrew Harclay protested at Edward's unmilitary division of the English forces." Jessie shook her head but could only be grateful for the English king's poor judgement. "Andrew warned him it would leave the English army unbalanced and short of archers."

"Aye," Bryce said, pleased. "Edward, backed by the Earl of Richmond, dismissed the only competent military leader he had."

"Which worked out great for King Robert I'd say." She met Bryce's grin. "Seeing how Andrew Harclay retired in a huff to Carlisle with his army and came to an accommodation with Robert."

"'Twas a good one too," Bryce said. "Leave me alone, and I'll leave you alone."

With Andrew out of the way, Robert moved fast and reached the Scottish border in late July where he immediately mobilized his forces.

By this point, King Edward occupied Edinburgh and Leith setting up home in Holyrood with Queen Isabella. Having been forewarned, over three-quarters of the populace had fled the city. The remaining quarter who remained, unfortunately, thought they would receive preferential treatment. Sadly, they did not.

Edward's army soon discovered foraging would be impossible. Foraging parties were ambushed by the moss-troopers under James Douglas. Food became so scarce that the English were beginning to eat their own horses. So Edward finally did what he should have done earlier. He organized supply ships to sail from the Humber, Tees, and Tyne to replenish his army.

Upon confirmation of this news, Robert the Bruce contacted Angus Óg MacDomhnaill.

It was time to cut off the English's supply ships.

So here they all were.

"Have you ever been on a ship?" Bryce asked as they drew closer to shore. "More than that, how do you intend to get a fleet of ships through bad weather?"

"With help from all of you." Her eyes met his. "Thankfully, we have the right people along on this journey." Her eyes went to Christina and Graham who stood on one of the docks. "A witch with superhuman strength and instincts as well as her wizard whose element is water."

He frowned. "Will that be enough though?"

"No." She shook her head as her eyes returned to his. "It's going to take all of us to get through this...including, quite possibly, yours and Sven's dragons."

He nodded slowly as he took her meaning. "You think we'll need to shift."

"It could very well come down to that."

Bryce eyed her for another moment before he nodded again. "Aye, then, lass, whatever you need."

They both knew it would be no small thing if he and Sven shifted. If nothing else, it would be hard to explain away to a fleet of Scottish ships afterward.

"You didnae answer my question," he prompted as they started down the dock. "Have you ever been on a boat let alone ships the likes of these?"

"No." She slowed, eyed the water and swallowed hard as it all became very real. "In fact, I have an unnatural fear of anything that takes me off the ground."

~Avenged by a Highland Laird~

Chapter Eight

UP UNTIL THIS moment, he thought they might just have a chance of seeing Angus safely around the north of Scotland. Now he wasn't so sure. Not based on how pale Jessie's skin had become as she eyed the ocean.

"Is it a fear of water then…or *anything* that takes you off the ground?" He frowned, surprised because she didn't seem frightened of the waterfall.

"It's all part of the curse," she said softly. "As I told you, I'm better protected by Earth and fire. Air and water are more difficult for me to navigate and make me more vulnerable to the warlocks." Her eyes stayed with his as if seeking comfort. "So it's rather ironic that sailing ships through a storm is part of my journey with you."

So it was more a fear of the warlocks than anything.

Or could it be something else?

Because for a moment there it almost felt related to dragons.

"Are you frightened of dragons, lass?" he couldn't help but ask though it made no sense considering her time spent with Ainsley. Rather than point that out, he referred instead to her disposition when they first met. "Back at the beginning, you didn't seem all that fond of us."

"I love dragons," she exclaimed. "I only acted that way because I've had to for so long. Anything MacLomain related must be shunned." Confusion lit her eyes. "Though you're right to ask because for a moment there I did feel something toward dragons…an unexplainable negativity." She shook her head. "Whatever it was it's gone now."

She said as much, but he sensed her emotions were overwhelming her. Fear of the unknown and at the forefront, discomfort that she had no control over the warlocks or even her own emotions.

Determined to help her in any way he could, he stopped, cupped her shoulders and made sure her eyes stayed with his. "'Tis normal to fear things in life that we cannae control. Yet remember this. You wouldnae be here if it wasnae meant to be and you couldnae handle it." He shook his head and reminded. "And you wouldnae be here with Sven, Christina, Graham and me if we werenae the people best suited to help you."

"And Aðísla," she whispered, her dark eyes never straying from his as she gathered strength.

"Aye." He grinned, hoping to make her smile. "If nothing else, she will keep Sven fiercer than he already is."

A small smile hovered on her lips. "True."

"You're far braver and stronger than anyone I've ever met." Caught in how good it felt to see her eyes lighten a little, he cupped her soft cheek. "And now you're not alone. You've got your friends and me along with you."

"Yes," she whispered as she bit her lower lip when it began trembling. She seemed to be gathering herself before she continued. "I'm sorry. Now that the warlocks are no longer part of me, I seem to have a great deal of trouble fighting emotions."

"Aye, 'tis just fine, lass." He couldn't help but pull her into his arms and offer her comfort. "'Tis understandable."

He enjoyed the feel of her in his arms. How she stiffened at first then softened against him as she realized she was safe. That though he wasn't as powerful as her in magic, he would always do his best to protect her.

Where some might tell her to rally her strength in front of Angus and his men to prove she could help navigate this mission, he would not. He would never tell her to stop feeling now that she finally could again. Instead, he would help her through all her emotions. He would support her any way he could but never in such a fashion that she reverted back to the emotionless creature she had to become with the warlocks.

After she had drifted off to sleep last night, he poured himself another ale, sat back against the wall next to his cot and simply watched her. He might have been overwhelmed by all she had shared, but it hadn't stopped him from staring at her for hours, his desire only growing. Though he knew it was likely the ring at work, a part of him rebelled at it being that simple.

While yes, he was initially frustrated with her for keeping more secrets, the fact remained that she was truly the most admirable person he had ever met. To have lived her life like she did even after she watched her mother fade away like that. To have pre-planned so much and kept these warlocks tricked for so long went far beyond what most would be capable of. Not just magically but mentally.

She had given up life as most knew it to protect Scotland. And she had done it alongside a warlock that offered her a glimpse of normalcy...of love. Though he still couldn't entirely wrap his mind around what that meant, he knew one thing for sure. The beast had exploited what should have only been between Bryce and Jessie.

And Bryce *would* exact his revenge.

He *refused* to be grateful to the creature.

Rather, he kept firmly in mind that though the warlock had given her some light within darkness, it was all a trick. It had used Bryce to give her a false sense of appreciation and love.

He fully intended to show her what real love was. How someone of her caliber *should* be loved. He wasn't precisely sure when he had come to that decision. All he knew was that he had. That he *would*. More so, he was surprised to realize as they sat together and chatted this morning, he *wanted* to. He wanted to show her the world in a whole new way. To help her see that there was so much more to life than then the tragedy she had lived up until now.

"It's good to see you two getting along so well," Christina said, interrupting his thoughts.

Bryce released Jessie when she pulled away and offered her friend a wobbly smile in greeting. Only then did he note the dampness in her eyes or felt the slight moisture on his chest where her cheek had rested.

She had followed his every thought.

"Are you okay, sweetie?" Christina said softly, her eyes alarmed as she noted Jessie's distress.

"I am." Jessie nodded, blinked away the moisture and gave Bryce a thankful look. "More so by the moment, actually."

Christina looked from him back to Jessie, clearly seeing what that meant, before she offered Jessie a warm smile. "Are you all right to come look at the ships?"

"Well, I better be because we're setting sail soon enough." Jessie nodded, indeed surer by the moment as she glanced at him one more time before she took Christina's offered hand and continued down the dock with her.

Bryce could tell by her confident stride as he followed behind them that she would be able to handle this. She was starting to see that there was life beyond the repressed place she had been for so long. That with the support of not only him but her friends, she could face anything.

Angus greeted them from the biggest galley of them all, waving for them to come aboard. "Ye'll travel on my ship until we've made it around the north of Scotland then ye can travel with John if ye like."

He wasn't surprised to find Sven and Aðísla already aboard eying the boat. As far as he could tell, they were impressed, and that was no small thing. Graham was there as well, not letting Christina too far out of his sight with so many men around. Or it could very well be that he meant to be readily available if she was in need.

He couldn't help but chuckle, aware of the overly amorous effects Christina suffered after she used her magic. Side effects only Graham could assuage. Following his thoughts, Graham met his grin. He imagined his cousin urged her to use her magic at every opportunity in light of such a thing.

"If it's all the same to you, Laird Angus," Jessie said. "I think it would be wiser if my friends and I split up and travel on three separate ships."

"Aye then?" He cocked his head. "Are ye sure?"

She nodded. "I am." Her eyes swept over his fleet. "Bryce and I will travel with you. Graham and Christina with John." Her eyes went to the Vikings. "Aðísla and Sven on whatever vessel seems the least threatening."

Angus frowned but didn't wear the condescending expression most chieftains let alone a captain might wear when a lass gave him orders. "Why?"

"Because when push comes to shove, they will be your best kept secret," she replied. "A back-up plan so to speak."

106

"I *do* like a good back-up plan." Angus looked from the Vikings to Jessie, pondering with a wicked gleam in his eyes. "Care to share more, lassie?"

She stood up a little straighter, notched her chin and never looked away. "Not right now."

He eyed her for a moment, stroking his beard before a sly grin turned into a wide smile. "Aye, then my wee lassie, 'twill be as ye wish."

Bryce didn't miss her slight slump of relief before she straightened again. He stepped close and rested his hand on the middle of her back in support. Some might say he should stay away and let her appear strong, but he was done letting her stand on her own all the time. If Angus or any of his crew saw that as a weakness, so be it.

They could bloody well deal with his dragon.

A soft smile came to her lips as her eyes met his. Again, she was following his every thought, and he was glad.

"Let's get the cargo loaded then all hands on deck!" Angus roared. "We depart within the hour!"

Soon enough, his words were repeated from ship to ship, and men sprang into action. The extra cargo's sole purpose was to weigh the ships down in preparation for stormy seas. A fully-loaded ship was safer than an empty one so long as the cargo was stowed correctly. That way the weight in the hull counteracted the force of the winds on the sails and rigging during heavy winds. This reduced the risk of the ship rolling on its side. If that happened, they were all done for.

Before he lumbered off, Angus looked at the sky, chuckled and winked at Jessie. "Ready yer sea legs, my wee lassie." Relish lit his eyes. "'Tis going to be the devil's own ride by the morrow's eve for sure."

She offered a surprisingly roguish grin. "Aye, aye, captain."

Christina's brows shot up with amusement as she looked at Jessie. "Just listen to you, darlin'. Already quite the seafarer."

Jessie grinned as Christina urged her to join her.

"C'mon sweetie," she said. "I met a nice seamstress that's going to provide us with clothing for the journey."

Jessie nodded, glanced at Bryce one more time with a warm smile, then followed. He was thrown off balance by how much that smile affected him. How much more of it he wanted to see. Particularly if it was aimed his way.

"Jessie's doing better by the moment, aye?" Graham said.

"Aye," Bryce responded as Angus insisted they make themselves at home and tour the ships. "As I told ye this morn, she's lived a verra lonely existence. So 'twill only do her good to finally have so much support and caring around her."

"Aye, then," Graham agreed. "Christina and I will help any way we can. Jessie isnae alone in this anymore."

Bryce nodded, grateful that his kin stood so readily by her side. While he knew it was in part because of their lasses, he also felt it was because they were simply a good, sympathetic lot. Especially Graham with his inherent need to save everyone since Fraser's death. They had talked at length while hunting so Graham knew they would know nothing more about their deceased cousin until her warlock was defeated.

No, not *her* warlock.

Not anymore.

A little under an hour later, having toured the ships and been given their own provisions for the journey, Graham and Bryce stood at the end of the dock with Sven. As it turned out, Angus had not only built a captain's cabin on his ship but even constructed a few small walled off areas for sleeping. One of which he had insisted Bryce and Jessie use.

"It was wise of Jessie to put us on three ships," Sven murmured, eying the sky with as much relish as Angus. An eagerness inherent to a man born to sea and adventure. "Jessie will do well on the open waters." He nodded. "She is a natural."

Bryce perked his brows at Sven. "Aye? How do ye know?"

"Because I watched her on Angus' ship." His steadfast eyes never left the horizon. "The sea has a good roll today, and the ships are listing more than usual." He shook his head. "Yet not once did she falter or lose her step." His eyes finally met Bryce's. "Her stomach will not grow uneasy even in the roughest of waters. She will be okay out there and keep a level mind."

He nodded. "'Tis verra good to hear."

Aware of her more by the moment, Bryce knew she was heading his way before she even made it to the dock. Not just him but his dragon seemed incredibly in tune with her. Yet she wasn't dragon, was she? Though he expected to feel sadness at that, he didn't.

"She is something just as good and just as powerful," Sven whispered, his eyes going to her as well. At first, he thought the Viking might be attracted to her but soon realized the way Sven looked at Jessie was similar to how he looked at Christina.

With respect.

Yet there was something else in Sven's eyes. Something beyond respect.

"What do ye know about her that we dinnae?" Bryce asked.

Sven's eyes lingered on her for another moment before returning to Bryce. "You must find that out for yourself, my friend."

When Bryce scowled, Graham clasped his shoulder, grinned and shook his head. "'Tis always an adventure with our lasses, Cousin. Enjoy it rather than fight it, aye?"

"Aye, then," he muttered but could fully admit as he watched her that there was plenty to enjoy. Though the dress she wore was simple in design, she had never looked more bonny with her hair blowing wild in the wind. It seemed by the very minute, she was becoming more and more alive as she laughed and smiled at something Christina said.

"Och, look at ye then," Graham said softly.

When Bryce managed to tear his eyes away from her and frown at his cousin in question, Graham grinned. "Ye just wore a smile to match hers, Cousin. And 'twas as wide as our country itself."

Completely unaware but not surprised, Bryce nodded then headed their way. "Aye then, let's go see to our lasses."

Less than a half hour later, sails with the black ship emblem of the MacDonald's unfurled and they were heading up the western shores of Scotland. The water was choppy and the wind gusty, but it was by no means a bad day for sailing. If anything, the wind worked in their favor as the day turned into evening.

"'Twill soon be a bonny sight if I'm reading my skies right." Angus, who had invited Bryce and Jessie to dine in his captain's quarters, rose his mug in salute and smiled broadly. "I foresee blackened skies and dangerous seas ahead indeed!" He narrowed one eager eye at Jessie. "So what are we facing then, lassie? What sort of evil wants to take down my bloody ships?"

In all truth, Bryce was starting to suspect Angus and his son were a wee bit touched. How else could it be when a chieftain remained this boisterously happy with such danger on the horizon? Had Bryce and Jessie been lured by the enemy in a way they never saw coming by sailing into a storm with a madman?

"It's an evil unlike anything you've ever seen," Jessie said gravely as she sipped her ale then shook her head, a little twinkle in her eyes. If he wasn't mistaken, the drink was going straight to her head as she leaned forward and narrowed one eye right back at Angus. "You'll have to trust me every step of the way." Her eyes narrowed even further as she challenged him. "Can you do that then?"

Their gazes held before Angus fell back in his chair, belly-laughing before he took a hearty swig of ale and nodded. "Och, aye, I see my son and me sailing straight into the pits of Hell for ye, my wee lassie."

"Good, glad that's settled." She nodded with approval as she twisted her hair into a rope then tied it in a sloppy but surprisingly becoming knot. "There." She smiled at them. "Much better."

Angus tilted his head and considered the stray pieces sticking up here and there on her head. "Aye, then, 'tis a good look for ye lassie!" Then they tapped mugs as he nodded. "Verra good look indeed!"

Meanwhile, Bryce fed Jessie random bits of meat and bannock without her overly realizing what he was doing. Not only was she small but new to alcohol. And while he reveled in the idea of her letting loose because she deserved it, he would not let this go on much longer. Though she might be a natural on a ship, he could guarantee that she would not appreciate a hangover on the morrow. Not on rough seas.

"So when will ye tell me what will be happening," Angus murmured, his chuckles dying down and his eyes sharper than expected as he looked between them.

When Jessie leaned forward, offered a lopsided grin and whispered with a slight slur, "That's on a need to know basis, m'dear," Bryce knew it was time to call it a night.

"*'Tis time to rest, aye, lass?*" he said into her mind, hoping she would agree and join him because he refused to control or force her. She had had enough of that for one lifetime.

Her eyes met his, and though he thought for a moment the ale might have gotten the better of her, and she would say no, she offered a soft, knowing smile and nodded. *"I see you're ready to seduce me then."*

"Och, nay, 'tis not like that," he muttered into her mind, well aware what she thought he wanted from her.

He stood, thanked Angus for his hospitality, and bid him goodnight.

"Aye, then." Angus chuckled, his merry eyes going to Jessie. "She's feelin' randy then, is she?"

"I am," she agreed, smiling widely as she took Bryce's hand and stood. "Not such a bad thing right?"

"'Tis never a bad thing, my wee lassie." Angus kept chuckling as he raised his mug in salute. "Sometimes 'tis best for a lass to walk bow-legged on a listing ship, aye?" He winked. "Helps keep yer balance."

When Jessie looked at him with confusion, Bryce promptly ushered her out.

"Bow-legged?" she asked as he kept his hands on her waist and steered her down the narrow hallway to their tight quarters. "For all my vast wisdom, I can't seem to figure that one out." She stopped abruptly and met his eyes over her shoulder. "What did he mean by that, anyway?"

"Nothing you need to concern yourself with tonight, lass," he assured as he shut the door behind them. The space was cramped but welcome enough considering most of the crew slept where they could find a spare spot.

"I *am* concerned though," she argued as she frowned at him. "Obviously it's sexual."

"'Tis time to rest, lass." He prompted her to sit on the small bunk they would be sharing then knelt and took off her boots.

"You know, I always knew you'd be handsome based on what I saw on the inside," she murmured, her eyes suddenly half-mast as she watched him. "But I had no idea how *very* handsome." She fanned herself with her hand and offered a sloppy grin. "As Christina would say, hot *damn!*"

"Och, lass," he muttered and shook his head, knowing full well that 'on the inside' meant his warlock double. "I never should have let you drink more than one mug of ale." He kept shaking his head. "Mayhap not even half a mug."

"Right!" she agreed, still grinning. "Because I've got no tolerance."

Despite being aggravated with himself for allowing her to get drunk, he couldn't help but be charmed. She was pouting and batting her lashes at him, clearly mimicking Lindsay as she tried to win him over. He bit back a chuckle as he urged her to lie back so he could cover her with a blanket.

"Not yet," she whispered and shook her head. "Please."

He frowned, confused. "What is it, lass?"

"I was hoping." She bit her lower lip, suddenly shy as she stared at him. "I was hoping I could do something."

"Nay, lass." He shook his head, under the assumption she wanted to try lying with him now. "I'll do no such thing with you for the first time whilst you're feeling the effects of ale." He urged her to lie back again. "Trust me, you'll thank me for it in the morn."

"No, that's not what I meant..." She shook her head. "Not really." Half a breath later, she leaned forward, cupped his cheeks and kissed him.

It was by no means an experienced kiss, but it was one he should have ended right away. She deserved to be sober for her first kiss. Yet he didn't pull away as her soft, warm lips touched his. Instead, he allowed it. He welcomed it actually, struck by how fire roared through his blood at the simple contact.

Their lips never opened, and their tongues didn't touch, yet her chaste kiss felt incredibly erotic. So sensual and arousing that he was moments away from taking her right then and there. She had instantly ignited a driving need that almost got the better of him.

"Nay," he whispered as he rallied all his considerable strength, pulled back, cupped her cheeks and shook his head. "Not like this, lass." He brushed his lips across her forehead then finally got her to lie back. "You need rest."

"So do you," she whispered, her eyes still on him. "You'll stay here with me, right, Bryce?"

"Aye, lass, of course, I'll stay," he replied as he pulled off his boots then lay down beside her the best he could on the small bunk. It was good she was so petite, or this might not have worked. As it was, he had to pull her tight against him, her back to his front.

"I'd rather face you," she whispered, her eyes already shut as she turned and curled up against him. She was just small enough that she managed it. Nonetheless, he wrapped his arm around her and kept her close as the ship swayed.

Moments later, she released a dainty snore then quieted.

Regrettably, he was so aroused sleep didn't come easy. When it did, he dreamt only of her. She was lying in a small, flower-ridden grassy clearing. Almost unblinking, she stared up at the trees so intently he swore she must be communicating with them. While it was sunny where she lay, he swore the forest was darker than normal and gathering ever closer to her.

Though he wanted to approach, he couldn't seem to get past the shadows.

"Don't then," she murmured. "Stay where you're comfortable."

Was she talking to him?

"I would prefer to be by your side," came a deep rumble. Startled, he realized the words had come from him.

"You are by my side." She finally dragged her eyes from the trees, turned her head in his direction and offered him a lazy smile. "You're only a few feet away."

He frowned. It seemed much further. "You are mistaken."

"No." Her eyes returned to the trees. "Remember, sunlight messes with your depth perception. Everything looks much wider or bigger in your eyes."

Suddenly, Bryce realized what was happening. She thought she was talking to a warlock. Based on how kind she sounded, he would say *the* warlock. He glanced down only to have his vision pulled back to her almost like a magnet.

"Another few weeks and the leaves will start changing," she murmured. "They'll be so beautiful." Then a flicker of sadness. "Then they'll die, and the branches will grow barren."

Something about that made him happy. But why? She soon answered that.

"Then these moments will be no more."

"I will keep you safe," he, *it*, responded. "They will not hurt you." He shook his head. "Never hurt you."

He felt the warlock's sentiment as if it were his own. How strongly he felt. How much he cared about her. Even loved her.

Then he felt something else.

A driving need to make her his. An unnatural desire to keep her with him always. What Bryce had thought was love moments before now felt twisted and dark. More like obsession and the need to possess.

Then those emotions vanished and became normal once more. It felt like love again. Goodness. He wanted to protect and keep her safe.

"You are too easily swayed," came a dark voice from beside him. "Too emotional." The voice grew even more grating. "You will never be able to do what you must when the time comes."

"I already have though," her warlock responded. "The time came and went, and I was there when I should be. I was successful."

What the bloody hell did he mean by that?

"Were you then?" said the other warlock.

"Yes," he responded as a disconcerting wave of dark pleasure rolled through him. "Though she doesnae remember it yet, she is already mine and will recall such when she least expects it."

Chapter Nine

JESSIE WOKE TO flames in Bryce's eyes. Though she should be terrified, something kept her calm. The ship still rocked back and forth as it had the night before, so they had yet to hit bad weather. So what had him so disgruntled? Enough so that his dragon reacted.

"What is it?" she whispered.

"I saw you," he said softly as he stroked her hair, clearly trying to keep her calm though he was the one upset. "And I saw your...*the* warlock." A deep frown settled on his face. "He knows something you dinnae, Jessie. He has something planned..."

She ignored the strange sensation that washed over her. Not just fear, but something undefinable. A memory just out of reach.

"But you don't know what," she said, finishing his sentence as his thoughts brushed hers. As she saw the dream as though she had experienced it.

"Nay, I dinnae know what but 'tis not good," he replied.

"I wouldn't imagine it is," she murmured, more aware of their intimate position by the moment. The size of his body. How close he was. How good he smelled. More than anything though, she recalled the brief kiss they had shared the night before. She hadn't expected to feel so much. So many emotions she was still trying to sift through.

"The good thing, though," she continued determined to remain focused on the matter at hand, "is that it seems you were part of the warlock and were recalling his memories which will be helpful."

Still stroking her hair absently, he considered that. "Do you think that we're forming a telepathic bond then? If so, might I be able to track him more readily?"

"It could very well be." Yet it troubled her deeply for another reason. "Which means it could work both ways...he would be able to track you too."

"Is there anything we can do about that?" he asked. "Anything I can do?" The fire might have dwindled from his eyes, but she knew he was out for blood.

"I don't think so," she said. "If I was still connected to him, maybe, but I'm not."

"And that's bloody good," he grumbled.

Was it? She wasn't so sure.

The distress must have been obvious on her face because his brows drew together. "What is it, lass?"

"I just worry," she murmured. "About growing weaker without their aid and letting all of you down."

"Och, nay." He cupped her cheek. "You've helped us out so much thus far that you are beyond letting us down at this point. Even if we were to fail, 'twould not be your fault. Not in the least."

She wasn't sure she would go that far, but she appreciated his kind words. Yet again, she did her best to swallow emotions as they tried to surface. They seemed to come fast and furious now that she could finally acknowledge them. Then there was his weapon-roughened tender touch. The way his large hand encompassed not just her cheek but a good portion of the side of her neck too.

"So how do you feel, lass?" he asked, his voice tentative.

"I just told you how I feel," she began before she realized what he meant and blushed. "Oh, you mean the ale last night."

"Aye." He grinned. "You were..." His grin grew. "Out of form."

"That's one way to put it." She forced a chuckle though embarrassed. "I feel okay." And she did for the most part. "I'm sorry I was so forward."

"Dinnae be sorry," he said softly, his hand still on her cheek. "'Twas verra good." His brows furrowed and his brogue thickened as he tried to be careful with her. "I hope ye ken why I didnae want to kiss ye, to begin with...or why I stopped anything else from happening."

"I do." She cleared her throat, more than ready to end the conversation. "And I appreciate it."

"Aye?" he asked, hopeful.

116

"Yes, of course." She managed a smile. "You were a gentleman."

"Aye," he whispered, a curious look in his eyes. "Would ye like another then?"

"Another what?" she asked like a fool, so caught in the golden flare of his eyes she barely followed.

"Another kiss," he murmured.

Though her first instinct was to say no because she was so nervous, she found herself being rather brave as she offered a single nod. Because she *did* want another kiss. Several more, if she were to be honest. But starting with one real kiss would be a good start.

"Did ye not think 'twas a real kiss last night then?" he murmured, desire clear in his eyes as they fell to her lips. Naturally, he was catching some of her thoughts.

"It was real," she conceded. Her cheeks were so heated they must be beet red. How was she supposed to tell him she was looking for something a bit more intimate? Deeper?

Thankfully, before she had a chance to formulate a word, he took the matter out of her hands and kissed her. At first, it was the same sort of kiss as last night. Warm and affectionate, it incited a thrilling rush of excitement.

Then it became more.

He wrapped his hand around the nape of her neck beneath her hair, tilted his head and began dropping small kisses in such a way that she barely realized she was returning them. She became so immersed in the feel of those kisses that she welcomed the sudden flick of his tongue along the seam of her mouth.

Eager to taste more, she opened her lips to the sort of kiss she always imagined. The sort of intimate, deep kiss two people could share. Initially, his tongue only danced lightly with hers before their tongues swirled and the kiss took on a life of its own.

She groaned as pleasure began spreading through her. Tingling warmth trailed down her neck and over her chest and arms until it became a fiery blaze that went lower. Not just fire but an instant aching need that startled her so much, she pulled back. That's when it occurred to her she could barely draw a breath.

"Are ye well, lass?" he murmured, his voice husky.

Just breathe, Jessie she kept telling herself as she offered a jerky nod.

"Everything yer feeling is normal, lass," he said softly, his voice soothing as he gently caressed the back of her neck.

As he kept murmuring things along those lines, she started to bit by bit relax. Even so, the aching need continued. A need she saw reflected in his eyes as he inhaled sharply and his jaw tightened. Well aware that dragons could smell the scent of arousal, she thought for sure she would be mortified but wasn't. Instead, she found it remarkably alluring. How his pupils flared, and fire sizzled in his eyes as he tried to fight it.

She was somewhat surprised by her utter lack of fear and brazen response as she didn't pull away, but kissed him *again*. It was as if another person was surfacing. One far bolder and more eager than she ever thought she could be.

This time *he* groaned as their tongues wrapped and the kiss grew more passionate than the last. By now, her whole body was alive in ways she couldn't put into words. Her breasts tingled in anticipation as did other things.

She wanted more.

All he had to offer.

She wanted to feel him between her thighs and finally experience what she had been fantasizing about for so long.

"Och, lass," he whispered against her lips before he pulled away and shook his head. "I willnae take ye on this ship. 'Tis not right."

"Why not?" she whispered, seeing no fault in it.

"It just isnae," he murmured. "Not here. Not now." He sighed as he sat up. "Ye deserve better."

In her opinion, better was being with him period. She didn't care where.

He took her hand and met her eyes as she sat up as well. "Ye deserve yer first time to be set apart from so many men, any of which could barge in here without a moment's notice."

Not only would they sense someone coming but she suspected privacy, in general, might prove a rarity on their adventure. Nevertheless, she didn't argue. If he felt this wasn't the right time, she would take his word for it. She could tell by the strain on his face, however, that it was taking him a great deal of strength to hold fast in his determination.

Yet he stood his ground as he cupped her cheek again, his touch gentle. "'Twill be soon enough and 'twill be somewhere better suited to ye. Someplace more memorable."

She could only imagine where he would find such a place but appreciated that he was determined to make it special. What more could a girl ask for?

"Come, let us change and see what's happening above deck, aye?" he said as he stood.

"Sounds good," she began, her words trailing off as he began undressing. She wasn't so naïve that she hadn't seen a man nude before. She often saw partial nudity when offering locals back home natural medicine. And she had seen Graham without clothes quite recently when she was time-traveling in spirit form. A fact she knew Bryce was aware of.

But Graham was not Bryce.

Though both were well-muscled and in remarkable shape, Bryce was more so somehow. Bigger. Harder. Her eyes trailed over his broad tattooed shoulders, down his chiseled abs to the ample bulge straining against his plaid.

"Though this is not where I wish to take you for the first time," he said softly, "I thought 'twould be good mayhap if you become more familiar with...me." His brows lowered in dubious amusement as a smirk hovered on his lips. "And aye, I'm built a wee bit different than my cousin." There was no missing his cockiness. "'Tis a dragon thing."

All she could manage was a nod, not complaining in the least that he was 'breaking her in' to seeing his nudity so to speak. The only real problem was that it was making her more aroused. He grinned, obviously pleased as he caught that assessment.

Though remarkably nervous she figured she might as well get used to showing off her nudity as well. So she stood and started to undress.

His eyes widened. "What are ye doing, lass?"

She stopped working at the ties on the front of her dress. "Getting comfortable with this...you and me." She lifted her brows, realizing that without meaning to she was giving him a taste of his own medicine. "You don't mind, do you?"

There was no missing his heavy swallow as he shook his head. "Nay, lass. Do as ye will."

She nodded and promptly set to removing her dress, more comfortable keeping her eyes on him rather than herself. Until that is, he yanked off his plaid.

"Oh, sweet Heaven," she whispered, not averting her eyes. "That's...you're..." She shook her head and finally managed to drag her eyes to his face. "It's okay." She shook her head. "Never mind."

Could she sound any more ridiculous? This wasn't the first time she had seen an erection. Men sometimes got them when she applied herbal remedies but not like that. Not so...big.

Meanwhile, his blazing eyes were trained on her body as raw hunger flared in their golden depths. Though certainly daunted by him, it suddenly occurred to her that perhaps *this* was the way to finally get what she wanted. To at last take the leap and experience the sort of passion she was eager for.

Then again, she wondered about his size...if she could handle it.

"Ye will," he said, his voice husky again as he wrapped another plaid and covered himself. "As I said before, ye will think of nothing but pleasure when the time comes, and ye will be ready for me."

She offered another nod as she crawled into her dress. If there was one thing she didn't doubt after those kisses it was that he could arouse her a great deal. And that was the key to good sex. With the right stimulation, people fit together comfortably no matter their size difference. She frowned at her own thoughts. More so that she knew all this from a purely medicinal doctor-like viewpoint. Not because she had experienced it herself like most women her age.

She downright scowled, suddenly angry at the warlocks because she had missed out on so much. Frustrated that they had stolen her life from her. And her anger, having been repressed for so long, only seemed to be growing more and more with each passing moment.

"'Tis good that anger," he murmured as they continued dressing. "'Twill help fuel you against what we face."

"I'm sure it will," she agreed as she yanked on her boots.

Before they headed up, he stopped her and tilted her chin until their eyes met. "Harness every bit of fury you feel toward them, lass. Use it then release it afterward."

"It's hard to imagine a day when I'll be able to do that." she murmured.

"You will," he said softly. "And I will be there to help you."

120

He really was turning out to be so much more than she had hoped for. Far more. She had imagined many things about this journey but not that he would offer her so much strength. That he would be so tenderhearted and sympathetic.

"Would you not have done the same for me had our roles been reversed?" He offered a soft smile as he responded to her thoughts. "We do share similar souls after all."

"I would like to think I would've done the same," she conceded. "I guess I worried for so long about how things might go that I started to assume the worst."

"'Tis understandable," he replied. "But you dinnae need to do that anymore. Instead, you need to see what's right in front of you so we can find what belongs to us. So that we can find this great MacLomain, Broun connection." He dusted her forehead with the pad of his thumb. "And dinnae keep all your thoughts and concerns locked away. Though it seems I can hear you quite readily I dinnae want to miss anything. I want you to communicate so that we better ken one another, aye?"

She nodded and offered a small smile. "I'll try."

"Aye, then." He brushed his lips across hers, took her hand and they headed upstairs.

Though the sky was murkier than the day before, the gusty wind and choppy sea had hardly changed. She knew that would not be the case soon enough though. What they faced ahead might be more than any of them could handle.

"Good morn to ye both," Angus said in greeting as men rowed, adding extra speed to that which the sails already offered. He tossed them each an apple. "To break yer fast, aye?"

They nodded thanks as Angus eyed the sky then the ships sailing alongside. "We've made good time and should be approaching the North of Scotland soon. With so many men under my command this journey, 'twould be best to avoid the Pentland Firth and mayhap travel round the north of the Orkneys or even further north around Shetland."

"No." Jessie shook her head, well aware of the timeline they were on even if Angus wasn't. "It will take too much time."

"Mayhap a day or two," he began before she shook her head again and interrupted. "I know the tide current in the firth is incredibly strong, but my friends and I will get you through safely."

Due to the shallow water through the firth, the tidal currents increased more than usual. In all actuality, they were some of the fastest in the world.

Angus' brows flew up. "Ye realize with a storm the likes of the one we're heading into the tidal currents alone could end us."

She nodded, amazed how calm she felt knowing full well those currents would likely be even stronger considering the strength of the warlock controlling the storm. Worse yet, the waves would be far taller. "We have to go that way." She shook her head with conviction. "We've no choice."

He frowned, crossed his arms over his chest and considered her. "Might ye give me a little history lesson then because yer asking a lot of my men and me."

She glanced at Bryce, unsure. While she might have hoped Angus would be convinced of the power behind them with Christina's actions the night before last, it seemed he needed more.

"What would prove my lass tells the truth?" Bryce said. "Me telling ye that ye might verra well lose our beloved Scotland to the Sassenach if ye dinnae do this?" He shrugged and allowed a flicker of fire in his eyes. "Or should I show ye what I'm capable of becoming?" He laid it on the line. "If I show ye right now, 'tis verra likely yer men might abandon ship. If I wait and only do it if 'tis necessary, 'twill be in the thick of it when yer men are busy trying to battle the elements. It could be verra distracting."

She had to give Angus credit for not flinching when Bryce gave him a glimpse of his inner dragon. Rather he appeared intrigued as he considered his choices.

"I suppose I need more information." Angus stroked his beard. "What precisely *is* it ye become?"

"A dragon." Bryce didn't sugarcoat it. "A rather large and ferocious one at that."

"Och, nay." Angus chuckled and shook his head as he gestured at a man nearby to do something for him. "I dinnae believe ye."

"I didnae think ye would but 'tis true," Bryce responded. "'Tis also why Jessie recommended Sven be put on one of yer most vulnerable ships as a back-up plan."

Incredulous merriment lit Angus' eyes. "So he's a dragon too?"

Bryce nodded, perfectly serious. "Aye."

Though Angus appeared to mull it over, it soon became clear he had already decided. Hence the gesture he'd made to his crewmate. John's ship had been signaled to come closer.

Angus jumped up on a bench, cupped his hands around his mouth and bellowed to his son. "Our wee lassie claims we must ride the storm through the firth if we're to help King Robert and save our country. What say ye to that?"

Lots of *nays* and '*tis a death wish*'s arose.

"Aye, that's what I said," Angus agreed, embellishing. "But, in addition to the certain mystical powers I know she and her friends possess, her lad here claims to be something fierce indeed. Something far more than the man ye see standing before ye."

"Aye?" John yelled, eagerness for a good show twinkling in his eyes. "And what is that?"

As Angus responded, he directed his words to his men as well. "The sort ye willnae believe until ye see it with yer own eyes." He made a grand flourish at Bryce. "Our new friend Laird MacLeod and his Viking friend, Sven claim they're mighty dragons." A wide smile split his face. "What say ye to that?"

Chuckles and nays arose on both ships.

"Aye, that's what I said too." Angus met their chuckles before he glanced at Bryce then back to his men, his countenance suddenly very serious. "Yet he claims 'tis true, and the wee lassie says he and the Viking will help us face what dangers await us in the firth so that we might save our beloved country." He cocked his head in question as he eyed his men. "What say ye again? If he can become something as mighty as a dragon and is willing to defend and protect ye, will ye travel those dark waters with me? Will ye sail straight into Hell? Because 'tis bound to be just that."

Some men nodded while others chatted amongst themselves before nodding as well. A man who was likely Angus' first mate responded for them all. "Aye, captain. We'll follow ye if we truly have dragons at our backs."

Soon after John and his men agreed it was relayed to the next ship then the next.

Jessie spoke into Bryce's mind. "*Are you sure about this?*"

"*I am.*" His eyes met hers. "*We'll figure out how to handle what they witness afterward.*"

123

She rested her hand on his arm and nodded. *"Be careful. They have a lot of weapons and who knows how they'll react."*

"All that matters is how you'll react, lass." His eyes searched hers. *"Are you ready for this?"*

"I am." I have to be. When his eyes held hers, she realized he was waiting for the whole truth. He wanted her to share her thoughts openly rather than try to keep them to herself. *"I fear for your safety not what you'll become, Bryce. I trust your dragon as much as I do you."*

She had left the village in Happrew before he shifted, so she never saw him embrace his dragon that day.

"Dinnae worry about me." She felt his gratefulness as their eyes held. *"The weapons these men possess cannae hurt me."*

"But maybe what the warlock throws at you eventually will."

He pulled her into his arms and murmured in her ear, *"'Twill be dangerous for us all, lass but we will defeat this creature then the next, aye? Because we've the power betwixt us all to do it. You've got the power."*

She nodded as she met his eyes again, glad to see such confidence there. Such strength. A strength that filled her before he pulled away and turned to Angus. "So I'm to show ye my beastie, aye?"

Angus nodded, skeptical. "Aye then, Laird MacLeod."

"And Sven?" Bryce asked. "Do ye wish to see him as well?"

When Angus glanced at his men, they nodded, so he roared it to John who relayed it to the others. She knew full well Bryce had already been speaking within Sven's mind though.

"Be safe Sven," she said to the Viking, thankful they could communicate this way. *"Please."*

"Do not worry about me," Sven assured. *"And do not be afraid of what happens next."*

She frowned. *"What do you mean?"*

No response.

Bryce met her eyes one more time before he set aside his apple, jumped up on the side of the ship then leapt overboard only for colors to swirl around him. Moments later, a massive black dragon launched into the air, his feet dragging in the water briefly before he gained altitude. The sheer power of his wings caused enough wind that the ship listed back and forth.

"Bloody hell," Angus whispered, in complete awe. "Will ye look at that."

Eyes were wide as some men fell to their knees and made the cross over their chest while others clutched their weapons. Others roared with approval while some scrambled back to the opposite side of the ship.

All she could do was stare as she walked to the railing closest to Bryce. He was absolutely stunning. Powerful. *Huge.* When his golden dragon eyes met hers a most unusual rush went through her.

What *was* that?

"Can ye hear me, lass?" he said into her mind. Though hearing his dragon's voice within her mind was titillating it was not the feeling she had just experienced.

"I can," she replied as Sven's dragon launched into the air as well. He was black too with icy blue eyes.

They flew alongside each other as they continued to gain altitude, up and up, nearly to the clouds, then they swooped down and around the ships. Men fell back in a mixture of awe, and roars of approval. Surprisingly enough, few screamed in fear.

This truly was a brave lot. Just the sort they needed for what lie ahead.

Seconds later, Bryce and Sven roared fire along the water leaving a row of boiling ocean and steam in their wake. The sharp scent of burnt salt gusted on the wind as they began to gain altitude again, clearly enjoying themselves.

"You should show them how you intend to help them in the storm," she said to what she hoped was both of them. Though it wasn't far-fetched that she could speak to Bryce's dragon, she was somewhat shocked when Sven's dragon responded.

"I think it would be too much right now."

"I agree," Bryce said.

She frowned, not in agreement at all. To her, it made perfect sense and *should* happen.

Moments later, it seemed they felt the same because both shot down, their eyes blazing. That same sensation that had rolled through her when Bryce first shifted rolled through her again. This time, however, it was far stronger. Powerful in a way she couldn't explain.

"Are ye all right, my wee lassie?" Angus asked.

"Of course," she murmured, watching the dragons closely. "Why wouldn't I be?"

"'Tis yer eyes," Angus murmured.

Her eyes were still glued to Sven and Bryce. "What about them?"

"They arenae right," he replied. "They glow a mixture of gold and blue. The exact shades of the dragons' eyes if I'm not mistaken."

"What?" she whispered, still watching the dragons as they landed on the backs of two ships, flapped their wings and began steering them.

"Och, they have great control of these vessels, aye?" Angus said, impressed. "Even in high winds, I imagine..." He frowned. "But we have several ships and only two dragons. What of the rest of my fleet?"

When Jessie finally tore her eyes away from them, the powerful sensation that had been building within her vanished. Half a breath later, both dragons launched into the air. All she heard were Bryce's frustrated muttered words garbled in her mind. Why was he upset? Better yet, what had just happened between her and them? Because something clearly took place.

"Lass, are ye all right?" Angus frowned. "I see yer eyes have returned to normal, but ye dinnae look like yer feeling all that well."

"I'm fine," she assured, swallowing hard as she gripped the railing. "I'm sorry, what did you ask me before?"

Angus eyed her with concern for a moment before he continued. "I was asking about the dragon to ship ratio."

"Oh, right." She nodded then shook her head. "It will only really be one dragon at first assisted by me, Christina, Graham and possibly Aðísla. Remember, Sven's your back-up plan. But don't worry, all your ships will be protected."

"Right," Angus said. "Against what exactly?"

"Very bad stuff," she murmured.

He eyed the sky ahead then her. "Worse than the weather?"

She nodded. "I'm afraid so."

He chewed on that information for a moment before he spoke. "Well, I suppose I'd believe anything by now." He sighed. "Witches and wizards and dragons." He shook his head. "Then ye with yer strange dragon eyes."

She frowned. "Dragon eyes?" She shook her head. "I'm not a dragon."

But Erin was.

He shrugged, muttering as he turned away and saw to his men. "Mayhap not but yer something along those lines, my wee lassie."

"Aye," Bryce said after he shifted and landed. "Something I didnae imagine existed until Sven just shared it with me."

She met his curious but troubled eyes and shook her head. "I'm sure that was just your mother's dragon magic coming through somehow."

"No," Sven said into her mind. "It was not Bryce's mother but your own inner dragon blood. A lineage that dates all the way back to the ancient dragon, Níðhöggr. Jessie, your bloodline makes you something very special." He paused for a moment, perhaps letting the enormity of what he had said sink in before he dropped the next bombshell. "You are without a shadow of a doubt, a controller of dragons."

Chapter Ten

THOUGH HE WAS frustrated that Jessie had taken control of his dragon against its will again, Bryce couldn't remain upset with her. Not when he saw the vulnerable, confused look on her face as Sven informed her of her lineage.

While he got the sense Sven had known about this prior, the Viking seemed just as disgruntled to have his dragon at her mercy. It went against their very natures to be controlled by another. Even their dragon mates didn't enjoy that luxury unless they gave it to them.

"I'm so sorry." Jessie shook her head, trembling slightly. "I had no idea. None at all." She kept shaking her head. "I never meant to…" She flinched as her eyes held his. "I just controlled you both against your will?"

"Och, lass," he murmured and pulled her into his arms. Surprisingly it wasn't just him but his inner dragon that was quick to forgive her and eager to offer comfort. "Sven will explain everything once we're past the danger ahead. Until then, ye must not overly worry about it, aye?"

"Worry about it." Her wide eyes met his. "I just controlled the most unbelievably beautiful, and independent creatures I've ever seen, and you tell me not to *worry* about it?" Her eyes widened even more as something occurred to her. "So does this mean I'm a dragon too?"

"We dinnae think so," he replied. "Though Sven cannae be one hundred percent sure now after having felt your essence so acutely."

"Oh, God," she whispered and rested her cheek against his chest. "I knew I was a lot of things, but that one would take the cake."

"Aye," he agreed.

As it was, she had a remarkable scent about her. Now he was beginning to wonder if there was more to it. Even if there wasn't, everything else about her drove him to distraction from the delicious taste of her kisses to her tempting wee body. He had never wanted to possess a lass as much as he did her. Pulling out of her welcoming arms that morning had been almost impossible. Seeing her smooth, soft flesh and dainty curves just about pushed him over the edge.

Well aware of his thoughts, she offered him one of those blushes he enjoyed so much. Unable to help himself and intending to do it as often as possible, he tilted her chin and brushed his lips across hers.

"So we'll sail through the firth then, aye laddies?" Angus roared to his men, interrupting what was fast becoming a much deeper kiss.

"Aye," his men roared in response.

Angus slid curious eyes Bryce and Jessie's way. "Normally, I'd have my men reef the sail at this point, but circumstances are a bit different this time." He arched a brow at them. "What would ye recommend?"

"We need all the speed we can get," she responded. Forty oarsmen strong, this ship might be larger than most, but it would need help. The sort of winds they would be facing would likely tear its sail to shreds. Unless... "Let me try something."

Angus nodded as she went to the mast, closed her eyes and murmured. As she had hoped, because both the mast and sail were of materials more directly connected to the Earth she could easily manipulate and strengthen them. Her eyes shot open when a strange warmth rolled through her. Someone else's magic was at work too.

Erin's.

Moments later not just her mast and sail glowed as it strengthened but the whole of the fleet's. As the glow faded, she smiled at Angus and nodded. "No amount of wind will rip these sails now."

Impressed, he eyed the material then roared, "Batten down the hatches, laddies, but keep the sail unreefed." A crazy sort of anticipation lit his eyes. "Men to oar because we'll be hittin' her with all the speed we've got!"

Bryce and Jessie stepped aside as men set to task and raced in every direction.

The skies ahead were black and crackling with lightning. White-peaked waves roiled beneath them.

Angus met Jessie's eyes. "By the sounds of it yer familiar with the Pentland Firth, aye?"

"I am…somewhat."

His bushy brows lowered sharply. *"Somewhat?"*

"Only what I researched here and there," she replied. "All I know for sure is with what you're about to face you won't have the benefit of some tides being stronger than others depending on the time of day."

"Nay?" He frowned. "But that's impossible."

"Nothing's impossible when it comes to dark magic," she said softly, her eyes steady with his.

Angus said nothing for a moment as he let that tidbit of information settle. "Och, then, I suppose that's all it could've been with the likes of ye and yers along, aye?"

"I'm afraid so." She impressed Bryce with how confident she sounded when he knew her inner thoughts were anything but. "Angus, you and I should stand at the stern of the ship for better visibility. You navigate the quickest route, tides or not, and my friends and I will handle the rest."

"Aye, then my wee lassie," Angus said, his mental wheels already spinning. "Either we can cut between the isles of Stroma and Swona, but that brings us over a sand wave field with the fastest tides and highest waves, dark magic or no." His eyes met hers. "Or we sail along the coast south of Stroma and ride the shores along Dunnet Head and Tang Head straight past Duncansby Head." He frowned. "Though that route brings us dangerously close to land on either side."

"Is one faster than the other?" she asked.

"'Twould all depend on the direction of the winds and the roll of the sea," Angus replied.

Jessie thought about that for a moment. "I think further away from land is better."

He nodded and said, "Aye, then," before he headed for the stern and started giving more orders.

"Why further away from land?" Bryce asked, sensing there was more to this. "Outside of the obvious risk of shipwreck, that is."

"The closer we are to land, the more threatening the warlock's influence," she explained. "And my guess is, the worse the weather and seas will be as well."

"'Tis a mighty amount of magic he's using to create this storm, aye?" he said as the winds picked up even more and the skies grew blacker still.

"All he has," she said softly as her eyes met his. "Angus is already ahead of schedule. If he gets through this as fast as we need him to, we'll want to convince him to drop anchor for the night so we can go ashore and find the warlock. He'll be at his weakest then after using so much magic. *That* will likely be our one and only chance to destroy him."

Bryce nodded as they joined Angus and presented the idea to him.

He frowned, perplexed. "We're to risk our lives in the firth because we cannae take an extra day or two to go north yet ye want me to drop anchor for a whole eve?"

"If you hope us to finish off the bastard causing all this weather, yes," Jessie said. "And we'll be back bright and early in the morning." There was a distinct warning to her tone as her eyes stayed with the MacDonald captain. "If I don't end my enemy he *will* end your country once and for all."

Angus eyed her for another long moment before he finally agreed. "Aye then, lassie. 'Twill be as ye wish."

She nodded as the oarsmen propelled them forward even faster.

"Keep them rowing until the last possible moment," she said. "Then, as I'm sure you already know, have them strap themselves down to whatever they can find." She glanced behind them. "You'll want your strongest man on the rudder. Maybe a few men."

Angus nodded and started barking more orders as he handed Bryce and Jessie leather straps. As the ship lolled, Bryce braced for balance on the slick deck and tied her off. When their eyes met, he didn't miss a flicker of fear for him.

"I'll be all right, lass." He shook his head. "But I willnae be tying off."

"So you can shift more easily, right?"

He could shift either way but wanted to be able to move more freely in case her bindings came undone.

When he nodded and offered no response, she narrowed her eyes and murmured, "It works both ways you know. I'd like to hear your thoughts aloud too."

"Aye, then, lass." He cupped her cheek and repeated what she already knew, his voice firm. "I willnae risk not being able to go after you if your bindings come loose."

"If that happens I'll likely already be overboard," she pointed out.

"Aye, and I'll be right behind you."

She sighed and frowned. "I won't be able to concentrate if I'm worrying about you."

"Aye, lass, you will because everyone's lives depend on it." He would not budge on this. "Dinnae worry. I'm verra strong." Then he reminded her just how strong. "Besides, soon enough I'll be shifting so you'll not have to worry anymore."

The skies darkened even more as they sped not just into the storm but the firth itself. Jessie's eyes went to the horizon then back to him, her words a warning.

"It's happening fast now." As their gaze held he felt her inner strength grow and her courage bolstered just from knowing he would be working alongside her. She also knew he would remain resolute in not tying off, and had no choice but to trust he would be all right. "Be careful, Bryce and remain vigilant at all times." Her voice softened. "I don't want to lose you."

He had just enough time to nod his assurance before she looked at Angus and gave the go-ahead. "It's time to pull the oars in."

As the men followed the order and strapped down, Bryce contacted his kin.

"*Are ye two ready?*" he said into Graham's and Christina's minds as day became night, and inky clouds swallowed the sky. The air became thick and oppressive and the sea murky and black. "*'Tis bound to be verra rough.*"

"*Aye, we're ready,*" Graham responded.

"*We sure are,*" Christina replied, a touch of excitement in her inner voice. "*Thanks to Graham's magical influence, I'm not nervous at all now.*"

No sooner did she respond than rain came in a thick, pounding wall of water.

Surrounded by so much water, not just in the ocean but in the clouds and rain, Graham was certainly the best wizard to have along right now. His power should be magnified a great deal. And though this wasn't particularly the sort of battle Christina's gift was designed for, he suspected her powers would amplify Graham's just as much as his did hers.

Bryce held on tight when the ship leaned back precariously, and they began climbing a wave that almost seemed to have doubled in height from the ones they had ridden moments ago. Blinding chain lightning electrified the air as it zig-zagged in every direction, webbing across not just the sky but the ocean.

"Bloody hell," Angus roared, his eyes wild as he offered an insane smile.

Wind speeds increased and jerked the ship forward even faster, causing it to grunt and groan as it crested another monster wave and they raced down the other side. The firth itself was a frightening sight to behold. Dark and foreboding, it seemed like they were racing into the gaping hole of Hell. The sound of its very water was both roaring and haunting. As though the ocean itself was crying out in pain at how harshly it was being treated.

Ear-piercing thunder cracked and boomed, vibrating the ships and even the seawater.

Rain slashed down from every direction, as the ships listed violently. Waves crashed over one side then the other, in a heavy, almost painful deluge. Though it was a tremendous strain on his muscles, Bryce never let go and certainly never left Jessie's side.

"*It's time,*" she said into his mind as her eyes met his and she repeated what she had said before. "*Be careful.*"

"*Aye, lass, you too.*"

Though loathe to leave her, he knew they had no choice. So he waited for the perfect opportunity between ship rolls, raced to the edge, leapt and shifted. His vision hazed with the red of his dragon as he struggled to gain altitude in the rough weather. No plane would ever survive this turbulence. Yet his dragon was strong. More than that, his need to keep Jessie safe and protect his country was even stronger.

Well aware Graham was already bonding his magic with Bryce's and manipulating the water around the fleet, Bryce looped around. Once he had a firm hold on Angus' ship, he began to steer it. As he did, Graham's magic ensured that all the other boats experienced the same. It would be as though Bryce were at the back of each and every one.

As it turned out, he had never experienced anything so challenging as navigating that firth.

The waves seemed like wild, shifting mountains. The rain was brutal and the icy winds ferocious. Even with Graham manipulating the water and trying to keep them heading straight into the waves, Bryce's dragon barely managed it.

If nothing else, this was an enormous show of power on the warlock's part.

"*Whatever happens,*" Jessie said into his mind, her inner voice remarkably strong and level. "*Keep doing what you're doing until every last ship and man is free from this storm.*"

"*I dinnae like the* sound *of that,*" he replied. "*What are you up to?*"

"*It doesn't matter,*" she responded. "*Just promise you'll do as I ask…not just for me but for your country.*"

Though he didn't like her vagueness one bit, he grunted, "*Aye, then.*"

That's when he spied the warlock in the far distance standing on the shore. His arms were raised in the air and his fury a twisting, rotten blackness around him. A fury Bryce sensed had more to do with betrayal than anything else.

By the looks of it, they were already about halfway through the firth.

Frustratingly enough, though he continued utilizing all his strength, his dragon was beginning to struggle. Everyone was as they tried to keep the fleet from being demolished. Graham and Christina's ring had ignited and threw forth as much power as it was capable of. Jessie was manipulating the air and grappling with getting the winds under control. Even his mother's and Aðísla's magic was wrapped up in this, as lightning was kept from hitting the ships.

Yet he sensed the storm overwhelming them anyway.

The warlock was winning.

"*It's time Sven,*" Jessie said into their minds, alerting Bryce as well that things were about to happen above and beyond the maelstrom they were already in.

Seconds later, Sven shot into the air and headed for shore.

Protecting himself, the warlock directed some of his wrath at Sven's dragon. That meant his full power wasn't directed at them anymore. This, it seemed, was when Jessie intended to make her move.

And what she did utterly shocked him.

Hands flung in the air, she manipulated all four elements at once and created a magnificent manifestation. A display only intensified by her own newly discovered dragon magic.

A monstrous wall of fire.

A barrier of roaring flames, it expanded across the entire firth and went as high as the eye could see. Strategically placed between them and the warlock, it crackled and hissed, steaming the ocean though it didn't put off much heat. Good thing because it would have likely turned the entire firth into one big boiling cauldron.

Moments later, a wave far larger than any before it swelled behind them and carried the entire fleet forward. By manipulating the wind, Jessie kept the fire away from them. And by manipulating the Earth, she kept the ships from cracking apart under the pressure of a wave propelling them forward so quickly.

Meanwhile, Bryce held on tight, braced his wings and kept them steady as they flew forward at an alarming speed. Men far and wide roared in what was likely a mix of terror, excitement and maybe even triumph.

By all appearances, they were going to do this.

They were going to make it.

Or so he thought until they were minutes away from clearing the firth. That's when his worst fear happened.

Jessie's strap snapped.

Though she initially fell forward as momentum dictated, she must have used her magic to veer right and go overboard instead. He roared in denial and was about to dive after her when her sharp words slammed into his mind. "*No, Bryce, see this through and keep them safe.*"

Infuriated because he was so helpless, he roared in denial again. She had used her dragon magic to order him. A magic so strong that his dragon literally could not break free from it. He became a puppet to her wishes.

And those wishes about broke his heart.

"*Hell, no,*" Christina said. "*Hold on, Jessie. I'm comin' for ya, honey.*"

He felt Graham's distress as Christina suddenly went overboard, somehow managing to dive off the side of the ship despite its momentum. She had embraced her godly magic, glowing brightly as she vanished beneath the dark water.

"*Bloody hell,*" Graham roared but kept steadfast and never stopped utilizing his magic. While terrified for Christina, Bryce sensed Graham's faith in her superhuman strength. His faith that she would be all right and save Jessie.

That, as it turned out, helped Bryce more than his cousin knew.

Determined, refocused, he helped his cousin and Aðísla keep the fleet on course, riding a wave the likes of which mankind had never seen. It was definitely a ride for the ages for Angus and his men. One that finally lost its momentum as they, at last, sailed out of the firth.

Half a breath later, the wall of fire fell, and a majestic stream of sunlight broke through the blackness. The rain stopped, and the winds died. Shortly after that, the wave dwindled down to nothing, dark clouds curled away, and the sun shone brightly.

Roars of happiness rumbled through the ships as ashen-faced men unstrapped themselves, cheered and clapped each other on the back. Wide smiles and laughter abounded as they continued celebrating.

Bryce wasted no time but tucked his wings and dove into the ocean, roaring Jessie's name telepathically. Fear struck him anew when he couldn't sense her at all. She was gone from his mind, leaving a gaping hole of intolerable emptiness. That's when he knew how incomplete he had truly been before he met her.

Though the ocean was calming down on top, the currents remained harsh underwater. Where were they? Despite his superior sight it was difficult to see through all the sediment being churned up from the ocean floor.

"*I've got her,*" Christina said. "*But I sure could use your help, sugar.*"

He noticed she didn't mention Jessie's status, but that was probably for the best right now. He needed to focus and get them to safety.

"*I'm coming, Christina,*" he responded, his dragon senses homing in on the direction her voice was coming from. "*Just keep talking.*"

"*You got it.*" He could hear the forced smile in her voice. "*You and I were in a similar position not too long ago, eh?*"

"*Aye, lass.*" She was referring to when she had been kidnapped and taken to Stirling Castle. No one but Bryce could hear her then. "*You don't have to describe things this time. Just keep talking.*"

So she did. About random things. Mostly how impressed she was with Graham. How well he used his magic. How happy she was to be with him. How she swore her unborn child helped them back there.

That would not surprise him. Yet he felt for Graham as he considered it. Just knowing how he feared for Jessie's safety before all this, Bryce couldn't imagine how much worse it would be if he knew she carried his bairn. Naturally, that brought him straight to thoughts of sharing a child with Jessie. How very much the idea appealed to him. How, for that matter, he couldn't conceive of it *not* happening.

So without meaning to, he managed to upset both himself and his dragon even further about Jessie's state of well-being right now. How she might be gone before they had a chance to experience the wonders of a child together. Infuriated at the injustice of it, he picked up his pace, eager to find her.

Fortunately, it didn't take long.

Christina was closer to shore than anticipated and pulling Jessie right along.

"*Jessie?*" he said into her mind. "*Are ye well, lass?*"

Dead silence.

Renewed terror filled him as he realized he was only detecting Christina's and her unborn child's heartbeat, not Jessie's.

"*Hold on to her,*" he roared into Christina's mind before he swooped below them, then surfaced the water with them on his back before he lifted into the air.

Thankfully, Sven was still alive and battling it out with the warlock on the craggy shore.

"Can you save Jessie?" he pleaded into Sven's mind. *"Is she dragon enough?"*

Unfortunately, Sven's magical abilities to heal only applied to fellow dragons.

"Maybe," Sven replied.

Maybe was better than nothing.

"Aye then," he responded. *"When I land, ye see to Jessie, and I'll battle the bloody warlock."*

Sven agreed. *"He's weakened a great deal but still very strong."*

Good. He was up for some vicious fighting before he ripped him to shreds.

The moment he deposited Jessie and Christina, he and Sven raced by one another. The Viking to save Jessie and Bryce to avenge his lass.

The warlock was a pathetic looking thing up close, his inky black skin hanging on a boney frame. Bryce roared fire at him as the warlock deflected and taunted him. "You think you'll ever truly get her, Scotsman? That my granddaughter will ever be free of us? Of *me* and all I created."

Bryce didn't bother responding but kept attacking him in every way he could think of. He used his wings and tail as a battering ram, his talons as non-stop blade thrusts and always his fire. But it wasn't enough. The warlock held him off, his raspy words challenging. "She will always belong to the darkness no matter what happens. You will *never* free her."

Like hell, he wouldn't.

He would free her if it were the last thing he did.

For a warlock who was supposed to be so intelligent, he wasn't very bright instigating a dragon. Especially one fueled by as much vengeance as Bryce felt.

With fresh fury in his heart and an undying rage for all Jessie had been put through, he roared fire at him again. This time, the stream of flames was even longer and more powerful than before. An inferno of searing death that seemed to get past the warlock's defenses enough to singe him.

Or so said the steam rising off him as he staggered back.

Bryce didn't back down but kept coming at him with everything he had and everything he felt. This warlock contained the essence of her grandfather. The man who was responsible for so much pain and heartache. The man responsible for stealing Jessie's life from her for so very long. Beyond angry, enraged, he roared fire again, and the ground shook.

This time, it burned the warlock even more, and he stumbled and fell on his back.

Yet still, he chanted, his voice weakening as he kept Bryce at bay.

"No more," a welcoming voice suddenly whispered from beside him.

Relief flooded him when Bryce glanced down at his side to see Jessie looking up at him. She was alive. Sven had saved her. While he was beyond grateful, he couldn't help but focus on something else.

Her gaze.

Better yet her eyes.

After all, what reflected in them was the very last thing he expected.

Chapter Eleven

S HE KNEW NOT only based on the red haze of her vision but the flare of Bryce's dragon's pupils, exactly what he saw when he looked at her.

Dragon eyes.

Something had shifted inside Jessie as she embraced so much magic on the ship. A magnification of her power she never could have expected. Almost a birth of sorts. Something brand new was awakening inside her. A sort of strength and magic so much more powerful than what she possessed before.

This wasn't Erin's dragon magic but her own. She might not be able to shift, but a dragon *did* exist inside her. Or remnants of one. She could sense it. Feel it. Much like a shadow, it was just out of reach but still there. Always a part of her though she could not embrace it.

"Finish him," she whispered as she touched Bryce's haunch, began chanting within her mind then looked at the warlock. "It's done. You have no more power over me."

Pain and blasphemous rage ignited in the warlock's eyes as her magic overcame his and left him completely vulnerable to Bryce.

"I know you'd like to make his death long and torturous," she said into Bryce's mind. *"But I need this to end now. The sooner it's finished the sooner I can move on."*

Though she couldn't be sure whether she compelled his dragon or if he simply abided by her wishes, Bryce did as she asked. Half a blink later, and a sharp slice of his dragon talon, the warlock was beheaded, and another piece of what had caused her a lifetime of torture came to an end.

She stepped back as Bryce reveled in the kill and tossed the body into the pounding waves. Clearly still furious and needing to take his anger out on something, he roared fire and seared the head until nothing but ashes were left.

She breathed deeply as the warlock's tether to her snapped away and freed her even more. Having destroyed the most powerful of them, the weight that lifted off her this time was so much more noticeable. She almost felt like she was walking on thin air. That she might very well float away.

Yet moments later, Bryce shifted back and pulled her against him, grounding her in a way she knew nobody else could. She pressed her cheek against his chest, more grateful for him than he could imagine.

"Bloody hell, I'm glad yer all right." Steam still rose from his skin as he stroked her hair. "Ye gave me a good scare, lass…many times."

"I know," she murmured, pulling back enough so she could meet his eyes. "And I'm sorry for that. I had no choice."

He nodded. "I know, lass."

There wasn't anger in his eyes but relief as he pulled her cheek back against his chest. It seemed for the moment he refused to have any distance between them at all. In agreement, she inhaled deeply, both comforted and aroused by his sweet yet smoky scent. It was a mix of him and his dragon she knew she would never tire of.

"And though my dragon doesnae like to be controlled," he continued, the emotion obvious in his deepening voice. "'Tis becoming verra clear that if anyone is going to do it 'tis *ye* he wants. 'Tis *ye* he respects."

"Well, I would hope so," Christina said, grinning as she came alongside them.

While Jessie would prefer to remain in Bryce's arms, it was time to acknowledge how thankful she was to those that were there for her. Beyond grateful, she hugged Christina then Sven.

"Thank you so much." Her eyes went between them, as unexpected tears welled in a rush of emotion. Not just because they had saved her life but because they gave her a chance to stay with Bryce. Something that had nearly been taken away from her. "I'm lucky you were both here." Before they could respond, a rowboat bobbing on the ocean caught her attention, and she managed a smile. "All of you, for that matter."

Christina waved and grinned as Graham and Aðísla drew closer. The ships had likely continued around the bend where they could anchor safely.

"I saw caves and woodland not all that far inland," Sven said. "It's a nice enough area to take shelter for the eve." His knowing eyes met Bryce's. "I do not see why Captain Angus needs to know the warlock is defeated until tomorrow morning."

When Bryce's eyes met hers in question, she nodded. She fully understood what that look was about. If she was able to harness so much power already, imagine how much more she might be strengthened if her and Bryce found their true connection. And that, as they all knew, would most likely happen once they came together.

Suffice it to say, they weren't doing too badly considering they had just defeated a warlock *without* the power of the ring. As far as everyone knew, that wasn't supposed to be possible. But then none of them took into consideration that she had such a strong dragon lineage running through her veins. Something she fully intended to ask the Vikings about once they found shelter.

Upon Graham and Aðísla's arrival, the Viking assured her any injuries Angus' men suffered were minor. Nothing their ship physician couldn't handle. So, though Angus was grateful for the offer, Aðísla and Jessie were not needed.

That in mind, they began making their way inland. Though the storm had fled the air was still crisp and gusty. Luckily, Aðísla and Graham had brought enough supplies from the ship to get everyone through the night including blankets, and a change of clothing.

"I'm ravenous," Christina mentioned, eying Jessie as they walked. "Don't you get hungry after using so much magic? Tired?" She shook her head. "Because you look pretty darn peppy."

Jessie shook her head and smiled. "I feel great actually. But then each warlock that's destroyed makes me feel better and better."

"Oh, honey, I'm so glad to hear that." Christina squeezed her shoulder and offered a sympathetic smile. "I just wish you hadn't been repressed like that all this time."

"You and me both," Jessie agreed. "But there's no changing the past." Her eyes went to Bryce who walked ahead with Graham. "Just the future."

Her friend nodded, her smile only growing wider. "So you two are really getting along well, huh?"

"We are." Jessie couldn't stop smiling. "Much better than I had hoped."

"That doesn't surprise me. Bryce is pretty great once you get to know him."

Jessie raised a brow at her. "Why just once you get to know him?"

"Oh, I just had some unfounded issues with him is all." Christina shook her head. "We got it all worked out though."

She nodded, sure she knew where this was going. "You mean about him trying to be with all of you at one point or another while he was promised to marry another."

"Well, yeah, that's exactly what I meant," Christina exclaimed, surprised as her eyes went to Jessie. "So you know about all that?"

"I do," she replied softly. "Remember, I've been with all of you one way or another since the beginning, so I'm well aware of Bryce's actions." She couldn't help a small knowing smile. "More than that, I know he was never attracted to any of you nearly as much as he is me."

"Aw, look at you go." Christina chuckled and winked. "I *like* the less repressed Jessie." Then she grew a little more serious. "So I'm dying to know a few things."

"I'm sure you are." Jessie squeezed her hand as they walked. "Things like why you were abducted and brought to Stirling Castle by one of the warlocks? Or maybe why I showed up in the woods after you and Graham were intimate?"

Christina nodded. "Yeah."

More than willing to share now that she could, Jessie took the time to explain everything to the best of her ability. For starters, how much influence Ainsley really had over Christina and Graham's adventure because she was trying to protect her brother.

"Convincing the warlock to take you to Stirling Castle was all me, though." She flinched, well aware of the poor treatment Christina initially received. "And I'm so sorry. I just didn't see any other way to keep things moving in the direction they needed to go." She frowned as anger flared. "As it was, I barely convinced the warlock to spare Lindsay's life."

Instead of being killed, Lindsay had taken a blade to the hand.

"How did you manage that, anyway?" Christina asked. "We were shocked Lindsay was spared."

"A lot of manipulation," Jessie said quite frankly. "As long as I kept convincing them we were working toward taking down an even greater threat, they played along." She fought a wave of nausea as she thought about what the warlocks were capable of. "And it didn't hurt reminding them they didn't have much time at that particular juncture to enjoy killing Lindsey." She suspected her eyes appeared haunted when they met Christina's "Not the way they would have wanted to."

Their eyes held for a moment as her friend got the gist of just how bad it could have been.

"Well, I know I speak for Lindsay and me when I say all's forgiven," Christina murmured, gratefulness in her eyes as they went to Graham. "Because just look where I am now. All I've learned about myself. Who I'm with." She put a protective hand over her womb. "What we created together."

Jessie pressed her lips together against yet another unexpected well of emotion. Not just happiness for her friend but the thought of having her own child. Something she most certainly never imagined would be possible. Bryce glanced over his shoulder and met her eyes. Just long enough for her to see the intense interest he felt at that particular thought.

"So I get the whole 'you steered everything along' part," Christina continued. "What I can't help wonder about is why the warlocks didn't figure out you were betraying them sooner. Especially when my abduction was so clearly a means to set history back on track."

"Like I said, I was always manipulating them and coming up with one excuse or another," she replied. "We've been together since their conception, so they assumed they knew me inside and out. If I kept secrets or my intentions worked against them, they would know it." She shrugged. "Not only that, but I worked hard over the years to gain their trust. Enough so that they trusted me to always have a master plan." A sour taste filled her mouth. "Though my grandfather was their creator I was something akin to a mother."

At least to four out of six of them.

A shiver rippled through her at how she had to convince them several times that everything was happening for a reason. How their eyes seemed to narrow more and more as time went on. How their dark whispers filled her nights warning her against deceiving them while at the same time still loving her in their own twisted way. It had been pure hell. A long, dangerous game she was glad was behind her now.

Well, mostly.

Only one warlock left to go. Her eyes went to Bryce. One *very* familiar warlock.

Christina didn't question her too much after that, but Jessie kept talking anyway, filling her in on as much as she could. Something she intended to do with Milly and Lindsay too when the time came.

Later, having found a rather pleasant mossy area sheltered by enough cave and thick trees to keep a warlock away, everyone sat around a fire and ate. At long last, the focus was off the warlocks and on something she was incredibly curious about.

What she was beyond an elemental witch and possible arch-wizard.

Namely, her dragon ancestry.

As it turned out, in Norse mythology, Níðhöggr—malice striker—was a dragon known for several ominous things. Some tales had it gnawing at the root of the world tree, Yggdrasill where others had it sucking the blood from the corpses of the dead on Náströnd in Hel.

"Those tales were but folklore carried down generation after generation," Aðísla said, her voice soft, and curious. "In truth, as far as we knew, the Níðhöggr bloodline never left dragon kind's home world of Múspellsheimr. They were a fierce and powerful lineage that had no use for Midgard's—Earth's—weak creatures." Her eyes met Jessie's. "Yet here you are. Proof that we were wrong."

"That's incredible," she murmured, more overwhelmed than she would admit and thankful when Bryce's hand slipped into hers to offer comfort.

"Do you have any siblings, Jessie?" Sven asked, still whittling away as his eyes lifted to hers. Somehow he had managed to keep the same little piece of wood with him from before.

As their gazes held, something flared in his eyes that made her vision go red for a moment.

He was connecting with her dragon. Or better yet her dragon magic. Because she wasn't really a dragon but merely carried the bloodline. Right? It was so hard to know because at times it felt like more. Like what she had felt on the shore. But that *had* to be hereditary dragon magic. It was the only thing that made sense.

"No, I don't have any siblings," she started to say but snapped her mouth shut when images started flashing in her mind's eye. Memories from what had to be her at a very young age. Or so it seemed. But why was her father there? That couldn't be right. As far as she knew he died in a fishing accident shortly before she was born.

Yet it appeared that wasn't the case.

Familiar with his image from a picture Mama kept tucked in a drawer, she recognized her father standing outside their house in Maine with her mother. By the looks of it, he carried an infant. A strange rush of familiarity blew through her as she tried to see the baby more clearly but it was impossible. The memory was too muted and the evident magic protecting and masking the three of them too strong.

Her parents talked in hushed tones, her mother sobbing before she nodded. Then she kissed him and the child before her father fled into the night. No sooner did he vanish then a burning dragon sizzled in the air then flickered away on the wind like a thousand fireflies.

It was the dragon on fire symbol.

What had she just witnessed? Who was that child?

"She was a little girl," Aðísla whispered, staring into the fire as Sven returned to whittling with a truly troubled look on his face. His expression was so intent that she knew his aunt's next words were going to be profound.

And they were.

"The burning dragon symbol was the result of you and that child being separated," Aðísla continued. "A protective spell wrapped up in prophecy. One that seems to be affecting a great deal now."

Baffled, amazed, Jessie frowned. "You mean the prophecy in your era affecting your people?"

"So it seems," Aðísla murmured. "One set in motion the moment your grandfather's curse first ignited."

"That's why it was so important to protect her," Jessie whispered, talking about someone else entirely as she suddenly remembered what her mind had kept from her. "Because she's going to help my sister when she comes. She's going to guide her and help your people."

Sven stopped whittling and narrowed his eyes as he sensed something. "Who?"

"I remember now," she murmured as her eyes met his. "I stopped in Winter Harbor on the way to New Hampshire. I knew I needed to go there but wasn't sure I ever did."

She blinked several times as the memory came rushing back.

White-knuckling the steering wheel, she had stared at the sprawling chalet on Frenchman Bay and knew this was precisely where she needed to be.

"You *can* do this," she whispered to herself. "You *have* to do this."

Courage rallied, she wrapped her hair in a tidy bun, grabbed her bag of cleaning supplies and got out. Determined to see this through, she put one foot in front of the other and headed for the front door, praying her magic was strong enough. No sooner did she get there and raise her hand to knock, when the door swung open.

Clearly not expecting to find her there, a beautiful woman around her age with a wild mass of curly jet-black hair and bright blue eyes stopped short. "Oh." Her eyes widened a little before she gathered herself. "I'm sorry, I was just heading out. Can I help you?"

Remain calm, she preached to herself, hoping the magic she had used ahead of time helped this go smoothly. Because the woman in front of her was very powerful.

"Yes." Jessie smiled warmly and embraced a false persona. "I'm with the cleaning service you hired. My name's Jessie." She cocked her head, sure to appear curious and light-hearted. "Are you Emily?"

"I am," Emily responded, a smile blossoming on her face. "But call me Em, everyone else does." She opened the door wider. "Come in, Jessie."

"Are you sure?" she said. "I can come back later if it's more convenient."

"Don't be silly." Emily ushered her down the hallway. "I just forgot you were coming. My fault, not yours."

That couldn't be further from the truth considering everything about this meeting was pre-planned by Jessie.

She eyed the sprawling chalet, trying harder by the moment to remain calm. This place was at the heart of so much. In *control* of so much. Her eyes went from wall to wall, imagining the pictures that once hung there. Ones she had dreamt of. Dragons.

And Emily? Jessie looked at her out of the corner of her eye. She was at the root of far too much. More than that, she was in terrible danger. Or at least she would be if Jessie didn't help.

That meant casting a spell to keep her off the warlocks' radar.

To keep her free from this God-forsaken curse.

Dangerous, not without risk, she knew she had to be quick about it. That Emily would catch on in no time if she hadn't already. So she whispered a chant within her mind then discreetly dropped a slip of paper from her grandfather's notebook as she set her bag of cleaning supplies down.

"Looks like you dropped something," Emily said as she scooped up the paper then slowed as she looked at it.

"What is this?" she whispered, shaking her head as she sank onto the stool at the kitchen island.

"Safety," Jessie whispered as she picked up her cleaning supplies, took the slip of paper out of Emily's hand and left.

As expected, Emily didn't follow. In fact, by the time Jessie shut the door behind her, Emily would have forgotten she was ever there.

Jessie's eyes fell to her drawing. A dragon on fire followed by a picture of Emily sitting on the couch, watching television in ignorant bliss.

"What did you do to her, woman?" Sven said through clenched teeth, ripping her from the memory. Based on his tight, borderline furious expression, he had followed her every thought. At least those that had anything to do with deceiving or controlling Emily. His eyes were fierce and fiery enough that Bryce had his hand on the hilt of his dagger.

"What did you do to her?" Sven ground out again, the distress in his deepening voice palpable.

"She kept her safe...is keeping her safe." Aðísla rested her hand on his arm and shook her head. "You should be thanking Jessie, not questioning or threatening her."

Jessie kept her gaze steady with his out of respect. It was clear he cared for Emily a great deal, and she should proceed very carefully. "She's all right, Sven," Jessie said softly. "Like your aunt said she's safe. I wouldn't let anything happen to her."

For a flicker of a moment, she allowed her eyes to drop to his carving. But of course, it was turning into a likeness of Emily.

"How did you keep her safe?" Sven persisted, still clearly distraught. "Safe from what?"

"The symbol is keeping Emily safe from the warlocks," Aðísla intercepted. "Just like it kept the warlocks from knowing Jessie had gone there, to begin with." His aunt's eyes stayed steady on him. "And it's doing that so she can face what's coming. What your father and King Heidrek are preparing for." Her eyes returned to Jessie's. "Prophecy first ignited by a curse." Her eyes returned to Sven. "Once this curse lifts and Scotland is saved, we will see the prophecy through with our own people."

A heavy silence fell as Sven's eyes, at last, turned to Aðísla's and held. It was hard to know if they were speaking telepathically or if he was simply weighing out his options. Because if nothing else held true about Sven, it was that he was a man of not only silent reflection but action. Based on the concern and determination in his eyes, the latter might take precedence right now.

He might very well abandon them and head for Winter Harbor this moment.

Would he truly? Better yet, would she blame him if he did? Had her and Bryce been in a similar position there stood a very good chance she might already be gone.

Yet as Sven's eyes slowly returned to hers, and their dragon magic reconnected, she realized she would not have done that. She would not have left despite how strongly she felt for Bryce. Any more than Sven would leave right now despite how much he cared about Emily. Like Jessie, he would put Scotland and her people above his own concerns and desires. Not only that but she sensed he had decided to trust her. And the faith he put in her was monumental because it concerned someone he cared about above all others.

Humbled by his trust, Jessie nodded that she understood without them ever exchanging a word.

"Thank you for protecting her," he said softly before he headed into the woods, off to deal with his turbulent emotions on his own it seemed.

She stared after him for several moments before Aðísla finally broke the heavy silence.

"Sven has loved Emily since she was a child," she murmured. "I'm sure it's clear to all that love has transformed into something far stronger with age."

Jessie nodded that she understood. Yet she sensed Sven and Emily weren't together and found that curious. Not curious enough, however, to question it. That was between him and Emily. Nobody else.

Now was the time to deal with her own heartbreaking revelations.

"Do you have any idea where my sister is?" Jessie asked Aðísla, unable to stop the moisture in her eyes as emotions welled up once more. Though the fiery dragon symbol was apparently part of a protective spell, what if it hadn't withstood the test of time. "How do you even know she's still alive?"

"Because the dragon symbol would not have appeared otherwise," Aðísla said. "You are one side of it with your curse, and she is the other side with her prophecy. Once you end your journey, she will begin hers."

"Will I meet her before then?" Jessie asked, ignoring the tear that slid down her cheek.

"I don't think so," Aðísla murmured. "Both the curse and prophecy will likely have to be fulfilled before you do." Her eyes were kind yet strong as they stayed with Jessie's. "Without either of you realizing it, she has helped you along your journey as you will help her." A soft, whimsical smile curved her lips. "While you are very strong, Jessie, even you were not strong enough to pull off the feat you did controlling the warlocks and manipulating so much all this time. She was there too, offering you insight and wisdom."

Silence again settled before Bryce whispered, "They're twins, aren't they?"

"Yes, very much so." Aðísla nodded. "That's the only way this would have been able to happen."

She had a twin? *Truly?*

Speechless, Jessie did her best to keep her emotions under wrap as Bryce stood and pulled her up after him. It was clear he realized she needed time alone to process everything. For that, she couldn't be more grateful. She felt like she was starting to lose her grip. That any control she might have reclaimed was slipping away under an onslaught of heart-wrenching information.

Yet it wasn't the massive weight it could have been, she reflected as she eyed Bryce. She wouldn't be alone as she came to terms with everything. Those days were over. Now she had someone to lean on. Help her. Offer strength as he did now bidding everyone a good night for them both, because she just couldn't seem to pull herself together. But she didn't need to as he grabbed a satchel and led her deeper into the forest.

"Not too far," she whispered, still a protector despite what she was going through. "Or I might not be able to keep them safe."

The truth was she knew the other warlock was nowhere near here but off licking his wounds. Where she had felt lighter after destroying the strongest of them, he would be devastated...and preparing.

"'Tis not all that far," Bryce assured, and he was right. They only walked for another minute or so before they ducked into a cave with a rather tight entrance even for her. When he murmured a chant, a fire flared to life, and she stopped short in awe.

The space wasn't overly large, but the soaring ceiling gave it a majestic feel with its thousands of sparkling bits of mica. They looked like twinkling stars as the firelight danced off of them.

Somewhere in the cave other than the entrance there had to be a small opening close to the ocean because the soothing sound of waves echoed off the stone. Her eyes went to the elevated shelf of rock on one side. Part of it included a small pool of water with steam rising off it. No bigger than a large bathtub, it was surrounded by soft, verdant moss.

Her eyes went to his, and she whispered, "You did this for me, didn't you?"

"Some of it, aye." He took her hand. "We can find another spot if the sound of the ocean is too much."

"Why would it be too much? I think it's wonderful."

He frowned. "'Tis just my concern over it nearly taking your life so recently."

She shook her head, touched that he obviously thought of everything when it came to this place. "No, I'm fine. It sounds soothing, and I could use that right now." Her eyes met his. "And if you don't mind, I'd rather talk and sift through my emotions later. Just being alone with you is enough for the moment."

"Aye then, lass." Knowing full well what she meant, he proceeded to take off his boots, spread a blanket on a grassy spot that shouldn't exist in here then set aside some skins of whisky. While he did, she pulled off her boots as well then wandered to the pool, watching him out of the corner of her eye.

Though most virgins would be getting pretty nervous right now, she wasn't. Instead, she was excited. She felt as if she was getting ready to jump off a ledge and spread her wings for the first time. That she was getting ready to soar.

"I thought you might like to bathe and get the salt off of you," he said as he joined her.

"Actually, I would," she began but trailed off as he reeled her closer and tilted her chin until her eyes stayed with his. She noticed he had a particular way of standing as though braced on a rolling ship, to better compensate for their height differences.

"I'd like to bathe as well," he whispered. "With you."

Then he kissed her.

Like before it was soft at first then more persistent. She loved how lost she became in a simple kiss. Well, simple was probably the furthest thing from it. More like masterful and sweeping. It almost took her outside of her body though she could still feel all the various ways her flesh responded. Eventually, those responses narrowed down to one very persistent need between her thighs.

Eager, wanting more, she wrapped her hands in his tunic and tugged a little.

Lust saturated his gaze as he slowly broke the kiss and whispered, "Not yet, lass. Not nearly yet."

When she frowned in what she knew was likely sexual frustration, a small, knowing smile curled his lips, and he began undressing her. Not quickly by any means but slow and tortuous, removing her clothing inch by agonizing inch. To elongate her pleasurable suffering, he gave his undivided attention to each bit of flesh he unveiled. Sometimes he kissed or even licked or nibbled while his fingers dusted here and there, intensifying the sensations.

First, he started at the tender lobe of her ear then worked his way down the side of her neck. The way he flicked his tongue then blew lightly on the indentation where her collarbone met in the center, made tiny flutters spread down her arms and torso. Then he worked his way over her shoulders down to her fingertips, all the while building the ache between her legs.

By the time he lowered her dress to her waist, she was so immersed in how he made her feel that her head had fallen back and her eyes were closed. Where some might be bashful at this point, she was the furthest thing from it as he began fondling her breasts. He was remarkably gentle, almost worshiping. So much so that she was utterly relaxed in a deep state of arousal.

Or at least she was until his tongue swirled around a nipple then pulled it into his mouth.

Her eyes shot open, and she groaned as a whole new type of pleasure shot straight to her center. She dug her hands into his hair, breathing heavily as he did the same to the other nipple. Thankfully, they were close enough to the ledge of the mossy area that when her legs grew rubbery, she could lean back.

But not before he had the dress completely down.

Before she knew it, he lifted her until she was sitting then urged her to lie back. Initially, she shook her head, feeling far too exposed. But then he focused on her nipples again, and all inhibitions drifted away as she gave in. Lost in sensual sensations she never knew were possible, she began to feel enticing and desirable. As such, she felt emboldened and unafraid when he kissed and nibbled his way down her stomach, then over her pelvic bone.

She shivered in anticipation as he bypassed her center and worked his way down first one leg then the other. Though she could barely crack her eyes open, when she did it was to find so much more than she anticipated. Not just desire in his eyes but wonder and pleasure as he appreciated every last bit of her. It was as though each centimeter of flesh from her thighs to her kneecaps to her toes offered him a new delight. If one were to guess, she would say he found her utterly flawless.

Seeing him so taken only made her feel more confident so by the time he made his way back up, spread her thighs and put his mouth where the ache was, she relaxed into it. At least for the first second or two. When sharp pleasure suddenly speared her, she gripped his shoulders.

"Bryce," she groaned, almost afraid of how good it felt.

"*Just relax, lass,*" he murmured into her mind. "*Dinnae fight it but embrace it. Let go.*"

She swallowed hard then clamped her upper teeth down on her lower lip as the pleasure only increased. It was one thing to imagine how something like this might feel and another altogether to experience it. Her lifelong fantasies were way off. A fact that became more and more evident as she twisted her hands in the material at his shoulders and hung on tight.

The building pressure inside her just kept growing and growing as though eager to encompass her whole body. As if determined to take away control entirely. Though fearful at first of the overwhelming pleasure, his soft words stayed with her.

"Embrace it. Let go."

So she let the sensations have her and didn't fight them as the pressure only grew. Then, just like she imagined, she hovered on the edge before she fell right over. She cried out and arched as she locked up then trembled as her body let go. Fresh waves of pleasure rolled through her again and again as she kept quivering.

She was only vaguely aware of him pulling off his shirt and plaid, perhaps intending to go bathe. But she didn't want that. Not yet.

"Now," she whispered, needing him close. She wanted more of this feeling though she was still immersed in it. Based on his rigid erection, he wanted it too. "Please...now...right here."

If he was at all undecided if this was the right time, it didn't last long as he swung her fully onto the moss then came over her. Then he kissed her again. Hard and passionately and with everything she knew he felt. As he did it combined the residual pleasure of her previous climax with fresh, desperate arousal.

She felt half human half animal in her instinctual need to be taken. In her relentless desire to have him closer still...to be filled. She was so entrenched in desire and arousal that she barely felt the stretching below then the pinch of pain when he finally took her. The look on his face was almost rapturous as he began to work his way in. Not quickly but slowly, giving her time to adjust.

Yet he was right. When he eventually seated himself fully, she was ready for him. More than ready for that matter. As was he based on his low moan and the way he trembled ever-so-slightly. Their eyes met one another's through a red haze of mutual understanding.

Their dragon magic was connecting.

Everything felt sharper than before. Every sensation ten times stronger. From the spicy heated smell of his skin to the sound of his racing heart. When he began moving, and his brows drew together in blissful concentration, she knew he was barely holding on. That the way she was making him feel was unique, new and intensely arousing.

He, in turn, was doing the same to her. Every part of her flesh and soul was responding to the glorious friction below. The acute pleasure of being close to a person that made you feel so incredibly good.

So astoundingly alive.

As he thrust and ground, she began to do the same, meeting him in a dance that felt as old as time. Anxious and racing toward a pinnacle both were desperate to reach, she wrapped her legs around him. In response, he didn't just groan but released a low growl as he thrust harder, his strokes longer and deeper.

Something about his near-ferocious response drove her over another kind of edge altogether. This time she might have even screamed her orgasm was so intense. One thrust later, he roared and locked up inside her. The feel of his heavy throb and release only seemed to intensify what she was already feeling.

Pure ecstasy.

She couldn't find better words to describe it. For that matter, she could barely form a coherent thought as the mica chips far above seemed to burst into a million different colors. She had never felt more alive and full of pleasure than she did at this moment. As her climax wrapped around her and seemed to bring her closer to him than she ever thought possible. In some ways, it was almost as if they became one. As if the pleasure they had found was equally matched and so much more than they realized it could be.

Seconds later, however, her blood ran cold when someone else's words whispered into her mind, "*Soon it will be even better.*"

Bryce's inner dragon roared in defiance and rage, silencing the warlock's damning words.

But not before he got his twisted point across.

"*Soon I will give you what you've always wanted.*"

Chapter Twelve

BRYCE COVERED JESSIE more securely, instinctually protecting her when he was ripped from pure bliss by his inner dragon's roar. Rare was the day his dragon was on such high alert. Someone, or *something*, had just made it into her mind and he was braced to defend her. His eyes swung around the cave seeking out anything that might be hiding in the shadows.

"He's gone," she whispered, her eyes wide as she trembled.

Bryce knew some of her physical response was because of the passion they had just experienced and some because of fear.

"I don't think he'll be back anytime soon." She shook her head. "Not like that. Not within my mind."

Of course, she was talking about the last warlock.

"The bloody bastard," he cursed as he cupped her cheek. "Are ye all right, lass?"

She nodded, the movement a little jerk-like. "Yes, just...feeling a lot at the moment."

He wiped the pad of his thumb across one cheek then the other, well aware of the numerous tears that had fallen throughout their lovemaking. Actually, from the moment he began undressing and kissing her.

"Oh, I didn't know," she whispered, surprised as she touched her cheek and caught his thoughts. "You must think I'm an emotional basket case."

"Nay," he murmured as he pulled back, lifted her and headed into the pool. "I think you've been denied emotions your whole life and now you're allowed to feel them." He lowered her into the warm water, his brogue thickening even more with his own emotions. "And I couldnae be happier that I'm with ye as ye do, lass." He shook his head. "Dinnae hold back. Feel everything and cry as often as ye like."

"I'm not sure that's really the front I should present to everyone as we move forward." A soft smile came to her lovely lips. "I mean what sort of arch-wizard with an ancient, powerful dragon lineage cries all the time?" Her brows rose. "That's not very intimidating now is it?"

He met her small smile. "'Twould disarm yer opponent if nothing else, aye?"

She chuckled softly before she grew more serious. "I'm so sorry the warlock took those last moments from us." Sadness warred with anger in her eyes. "He had no right."

"He's evil," Bryce reminded as he began bathing her. "And he didnae take anything from us." He cupped her cheek again and met her eyes. "That was unlike anything I've ever experienced, lass and 'twas ours alone, do ye ken?"

He had never meant anything so much. Every part of her was exceptionally beautiful both inside and out. While he had found her body alluring on the ship and knew it would be no hardship seducing her, he had no idea how much pleasure and even joy he would find in it. Every inch of her flesh enthralled him. Every sound she made thrilled him. Her every movement and facial expression drove him to distraction.

No lass had ever enjoyed his attentions so avidly and he sure as hell had never enjoyed a lass half as much as her. If true love could be found in the mere act of lying with a lass, then he had found it with her. Their connection had been powerful.

It had been, without question, life changing.

Where that might daunt some, he very much liked it as did his dragon. His inner beast felt like it had possessed its mate and the man just fell head over heels into something he suspected was indeed very much love.

"It *was* ours alone," she agreed softly in response to his words. Her eyes were on his as she broke into his thoughts. Musings he knew she followed and evidently liked based on her dewy smile. "Thank you, Bryce. Thank you for being so…" She shook her head and blinked away fresh moisture as she searched for the right words. "For making my first time so memorable."

"You made it verra easy, lass," he murmured as he ran his fingers through her silky hair beneath the water. "'Twas truly a privilege *and* a pleasure."

A becoming blush stained her cheeks as her eyes dropped to his chest then began to slowly roam over him. She had little time to look at his body let alone touch him but seemed inclined to do that now as she ran her fingers along the path of her eyes.

"You're amazing," she murmured, fire flaring in her eyes in appreciation. "I didn't think with our notable size differences that we would fit together so well..." Her eyes rose to his as her fingers drifted down his abdomen. "But you were so gentle..."

"Not toward the end," he reminded, unable to stop himself. Eager to see what she'd make of the truth. "I was rougher than intended, lass. My dragon got the better of me, and for that I'm sorry." He shook his head. Because of her delicate frame, he tried his best to take it easy but knew he had failed miserably. "'Tis the way of my kind to grow somewhat rambunctious when overly aroused."

"You were rough?" Her brows shot up in surprise. "Rambunctious?" Amusement suddenly lit her eyes. "Really?" She cocked her head, truly curious. "When?"

He couldn't help a chuckle. Was she serious? "Toward the end, lass. 'Twas actually rougher than I've ever been with a..." He realized talking about another woman probably wasn't appropriate at the moment. "Let's just say there was a lot of my inner beast taking part."

"Well, then I guess I like your inner beast." She grinned. "Because I didn't think it was rough at all." She shrugged, another blush warming her cheeks. "Actually, I wouldn't have changed a thing and..." Her hand drifted even lower. "I look forward to experiencing your inner beast again."

"Och," he whispered as she found what she was looking for.

"Oh," she whispered in return as she wrapped her small hand around him. Well, as much around him as she could manage. It might have been mere minutes since they came together, but he was more than ready for her again.

Though he immensely enjoyed how brazen she was becoming, he also knew she was going to need time to heal and told her as much.

"I don't think so," she murmured as she continued fondling him. She might have been a virgin, but she had the benefit of reading his mind and knowing precisely how he liked to be touched. "I don't feel any pain at all or even tenderness."

"Nay?" He looked at her curiously, his voice thickening with arousal. "'Tis odd that." He kept considering her, struggling to keep his thoughts in order as she stroked him. "'Twas also somewhat odd you didnae feel a wee bit more side effects from your whisky last night...or that you wernae more exhausted after the battle on the ship, then yer near death experience."

"Honestly, I think it all might have to do with my gift," she replied, her touch growing more fervent, her pleasure in his pleasure obvious. "I've always healed faster than usual and never caught any illnesses after being around sick people." She shrugged. "I've never been sick at all for that matter."

"Interesting," he said hoarsely, so aroused now he envisioned turning her, bending her over the side and taking her in a way unbefitting a lass so new to sex. "So you're truly not feeling any pain?"

"Not the kind you're talking about," she said softly, her voice not quite right either as she turned, stepped up on a small stair-like incline beneath the water, bent forward and glanced at him over her shoulder. "And I don't think what you want to do to me is unbefitting at all."

"Bloody hell," he managed, well aware her dragon magic was at work here. Or at least it certainly felt that way. It was as if she did, in fact, have a dragon lingering inside of her.

A lusty little dragon at that.

"Well?" she murmured, fire flaring in her eyes. "Do I have to tell you twice that I'm not in any pain?"

He probably should have questioned her more or flat out denied her just in case, but he was thoroughly incapable. Not just of denying her but of even taking it slow. His inner dragon was wide awake and eager, as were other parts of him.

His vision hazed red as he spread her legs, gripped her shoulder and hip then thrust deep. At first, when she cried out, he thought he

160

had hurt her but soon realized it was a cry of pleasure. Bless the gods because he wasn't sure he could stop. She felt far too good, her tight heat welcoming as he began to move.

She dug her nails into the moss, arched her back and began making all sorts of sounds that revved him up even more. Sometimes she moaned and grunted where other times she mewled and even whimpered. Yet it was all in unabashed enjoyment as new feelings swept over her.

It was impossible to hold back as he thrust, his dragon eager to dominate in direct response to her 'dragon' wanting to be dominated. It was an intoxicating ride far beyond anything he had ever experienced. She was receptive and eager and so damn enticing he knew he was going to find his pleasure far too soon *again.*

Moving closer, he braced his arms on either side of her, covering her body with his, and all but wrapped around her when he knew there was no more time. Self-control was clearly a lost cause when it came to her. She just felt too bloody good. Thankfully, like before, they synchronized because no sooner did he press deep, roar and let go, she did the same.

Her roar turned into a long, low groan as her inner muscles clenched tight, and she quivered then melted onto the ground. Meanwhile, he hung his head, his heart racing and his breathing ragged. She brought out an incredible amount of energy in him. Potent enthusiasm he had never felt before.

"You still didn't strike me as rough," she murmured into his mind, the smile in her voice obvious.

He smiled in return, scooped her up and brought her back into the water to finish bathing. She was far drowsier now and not all that coherent by the time he lay her down on the plaid, pulled her into his arms and covered them. He whispered a chant to ensure the fire remained lit, checked in with his cousin to make sure all was well then found himself yet again watching her sleep.

Her ring still didn't glow, but he couldn't care less. While yes, it would certainly be helpful, it was by no means necessary to help define how he already felt about her. His dragon fiercely wanted to keep her, and he was in complete agreement. While he had been somewhat disbelieving as he had watched his cousins fall far too quickly in love with their lasses, now he understood.

It really did happen that fast, didn't it?

The next morning, when Jessie's eyes drifted open, and she smiled at him, he suspected she felt it too. How close they were becoming. How it truly seemed that love was igniting between them.

He had slept some but not much. Though she had assured him the warlock was nowhere nearby, he felt better remaining alert.

"Good morning," she murmured as she stretched and kept smiling. "I hope you slept."

"Aye, enough so." He brushed his lips across hers then dropped a few more kisses on her before he forced himself to stop. "We should join the others soon and get back to Angus."

"How soon?" she whispered, the devil in her eyes.

He chuckled and stood before she got the better of him. "While I more than appreciate your insatiable nature and fully intend to satisfy it as time goes on, I'll feel better once I have you safely back with the others."

The truth of it was he would much prefer to stay here for an indeterminate amount of time and continue enjoying her body. He knew he would never tire of her. Not for a moment.

Though tempted to dress her himself he had no doubt that would only lead them back to bed, so he handed her fresh clothing and got dressed. As he did, he felt her thoughts shift back to things she had set aside last night. Not just her newfound sister but the warlock.

"I'm just surprised I never sensed her," she said softly, clearly referring to her sister. "I sensed Iosbail but not my own blood." She sighed, muttering, "Then there's the warlock. I wish I knew what he was up to." She shook her head. "I wish I could better prepare us."

He gripped her shoulders lightly and made sure her eyes were with his when he spoke. "All the preparation we'll need is the strength we find together. I know that doesnae sound overly reassuring at the moment, but 'tis true." Confident he was right, his eyes stayed with hers. "I have never been more sure of anything."

How else could it be considering what they had found together? How quickly their feelings toward one another were growing?

"As to your sister," he continued. "Dinnae focus on the connection you never felt, or the years you lost with her but on what you know about her now, and that there *is* a future for you both."

"How can you be so sure?" she murmured.

"Because she has seen you through this journey and we will succeed," he replied. "Then you will see her through her journey,

162

and she will succeed." He shook his head, never more serious. "I dinnae have any doubt that once all is said and done that you two will come together. That you *will* have a future."

"Yet it sounds like hers might be in ancient Scandinavia with Vikings." Her eyes remained with his, and her next words warmed his heart. "Where mine will very much be here with you."

He offered a lopsided grin. "Have you not heard of time-travel then?"

A small smile wobbled on her lips. "Good point."

"Aye." He kissed her again then packed up their satchel. "'Twould be nice to travel through time just for friendly family visits rather than to deal with all the strife happening now."

She nodded, but he could see the flicker of worry still in her eyes as they began making their way through the woods back to the others. "Something else occurred to me too," she said. "Something I probably should have figured out sooner."

When he looked at her in question, she continued. "While the warlocks definitely haven't been behind all the time-traveling with everyone, I'm beginning to think this last one has when it comes to you."

"Aye?" he said.

"Yes." She appeared troubled. "Twice now you've ended up in dangerous positions when you traveled through time. The first when you traveled to Bannockburn with Christina and Graham and this time by the waterfall." She shook her head. "It's too coincidental in my opinion." Her eyes met his as she took his hand. "So please, if...*when* we travel through time again, be extra vigilant okay? I'm starting to suspect the last warlock is very jealous of you."

He nodded, seeing the logic in that. "You have my word, lass. I'll be verra careful."

She nodded as well and was about to say more when she stopped short and whispered, "Samhradh," as if it had just popped into her head.

"Summer," he repeated, narrowing his eyes.

She had just said the fourth seasonal word that had been a part of everyone's adventures.

"A spirit comes," she whispered a few moments later.

Her eyes began to glow not with dragon magic, but her own unique magic as a slender, beautiful but very transparent woman appeared through the forest. She wore trousers and appeared ready to fight.

"Aye, then, ye've nearly made it," the spirit said in greeting, pleased as her eyes lingered on him with appreciation. "But how could ye not with the likes of ye along?" She eyed him up and down. "The MacLomains do make some fine lookin' lads."

Jessie's eyes widened as she whispered, "You must be her..."

A ghost that knew he had MacLomain blood and looked, acted and spoke like this one? He could only think of one woman that fit that description. A woman at the heart of many stories told around the campfires of his youth.

"Has my brother not figured it out yet then?" The spirit rolled her eyes. "'Tis no wonder I suppose, being reborn such as he was." Her brows flew up. "And without me along no less!" She winked at Bryce. "Though as ye all verra well know I've been along aplenty and enjoyed the ride."

"Iosbail MacLomain," Bryce said softly.

He dropped to a knee and lowered his head in respect. A very long time ago this lass had once been immortal and birthed the Broun clan. Like her brother Adlin, she had done a tremendous amount for Brouns and MacLomains alike.

"Aye, Iosbail MacLomain," came a deep voice as none other than Adlin and Milly appeared through the forest. His eyes were moist as they met Iosbail's. "I cannae tell ye how good it is to see ye again, Sister. I've missed ye something fierce."

"Aye, Brother." Her voice softened as Adlin stopped in front of her. "'Tis hard being separated but I've kept a close eye on ye over the years." She grinned. "Especially lately."

"And I'm verra thankful...and impressed."

It was clear he had many things he wanted to ask her but held back. Perhaps because he didn't want to overwhelm her or because he was waiting for her to continue which she readily did.

Her knowing eyes lit with amusement. "I see you're curious about many things, Brother."

"Aye, we've accomplished much." His pride was obvious as he considered her. "As have ye." His eyes lit with curiosity. "How is it ye were able to influence this whole journey because ye did, aye?" He shook his head. "And without Grant and I sensing your presence." He continued looking at her thoughtfully. "And why the seasonal words in Gaelic? Though they lined up with the battles we've been to, how could ye have such accurate foresight?"

"Och, ye forget how powerful I can be, aye?" Though it might have sounded like she took insult, the sparkle in her eyes said otherwise as she went on. "My presence and magic are now of the spirit realm. 'Tis why Jessie could more easily sense me. And because Jessie has such a connection to the fifth element, that of spirits, I've been able to follow her intentions since the curse began unraveling." Her eyes went from Jessie to Adlin. "Therefore I could give her a little nudge here and there if her plans took any of ye off the course I knew would be best."

Adlin eyed her for a moment before he figured something out and a knowing smile formed. "And that little nudge ye gave, without question came from ye using your Irish roots in conjunction with the magic of the rings themselves." He cocked his head. "Which leads me to believe the curse has no connection to the Celts. Hence your ability to navigate around the warlocks."

"Aye, Brother, 'twas the magic of me birth home Eire that helped me." She looked at everyone "That helped all of you." Her eyes flickered from Jessie's ring to Adlin. "But then how could Ireland not fight on behalf of her Claddagh?"

"How could it not indeed," Adlin said softly as his eyes stayed on hers. "I know I speak on behalf of us all when I say thank ye, Sister. Ye have well and truly protected your kin and country."

"Aye." Iosbail chuckled as she teased him. "'Twas verra clear ye and Grant needed my help from the get go." She shook her head. "I dinnae think I've ever seen anything elude ye two like this curse." She shrugged. "But then 'tis not every wizard that tries to create the Claddagh rings. 'Tis supposed to be an impossible feat for mere mortals, whether magic is involved or not."

Her eyes were fond as she continued. "So thank ye both on behalf of my kin and country that ye were able to do it as well as ye did. 'Tis no blame of yers that ye couldnae control every aspect of it this time." She gave him a pointed look. "Because if I know anything about ye and Grant 'tis that it must have been bloody hard to have so much taken out of yer hands through all this."

"'Twas not easy," he conceded. "But we didnae lose control when it came to steering the couples closer." His grateful eyes flickered to Jessie before returning to Iosbail. "And we have more faith than ever that each and every couple that's come together will see this curse through and save Scotland." He had a look of both pride and resignation on his face. "The time was bound to come that I couldnae be as all-knowing as I once was."

"Aye, times are changing indeed," Iosbail agreed. "But we've created good Scottish bloodlines, strong witches and wizards all, that will keep Scotland on track. And though we might not always be there to guide them, I'd say we taught their predecessors verra well. So well that both MacLomains and Brouns will always be as courageous and persevering as we ever were." She chuckled and winked again. "And naturally, like us, verra clever and not hard on the eyes."

Adlin grinned, back to his chipper self in no time. "We *are* verra clever on occasion."

She eyed herself over, grinning as well. "And verra attractive." Then she shook her head. "Even if one of us is transparent."

Both chuckled, smiling as their eyes held and they reconnected in a way long lost to them.

Yet all good things must come to an end.

"I'm afraid the time has come that I say goodbye to both ye and me beloved clans," she said softly, "and remain in the afterlife with me king."

Like Adlin had when he met Milly in his previous life, Iosbail had met and fallen in love with King Alexander Sinclair and begun her aging process. Though Bryce was curious why Adlin had been reborn and not Iosbail, now was certainly not the time to question it. In all likelihood, the answer was as simple as wanting to remain with her one true love.

Iosbail's eyes went to Jessie, impressed. "Ye have done verra well by my country, and I couldnae be more proud." Her voice lowered in respect. "Neither could yer mother, lass. She sends her love and strength and will see ye again someday."

Jessie's eyes welled, and she nodded as Iosbail's gaze turned Bryce's way. "And yer sister feels the same about ye, lad. Know that someday we'll all be reunited as we should be. Until then, continue to protect yer clan as valiantly as ye already have."

Bryce nodded, more than grateful for the kind words and the sense of comfort she offered.

She nodded, clearly pleased with Bryce and Jessie "Ye saw through the last of my influence over this curse when ye aided Laird Angus MacDonald and set history straight again."

Something in her eyes told him it wasn't quite over yet though. History would still need some help, but it was out of her hands.

At last, her attention turned Milly's way. "I couldnae be happier that ye and Adlin are reunited, Mildred. Ye share the truest of love and 'twill always keep ye both strong."

"Thank you, Iosbail," Milly replied, her eyes fond as she obviously recalled Adlin's sister from a previous life. "Thank you for everything."

Iosbail nodded before her eyes, at last, settled on Adlin, her words emotional. "'Twill be some time before we meet again, Brother. Until then, I wish ye the verra best and love ye verra much."

"Aye, Sister," he replied, just as emotional. "And I love ye."

Their eyes held for a long moment before she began to fade then vanished. Nobody said a word as Adlin stared at where she had been for a few moments longer before he nodded as though accepting that she was, indeed, officially gone.

"Well, then," he finally said, breaking the silence as his eyes went to Bryce and Jessie. As only he could, he set aside melancholy and smiled. "It seems you've been busy in our absence!"

"Aye," Bryce replied, truly glad Adlin had arrived. He had wondered if either arch-wizard would make an appearance on their adventure. "It's been verra entertaining."

A knowing little smile hovered on Milly's lips as she looked between Bryce and Jessie then hugged Jessie hello. As they started back toward the others, Milly said, "We brought someone along that's eager to see you, Jessie."

Jessie nodded, not needing to ask who. Minutes later, they joined his kin, and Lindsay was embracing her tightly. Neither had a dry eye by the time Lindsay pulled back, held Jessie at arm's length and gave her the same sort of knowing look Milly just had. "Well, look at you, darling." Her eyes flickered to Bryce then returned to Jessie. "You're blossoming before our very eyes, aren't you?"

Though pink stained her cheeks, Jessie managed to smile. "So it seems."

After that, Lindsay took her hand and walked off to spend some time alone catching up. Already packed and ready to go, everyone followed at a distance. Conall handed him two sticks with meat on it, explaining one was for Jessie.

"Since we learned the truth, Lindsay's been verra eager to reconnect with Jessie," Conall said as he, Adlin and Bryce walked together. "'Tis bloody amazing how much Jessie's accomplished."

"Aye," Bryce agreed. "I'm verra proud of her."

Adlin eyed him. "I'd say yer more than that when it comes to the lass."

Bryce shook his head. "I've never met anyone like her."

"'Tis safe to say none of us has," Adlin murmured. "She's exceptional." He grinned at Bryce. "Though ye know verra well I wasnae referring to her magic but the love already betwixt ye."

"Aye," Bryce said softly. "'Tis...remarkable."

"Aye," Conall replied. "There is nothing like coming together with our lasses." His eyes remained on Lindsay. "The love is verra strong verra fast."

"Aye," Bryce agreed. "'Tis unlike anything I've ever felt."

"And that love has already made a difference," Adlin said. "Though I cannae help but wonder why I was compelled to come here when 'tis obvious ye've things well in hand. I would have thought ye'd be on to the Battle of Byland Moor by now." He shrugged. "Mayhap 'tis as simple as making sure Lindsay works her magic on Angus' fleet, so they dinnae remember seeing dragons."

Bryce had been wondering the same thing about their arrival. More than that, why they were still here. Two rowboat trips later to get all of them back aboard the ships, he continued to wonder. As far he could tell, all was as it should be as they set sail down the eastern shore of Scotland. The weather was temperate and the North Sea fair. Too fair actually with far too little wind.

"Mayhap 'tis as simple as needing Conall along to manipulate the wind, hence ensuring Angus and his fleet arrive on time," Adlin pondered as he, Milly, Bryce, and Jessie stood at the railing and enjoyed a vibrant sunset rich with deep reds and oranges.

Because Angus had the largest boat with the most space, he had taken the extra travelers aboard his ship. As it was, Lindsay had to be on the same vessel as Jessie so that his lass could amplify her friend's gift of enchantment to the entire fleet when the time came. The others had returned to their original ships, confident Adlin would make sure all traveled on to the next battle together.

Bryce suspected Angus had insisted Lindsay be on this ship for more selfish reasons than anything. Where his son seemed to have a taste for petite brunette's it appeared the MacDonald Laird enjoyed blonds. But then Lindsay was, at heart, an actress and seemed to only boost the morale on the ship with her enigmatic ways. Of course, this was much to Conall's chagrin who remained by her side and manipulated the air so well that wind helped the rowers move the ships right along. The truth was Lindsay only had eyes for Conall, and he knew it. Moreover, as Adlin pointed out, a boost in morale could only help their cause.

As it turned out, everything worked perfectly.

Lindsay used the opportunity to enchant the men into forgetting that they ever saw dragons or witnessed any magic at all. Rather, she convinced them they were such mighty sailors that they had single-handedly weathered the most powerful storm in Scottish history. And all for the love of their king and countrymen.

Though Bryce and his kin knew full well those extras Lindsay threw in would be lost to history, it helped the men tremendously. And where it might have taken too long otherwise, thanks to Conall and their current speed they should arrive right on time. Not to say Jessie couldn't have managed it, but she seemed just as happy to take a break.

"And what harm can it do to be a part of such history as what lays on the morrow, aye?" Adlin asked.

Bryce grinned. "Aye, I hope we're around long enough to see King Edward's face when Angus sails by with three of his ships."

Jessie was about to speak but stopped when she seemed to see something they couldn't.

"What is it lass?" he began, but trailed off when she put her hand on his arm, shook her head and whispered, "Look…"

The moment she touched him, not only him but his cousins and their lasses saw the same thing.

A ghost ship was sailing by in the opposite direction, its black sails revealing what it was. What truly startled them, however, was the bearded man who stood on the side closest to them, his narrowed eyes locked on theirs.

"'Tis Fraser," Bryce murmured, shocked. "And bloody hell if that's not a fifteenth century pirate ship!"

~Avenged by a Highland Laird~

Chapter Thirteen

WITHIN MOMENTS, THE pirate ship faded but not the inner turmoil Jessie felt within every MacLomain who had just connected with her via Bryce.

"I dinnae ken," Bryce growled, fire flaring in his eyes as he stared at the sea where the mighty ship had just been. "Is Fraser dead or alive?"

"Alive," Jessie said softly. "Though he appeared to be a ghost, and I certainly accessed the spirit realm to see him, it was more of a time flux. Similar, actually, to what Christina and Graham experienced the first time they met at Mystery Hill in New Hampshire."

"Bloody hell," Adlin muttered, echoing Bryce's earlier sentiment. "How can he be alive when Grant and I cannae even sense him? 'Tis frustrating!"

"Don't forget what you and Iosbail so recently discussed," Milly reminded, squeezing his hand. "A lot's been taken out of your hands because of this curse." She shook her head. "You can't blame yourself."

"That's right," Jessie said as her eyes met Bryce's. "As I told you, I'll know more once the last warlock is defeated. Until then, you need to focus on the fact that Fraser *is* still alive."

"Aye," Bryce murmured as his brows drew together. "Yet he seemed changed...different."

"*Just like Kenna warned us,*" Christina said into their minds.

Bryce and Adlin scowled at that. Kenna, who once loved Fraser, claimed that where he went changed him. That he was hardened in ways he had not been before. Kenna, sadly, had lost her life on Christina and Graham's adventure.

"*I sensed something else from him too,*" Adlin murmured. "*Something even more out of character.*"

"Aye," Conall replied. "*'Twas a bit of roguishness, aye?*"

"*Aye,*" Graham agreed, the frown obvious in his inner voice.

It was hard imagining any man with MacLomain blood being unprincipled, but Jessie had caught the same thing in Fraser's hard icy blue eyes. Or so it appeared.

"*I wouldn't trust anything you see just yet,*" she said to them all. "*Right now, he's still under the influence of the warlock, and that could very well be messing up everything. Not just how he's acting but how we perceive him.*"

Adlin nodded, his eyes grateful as they met hers. She knew the struggles he had experienced coming into his powers this lifetime. The man he had to measure up to. His previous self. On rare occasion he still battled to get back to that person. Especially at times such as this when sound, reassuring words weren't coming from him but her. Still, he was a reasonable man who was wise enough to be thankful when the moment warranted it.

Adlin might have been part of creating the rings, but she had all but created the warlocks. Or at least that's how she looked at it. She might not have been the evil behind them, but she had helped direct them and knew them better than anyone. More than that, what each and every one was capable of.

"Come," Angus said in passing, totally unaware of what had just transpired. "I invite ye all to dine with me."

They nodded, more than ready for a drink.

Angus raised his mug of ale in salute a while later. "Here's to me and my men navigating the most dangerous storm in history yesterday!" He grinned broadly. "'Twas one hell of a ride!"

She didn't miss it when Bryce winked at Lindsay.

Jessie was so much a part of his mind now she followed nearly every thought. How impressed he was with Lindsay's magical abilities of enchantment. She had done a stellar job with Angus and his crew.

Though she tried to repress a twinge of jealousy, Bryce didn't miss her reaction to the brief connection between him and Lindsay. The truth was he and her friend had shared several connections since the curse began unraveling. Most importantly, when Lindsay saved his life in Stirling. Thanks to her, though he had been beaten within an inch of his life in the English encampment, they didn't end him altogether.

It had been a horrible thing that Jessie imagined would always haunt her. How helpless she had felt at the time. How pleased the warlocks had been at his suffering. Soon enough she would use that memory against this last warlock. She would keep it firmly in mind and have her retribution.

Yet despite how grateful she was to Lindsay, she still had the nerve to feel jealousy. Shame on her. Even if she understood the root of her response, there was no excuse. She should be better than this. If for no other reason than she knew Lindsay was no longer a threat.

When Bryce rested his arm on the back of Jessie's chair and stroked her shoulder in reassurance, she knew he realized her reaction wasn't just remorse over his poor treatment. It was jealousy too.

"*I'm sorry...for all my emotions right now...*" she murmured into his mind. "*You can't imagine how difficult it was knowing you were hurt so bad...*"

When she trailed off, he prompted her to continue.

She said nothing at first as everyone chatted yet eventually came clean with him in a way she had not intended to. Yet she supposed she wanted to better explain herself. Why she had felt jealous, to begin with.

"*Though we all have one true love, sometimes there's a second person out there whose soul is compatible enough that deep love can form.*" Her eyes remained on the others in avoidance as she sipped ale. "*It doesn't happen all the time. It didn't with Milly and Adlin or with Graham and Christina.*"

Bryce waited patiently for her to continue when she paused, considering how to phrase things.

"*Had Lindsay not reconnected and found Conall, the two of you would have been compatible...you might have found love.*" Her eyes finally turned to his. "*Hence her attraction to you before she came together with Conall.*"

Though she knew he was tempted to deny it, he *had* been aware Lindsay was drawn to him at one time. Men knew such things. Especially men with MacLeod and MacLomain blood.

"*Yet I wasnae drawn to her,*" he replied, absolutely truthful. "*Shamefully enough, as soon as I knew she was meant for Conall and couldn't possibly be the one to free me from a loveless marriage, I focused on the next Broun lass.*"

"*I know,*" she replied. "*But had things gone differently, namely her and Conall not coming together, then us, you would've been drawn to her eventually. It was inevitable.*"

"*'Tis a bloody odd thing to consider,*" he replied frankly as he dusted his fingers along the side of her neck. Based on the flare of his pupils, he clearly enjoyed when she shivered with awareness.

"*No offense to Lindsay because she's a kind and bonny person,*" he went on, "*but I think 'tis safe to say she and I are glad that you and Conall exist.*"

She offered a small smile. "*Me too.*"

"*And 'tis perfectly normal to feel jealousy.*" His inner voice remained gentle. "*Dinnae forget that you're human before anything else, lass.*"

She sensed that some small part of him actually liked her response. Her possessiveness. How strongly she felt. Which told her where his mind was when it came to her. His love. Which in turn made her hope that the conversation would end here because there was more. Something now irrelevant to their situation, but information she might want to know if she were in his shoes.

Not surprisingly, he sensed the thoughts she was trying to repress and narrowed his eyes. "*What is it? What aren't you telling me?*"

"*Nothing that much matters now.*"

"*Och.*" He leaned closer and murmured in her ear, "When it comes to you, *everything* matters, lass."

Another shiver of awareness went through her as their eyes met. Though hesitant at first, she finally gave in and told him.

Almost as if he knew what was coming, Adlin's eyes suddenly turned their way. It seemed, perhaps, their private conversation had become too important for an arch-wizard to ignore.

"*Weren't any of you ever curious why there were only four rings,*" she asked Bryce, "*when there are five MacLomain men?*"

"Adlin and Grant were curious but had no way of changing the fact their magic was only determined to make four rings," he replied, frowning. *"Then when Fraser and Kenna fell in love they assumed he was the one who wasn't meant to make a MacLomain, Broun connection."*

"That's always a possibility." Her eyes stayed level with his. *"Though I strongly suspect that's not the case based on how thoroughly Fraser has been removed from the picture by this last warlock."*

As their eyes held it suddenly occurred to him what she was trying to say.

"You cannae mean Fraser..." His brows slammed together in a look of incredulousness. *"And you..."*

When he trailed off in shock, she nodded. *"My guess is though he's clearly not my true love, we would have been compatible...we would have found love."*

"Bloody hell, why didn't we see that one coming?" Adlin muttered aloud as he shook his head and took a swig of ale.

Bryce frowned and took a swig as well, his every thought coming through loud and clear. To his mind, it all made perfect sense now. The warlock contained a piece of Bryce's essence and as Jessie surmised, was jealous enough to try to kill Bryce during every time shift. Along those lines, would he not have removed anyone else he considered a threat? His eyes slid back to her. And—though he tried not to think it, but focus on being grateful his cousin lived—was Jessie not Fraser's type physically? After all, Kenna had also been petite and brunette.

"Ye didnae see what coming?" Angus responded to what Adlin had said.

On the ball, Adlin shook his head, raised his mug and offered a wide smile. "Enjoying myself so bloody much aboard yer bonny ship!"

"Aye!" Angus roared as everyone held up their mugs and did the same before taking another swig.

Thankfully, with her affectionate assurances that he was the only one she wanted, Bryce set aside his jealousy, and they enjoyed several more hours in Angus' company. Most of that time the captain made eyes at Lindsay, Conall be damned. But then what sort of pirate in their right mind cared a lick if her man was sitting right there? Because if nothing else could be said about Laird MacDonald, it was that the historical rumors about him being a pirate were absolutely true. So said the tales his men told of their thieving ways. On behalf of the Scottish crown, of course.

Later, when Bryce and Jessie finally made it to their quarters, she was still chuckling at that fact.

"Oh, he's a pirate all right!" She shook her head, grinning. "Heck if Conall doesn't have his hands full with Lindsay though. She's always been a diva, that one. How could Angus *not* fall head over heels in love with her?"

"Aye, but she doesnae return her admirers' affections." He grinned and shrugged. "And we *are* dealing with a ship full of men at sea for days." He shook his head. "So she was bound to stir things up." He gave her a pointed look. "And she's not the only one. You and Milly have been turning plenty of heads on this ship."

She didn't comment on that as she pulled off her boots. "Either way, we're lucky to have you MacLomains," the corner of her mouth hitched, "or should I say a *MacLeod* watching over us."

"Aye," Bryce agreed as he backed her up against the door before she could undress any further. "And we're just as lucky to have you Brouns to watch over." He pinned her wrists by her head and came close. "Verra lucky." His voice lowered. "I'm grateful you're mine, lass."

They both knew he was referring to the remote possibility she might have ended up with Fraser.

"But I didn't," she whispered, her heart racing as their eyes held. She was so turned on she could barely think straight. "Nor would I have wanted to."

He brushed his lips across hers, then pulled up her skirts and hoisted her so she could wrap her legs around his waist. Again, his thoughts came through loud and clear, and she could only be grateful for his reasonable mind.

Though some small part of him wondered if he should feel guilty about the warlock's part in Fraser's fate, he knew better. Evil had been at the root of what happened, not Bryce. He was just a victim too. And the gods knew Fraser was just as much a victim. Not just because of where he was and what he had become, but because he hadn't ended up with Jessie.

When she wrapped her arms around Bryce's shoulders, and their lips met again, thoughts of his cousin faded. Instead, he became as lost as before not just by the feel of her lips but by the confident way she moved against him.

Though she should probably try to block their mental connection a little, she found following his thoughts and emotions enthralling.

His arousal and need screamed up so fast inside him that he thrust against her instinctually. When she groaned her approval, he only grew more desperate. So desperate that he took immediate action.

Rather than waste a few precious seconds falling to the bunk, he yanked off his plaid, shoved her dress higher and took her right there. She released a ragged cry then bit down near the nape of his neck. Fueled by her animalistic response and the exquisite feeling of being inside her, he began thrusting.

It didn't matter if the ship was swaying, he had never felt more steady and driven. He wanted to feel her over and over and push her to peak again and again. He wanted to hear her cries of pleasure as she found her fulfillment.

Which, as it turned out, happened rather fast.

She bit harder when her body began to shudder then she let go with a strangled moan. He paused, enjoying not just the pinch of her passionate bite, but the feel of her climax. As soon as she began to relax and her teeth let go, he resumed kissing her.

Then, still inside her, he lowered her to the bunk and started moving again. This time, he seemed determined to draw out her experience as he took it slow at first. But that only lasted so long. They were too eager. Greedy. Desperate.

Sweat slicked them as their passion increased. He particularly liked when she rode him, so she spent ample time doing just that. Not tentative in the least, it took her no time to move her hips just the way he liked. She felt emboldened and pleased as he imagined he would like anything she did and any way she moved.

She offered a womanly smile at those thoughts. The sort of smile that promised she would offer him far more. That she had no doubt of the pleasure she could give.

In fact, she did such a good job of it that she never made it beneath him again before he gave into her feminine powers and released hard. Soon after, she followed, digging her nails into his chest as she locked up and then melted down against him.

Neither said anything for a while as he stroked her back languidly.

Eventually, she murmured, "I think I'm making up for a lot of lost time."

"Aye," he rumbled, smiling. "'Tis verra good for me that ye are. I particularly like the feel of ye in my mind so thoroughly too. 'Tis even more arousing somehow."

In agreement, she chuckled as she remained focused on making up for lost time. "I hope you still feel that way a year from now because I have a feeling it might only get worse."

"Worse?" He shook his head. "It could never get worse but only better."

She smiled as she whispered, "I have a feeling you're right."

They talked for a while after that and continued getting to know each other better.

"You're a verra dynamic person considering you've lived such a lonely, sheltered existence," he said softly, flattering her not just with words but with his thoughts. He appreciated her intelligence and her zest to always learn more.

"Thank you. I read a lot," she explained. "The warlocks thought it was all in preparation for destroying Scotland and learning about herbs and such but it wasn't." She remained on top of him, her chin propped on her hands as she looked at him. "While I certainly loved learning things, especially history, I enjoyed fiction too."

He continued running his fingers here and there over her back, renewing her arousal all over again as he murmured, "Aye?"

"Sure. Just about every genre too." Though she smiled, she knew a touch of sadness reflected in her eyes. "Even romance."

"'Tis good," he murmured, well aware her sadness came from the loneliness she had felt. The love she never thought would be hers. "Romance is good, aye?"

"Yes it is," she whispered as their eyes held and fire flared. "Better than any book portrays it actually."

As to be expected from that point one thing led to another, and they made love again before they drifted off to sleep. Then dreams came and went, but she always seemed to return to the same one.

A memory from her past.

She stood in a small clearing in the Maine forest of her youth wishing it could stay summer forever. She wished she could stay in this spot. But winter would come, and with it, the trees would go to sleep. When they did, though their barren branches would allow more sunlight through, it wouldn't matter. The warlocks always moved around more when the trees rested. When their Earthly protection waned. That's when they got even closer to her.

More so, the one that wanted her in a different way than the others.

"Do you not like when I can come closer?" he said softly from the shadows. "Does it no longer please you like it once did?"

A strange mix of chills and longing rippled through her as their eyes met. This was always when she lost perspective. When he looked at her the way she imagined his other half would. The man whose shadow he seemed to have stolen.

"I *do* want you to come closer," she whispered. "Just not them." She shook her head. "Not the others."

"But they love you," he responded, his dark eyes narrowed against the sunlight. "Just like I do."

Though it might seem it to them, she knew love was the furthest thing from what they felt. She wasn't about to say as much though.

"Come, be with me," he urged, using the voice that tempted her. That made her imagine he was someone else. That normal desires were possible. "Why stand alone in the sun when we can be together in the shade?"

The way he said it, the genuine need he felt, called to her.

He was her other half.

Her soul mate.

"Yes," he whispered. He seemed to follow her thoughts as he held out his hand. "I am he. I always have been. Come to me, lass."

He did that sometimes. Spoke with a particular brogue she knew belonged to another. Lured her into a trance as she envisioned the man he could never be. Yet, at that moment, in that memory, he *was* him. He wasn't dark and foreboding but tall and muscled and handsome.

Bryce...

She never said his name out loud, but she went to him, leaving the sunlight behind. Suddenly, just like the memory itself, she fell into nothingness, the dream ended abruptly, and her eyes shot open.

179

Bryce's did as well, and his arms tightened around her momentarily as if he was catching her. As though he had just experienced the same dream or memory.

"You were there, weren't you?" she whispered. "Back at the clearing in the woods in Maine."

"Aye," he replied as they sat up. "I was part of the warlock again. Part of…"

When he trailed off with a frown, she looked at him in question. "What happened when I came to you?" She shook her head. "Because though that actually happened, I have no memory after the moment I headed for the warlock and entered the shadows."

Troubled, he sat on the edge of the bunk and pinched the bridge of his nose. "I knew a moment ago…upon awakening, but it's fading so fast." He shook his head as he concentrated. "He pulled you into his arms then he did something to you."

Frustrated, he stood and scowled as he braced his hand against the wall. "Something you didn't expect. Something that bonded you to him in a whole new way."

Just as frustrated, she stood and began dressing. "What we just dreamt happened before the other dream you had. So I think the moment we just shared was what the warlock was referring to. What he meant when he said that though I don't remember it yet, I'm already his and will recall it when I least expect it."

"Aye, I think you're right, lass," Bryce agreed as he pulled on a dark tunic and wrapped his plaid. "'Twould do us both good to give this a great deal of thought as we continue our journey. Because I sense whatever he has planned will be happening verra soon."

She nodded. "You're sensing him more and more, aren't you?"

"I am," he replied as they put on their boots. "I had several dreams last night." His eyes softened as they went to hers. "Dreams of you when you were younger. Moments we shared."

Though she knew he struggled with the idea that he and the warlock were so connected, it was good that he was starting to accept it. He needed to embrace it as much as possible to better their chances of staying one step ahead of their enemy.

Before they headed upstairs, he cupped her cheeks, brushed his lips across hers and murmured, "I *am* glad, however obtuse, that I was somewhat there for you, lass. And though I dinnae like that evil was so close to you, I look forward to remembering more. To seeing you grow into the woman you are today."

His words meant more than he knew. That he wanted to be a part of her life, no matter how dark it had been. In turn, she was grateful that thanks to Erin, she had so many memories of his upbringing as well.

Speaking of family, his was rather upbeat by the time they joined them. But then this was a day none thought they would be part of. Graham and Christina had come aboard earlier, choosing to stay with them rather than continue the journey with John.

Soon after, he and his men waved goodbye, their spirits high as they left. The day Aðísla had been so concerned about arriving was here, and things were going as they should.

John was heading up the Forth to Culross to report that Angus Og's fleet was in the Tay and had already sent scouting ships down to the Farne islands and the Bass Rock with more galleys sent on to blockade the Humber, Bridlington, Whitby, Hartlepool, and Tynemouth.

It seemed the bulk of Angus' fleet had continued south early that morning to prepare for battle. As it was reported, they enjoyed fair winds so should make good time.

"'Twill be a good day for John when he arrives," Bryce commented.

"Aye." Graham grinned. "'Tis not every day King Robert is so delighted by news that he knights its messenger straightaway."

Everyone smiled, sure to keep the news from Angus who would find out eventually.

"Aye, then," Angus roared to his crew. "Let's go join our brothers-in-arms and see if we cannae capture a Sassenach ship or two for our good King!"

A huge roar of approval followed as men began to row. As it turned out, the winds had died off a few hours ago, so Conall again came in handy as gusts filled their sail and they were off. Like before, Angus tossed them each an apple then tried to pry information out of them. What could they expect from the upcoming battle? Would they be victorious?

"We'll not be telling ye a thing," Adlin replied. "Only help ye however we can."

Angus grinned and shook his head, clearly confident enough in current events that he would do just fine. And it truly did prove quite favorable that Conall created his winds and moved them faster because as they approached Bass Rock, an English fleet appeared on the horizon.

That in itself wasn't so alarming.

They were supposed to be there.

What was daunting and unexpected, however, was the sheer amount of battle hardened Englishmen aboard.

Chapter Fourteen

BRYCE AND HIS cousins couldn't contain their anticipation if they tried. Though it hadn't been all that long since battling in Bannockburn, they were eager for more Sassenach blood. Still decades away from cannons on ships, it would come down to naval prowess and hand-to-hand combat. By the looks of it, the ships would be coming in close enough to each other for a bloody good battle.

Though the English fleet counted more than Angus anticipated, it likely would not matter. Especially with his newfound friends along including, undoubtedly, Christina and her godlike warrioress abilities.

"I dinnae think magic will be all that necessary this time," Adlin remarked, grinning.

"But if it is," Lindsay chimed in. "I can always take care of it afterwards."

"Aye, lass," Conall murmured, pulling her close. "But mayhap 'tis best this time if you dinnae have to."

Bryce winked at Jessie and chuckled. Truth told, his cousin probably wanted to take a rest from so many men adoring his lass.

"Archers take up positions," Angus roared at his crew as he drew his sword. "Weapons at the ready! We'll be on 'em soon, lads!"

Though the rest of his fleet had already arrived and were prepared for battle, it clearly bolstered them that their chieftain had joined in the fun.

"Have ye a spare bow and some arrows around, Laird MacDonald?" Bryce said, missing his favored set. "Though I fight well with anything, 'tis my weapon of choice."

"Aye, laddie." He gestured at a compartment beneath a bench. "Help yerself." Then he nodded at another location. "Ye'll find a variety of blades over there."

Bryce nodded and found a bow suited to his size, a sword, and some daggers before he focused on Jessie. "As ye've no experience fighting, I think ye should stay below deck."

She only smiled and shook her head.

Christina, it seemed, decided to answer for her. "Seriously, Bryce? Fighting aside, you *did* see what she was capable of in the firth, right?"

"Aye," he said proudly before he shook his head and frowned. Like it or not, Christina was right. Jessie could more than handle herself. Yet his rapidly growing love for her disallowed him from feeling anything but protective. What if she got distracted and an arrow slipped by her defenses? What if worry over her friends drew her attention away long enough that a blade ended her?

What it all broke down to was one simple fact.

He couldn't bear losing her.

"You won't lose me," she said softly as she rested her hand on his chest and met his eyes. "I've come *way* too far to finally be with you to let anything take me away from you now."

"Aye, then," was all he could manage, touched by the raw emotion in her gaze. For a moment it felt like those dark eyes of hers wrapped right around his soul and pulled him even closer.

There were a hundred different ways he wanted to say how he felt but couldn't come up with a bloody word. So he pulled her into his arms and kissed her soundly. As usual, that wasn't the best move to make when he should be focusing on other things. She had a way of making everything else fade away. Of taking his mind somewhere soft and warm and very, very arousing.

Seconds later, however, he had no choice but to snap out of it as an arrow whizzed by.

"Bloody hell," he grumbled as he spun, leapt onto a bench, focused and began shooting arrows at the oncoming ship.

After that, the battling began.

Weapons drawn and roars aplenty, men leapt from ship to ship and began fighting one another. Graham, Conall, and Adlin crossed blades with several men at once as Bryce kept shooting off arrows. He took down one, two, three, four Sassenach in rapid succession before he lost a clear shot.

He needed more visibility.

"Go!" Christina roared as she crossed swords with an oncoming soldier. "I'll stay close to Jessie. Don't you worry about that, darlin'."

Bryce glanced at her, wishing for a split second that they still possessed the amplified magic they had shared in the last battle thanks to Ainsley. Yet that was over now. But that was okay because Christina was a remarkable fighter, and he knew she would never let anyone hurt her friend. That was more than obvious when she jumped into the raging ocean to save her. He noticed Lindsay and Milly weren't far off either. They would stick together and protect each other.

When his eyes went to Jessie, she nodded in reassurance and spoke within his mind. *"Go, Bryce. Help make history."*

Confident that she would be all right, he nodded, grabbed more arrows, and leapt onto the English ship. Ever the berserker, Graham laughed as he ran his sword straight through a man's neck then kicked another overboard. Adlin and Conall had already leapt onto another ship and were grinning like madmen as they fought.

Bryce chuckled and shook his head before he whipped a dagger into one man's gut before he notched an arrow and took another Sassenach down as he tried to sneak up behind Angus. The captain nodded his thanks as he resumed battling.

Wasting no time, Bryce pulled his dagger free from the man's gut then punched him so hard he stumbled back and cracked his head open on the deck. Always aware of what was happening around him, he set aside his bow and fought by sword for a bit, dropping three more Sassenach before he glanced back at Angus' ship. He couldn't help a small grin. As far as he could tell Christina wasn't letting her friends battle at all. Instead, she took down any enemy the minute they set foot on the boat.

Well satisfied with Jessie's safety, he grabbed his bow, leapt a few more ships and joined Sven and Aðísla who were thoroughly in their element and enjoying themselves. Sven was a particularly

185

vicious fighter who tended to have men scrambling away from him in fear rather than battling. This, it seemed, pleased him greatly as he let them wait in the wings while he engaged others. That, naturally, only intensified the terror of those who knew their turn was coming.

Bryce got the sense Sven used his fighting as an outlet for deeply rooted feelings that were bothering him, be it kin or something more. If he were to guess, he would say a lass was at the heart of it.

Emily, to be precise.

Bryce fought alongside the Vikings for a time, sometimes choosing to use his sword, other times simply punching or kicking. All the while, he continued shooting arrows and taking down men. One after another after another until there were no more to face off with.

By that time it was clear history was going precisely as it should as the vast majority of Sassenach had fallen. Three ships heavy with supplies for the depleted English army were now under the MacDonald's control. Some ships had fled, but as Bryce very well knew, Angus' galleys would soon drive those ashore to be wrecked on the Northumbrian cliffs. Other less seaworthy ships would be lost at sea in severe gales.

Everything seemed to be going just as it should. That is until the unthinkable happened.

Almost.

A furious Sassenach who knew his time was coming to an end, managed to get off one last arrow. An arrow, as it turned out, that nearly landed in the center of Angus' forehead if Bryce hadn't acted quickly and shot off his own.

Not only was his arrow pinpoint accurate and intercepted the other but Jessie, just as quick, redirected the arrow so that it landed in the enemy's forehead instead.

"Bloody hell!" Angus swore before he flung back his head and roared with laughter.

Bryce and Jessie locked eyes and smiled from across two ships before the unmistakable pull of time-travel swept around him. Though he tried to get to her first, it was too late. The deck dropped out from beneath him, colors swirled, and oxygen grew sparse.

Moments later, he landed in a most unfavorable position.

"Och," he muttered as he slid past trees down a rain-slicked muddy hill straight toward what looked to be a cliff. Seconds later, he learned that was precisely what it was as he tried to stop but ended up sliding to the end, teetered then tumbled right over. Worse than that? He couldn't seem to shift but fell toward dangerously jagged rocks from a distance far greater than he anticipated.

Seconds later, thank the gods, Sven's dragon caught him.

Though grateful, he muttered at the indignity of being carried by another dragon. *Especially* a male. Bryce continued grumbling as Sven landed and he got off, even more mortified to find he had an audience. Sven, likely well aware of Bryce's state of mind, was gracious enough to act as though nothing embarrassing had just happened as everyone joined them.

"I'm so glad you're okay," Jessie exclaimed as she flung her arms around Bryce and pressed her cheek against his chest. All his aggravation fled as she trembled and he realized how much that had scared her.

"I'm fine." He finally did the right thing and nodded his thanks to Sven as he held Jessie.

"Bloody hell." Graham shook his head and eyed the cliff Bryce just went over. "You really do have awful luck when traveling through time, Cousin."

"Aye," Bryce murmured.

It seemed they were not going to witness King Edward's infamous anger at King Robert after all. Because days later, Angus would sail those three English ships laden with foodstuffs right past Edward in Edinburgh, and up the forth to Culross. There they would unload their contents to the Scottish Army which was reported to number around twenty-five thousand.

At least Bryce and his kin had the satisfaction of knowing they had helped make that happen.

"We should tell everyone what's going on," Jessie said softly as she pulled back.

Her fear over his safety had turned to renewed anger at the warlock and his influence over Bryce's time-traveling. She wanted to tell everyone about his connection to Bryce, and he couldn't agree more. So he nodded as he brushed a tear from her cheek. It seemed he had indeed terrified her with yet another near death experience.

"Oh, my darn emotions," she muttered under her breath as she rubbed her eyes, removed the last of the moisture then proceeded to fill everybody in on what was going on with the warlock.

Adlin sighed as he considered that. "I can see why they left this warlock for last then."

Jessie nodded. "It was a clever move."

"Aye," Adlin murmured. "A true test of love if ever there was one."

Bryce narrowed his eyes, wondering precisely what Adlin was getting at. "Hasn't this entire journey been that one way or another?" His eyes swept over the others. "For us all on our adventures."

Adlin nodded. "Aye, but some tests are more difficult than others and none, I suspect, as hard as what you and Jessie still face."

"We're ready for it, though," she replied as her eyes went from Bryce to Adlin. "Though my ring doesn't shine yet, we love each other very much."

Bryce nodded, in full agreement. It might have happened fast, but it was absolutely true. "I know it's only been days, but we feel verra strongly." He squeezed her hand. "Mayhap not just because of the time spent together now but because I'm beginning to remember parts of her life...parts that the warlock remembers." He scowled. "In truth, parts that are actually mine to remember."

"Aye," Adlin said softly, a touch of worry and sadness in his eyes as they met Jessie's. "If 'tis as you say and this warlock took a piece of Bryce's soul or essence before he was ever born, then 'tis verra much Bryce himself though not whole, right?"

"That's right," she said, clearly glad that he understood the dynamics so well. "And that's what I explained to Bryce."

Adlin nodded slowly. "Lass, has it ever occurred to you that the love you feel for Bryce can only ever be in its entirety when a true MacLomain, Broun connection is made?"

"Yes, of course." She nodded. "And I do." Her eyes went from Bryce back to Adlin. "I love all of him with all my heart."

"All of him," Adlin said gently. "Is not standing right here, Jessie."

Bryce felt her flare of distress at that. "But he will be once the warlock is defeated."

"Will he?" Adlin's brow furrowed in uncertainty though his voice remained gentle. "Because if this warlock does indeed possess a part of Bryce then 'twill be Bryce himself that you must kill in the end. After all, you cannae truly be in love with Bryce without loving the warlock and vice versa." He shook his head. "Because they are deeply interconnected if not one and the same."

Silence settled as Jessie blinked, swallowed hard and shook her head as she clearly tried to wrap her mind around that.

"I suspect love has as it sometimes can, blinded you to this fact," Adlin murmured. "Though on some level, you were always aware of it, weren't you?" His eyes flared light blue as his magic ignited. "You often saw Bryce in the warlock. Not just his soul but his appearance."

Jessie pressed her lips together and nodded once.

"'Tis a verra difficult thing." Adlin closed the distance and took her hand, his eyes never leaving hers. "Yet 'tis something you will have to face." His eyes flickered from Bryce to her. "Both of you." He squeezed her hand. "But you will be together, and in that, you will find unparalleled strength. Not just you but Bryce. And 'tis in that, your mutual strength and a love so strong you're willing to let it go, that I believe you'll find freedom."

Though Adlin could be as cryptic as Grant, the gist of his words was more than apparent. This warlock might mean Bryce's death, but they had to face it to see what was on the other side for them. It was the only way. And they had to trust in that to find out if their love would survive…if it was truly meant to be.

Jessie blinked away moisture, stood up straighter and nodded. "I have not quit being strong since I was ten years old and I don't intend to start now." Her eyes went to Bryce. "I'm more than willing to go to Hell and back if that's what it takes." She flinched. "And I'm not speaking figuratively."

"Aye, lass," he said as their gazes lingered. "We'll fight together until the end."

"A good ending," Christina declared. "One you won't be facing alone because I'll be damned if we're not all there helping you."

Everyone agreed, and they meant it. They had all come too far not to stick together now.

Ready to seek shelter and food, they headed into the woods under Aðísla's direction. It seemed she sensed a more discreet location where they could make camp for the night and perhaps wash off the blood of battle.

Though they couldn't be entirely sure where they were, Adlin felt confident it was close to where they should be. That meant it was a little over two months after the sea battle and they now stood in Northern England. On that note, he remained hopeful Grant might already be here aiding Robert the Bruce.

As it happened, they settled for the evening under a massive slab of rock which Jessie felt would help protect them from the warlock. Not only that but it better insulated them against the damp chill of autumn. There was a small pond nearby that suited their needs, and within a few hours, they were clean, roasting game and sitting around a fire. Though they had no change of clothes, they used a wee bit of magic to clean their current clothing well enough.

Aðísla had volunteered to keep first watch and was somewhere out in the darkness.

"You know what I keep wondering," Milly remarked as her eyes met Jessie's. "How come the warlocks have a Scottish accent? I get why the one with a piece of Bryce would but not the others."

Jessie shook her head. "I'm afraid I have no explanation for that and always found it strange considering my grandfather created the curse and he was so opposed to Scotland." She frowned. "Or should I say angry at all things Scottish."

When she clenched her hands together on her lap, Bryce knew she was thinking about her little notebook. It was officially gone. Left behind on Angus' ship.

"*'Tis okay*," he said into her mind as he rested his hand over hers. "*Though you might not have the book now, you possess strong dragon magic as well as Ma's magic.*" He squeezed her hand. "*Not to mention me. All of us for that matter. A family unlike any other who will always stand by your side and fight for all they're worth.*"

A grateful glint lit her eyes as she nodded.

"Your grandfather was opposed to Scotland because of your grandmother's death, aye?" Adlin murmured, his eyes on Jessie as he drew them back into the original conversation. "And she died giving birth to your mother?"

"Yes." She shook her head. "After that Grandfather hated all things Scottish presumably because it reminded him of the woman he lost. Or so my mother surmised." Her eyes narrowed. "I've always thought it went deeper though. That there was a bigger picture."

Adlin pondered that. "The enormity of what he did certainly implies such."

Jessie nodded.

"'Tis your mother's side you inherit your Broun blood from aye?" Adlin said.

"Yes." She seemed surprised. "How did you know that?"

"I might seem off my game lately with certain things, but my magic has indeed grown stronger since I came together with Milly." He squeezed Milly's hand, love blazing in his eyes as he looked at her before focusing on Jessie again. "I can sense your mother's Broun blood in you as I can sense what must be your father's blood." His eyes narrowed. "A bloodline I couldnae sense before you and Bryce came together. 'Twas well masked and even still verra hard to see."

"That must be because of the warlock," Jessie replied.

"Aye, mayhap in part to be sure."

"In part?"

He nodded as he kept giving it some thought. "I think I know how you might be able to get more answers about your grandfather's anger toward Scotland."

Jessie cocked her head. "How?"

"Well, I've been observing your connection to the spirit realm and 'tis far stronger than mine or even Grant's," he replied. "Where we can see ghosts more clearly and communicate with them, I think your magic attracts them." His voice softened. "I think, in a way, like you do with the warlocks, you can control them...which means you can summon them."

Her eyes widened slightly. "You can't mean for me to summon my grandfather." She shook her head. "Because I absolutely will not."

"Not your grandfather," he said gently. "I would never ask that of you, lass." He looked at her in question. "But mayhap your *grandmother*. She who is at the root of all this."

~Avenged by a Highland Laird~

Chapter Fifteen

12 October 1322
Northallerton, England

JESSIE WASN'T SURE what to make of Adlin's suggestion. She had never purposefully summoned a spirit before and wasn't sure she wanted to now. Yet she understood the logic behind it. Perhaps even the necessity.

"What if my grandfather shows up?" she whispered aloud without meaning to. She frowned, embarrassed that she was still so terrified of the man. That he still had that kind of power over her.

"We will all be right here with you." Adlin's eyes never left hers. "And though I'm not as strong as you in that realm, I can use my magic there and *will* protect you, lass."

"As will I," came a soft voice before Grant appeared out of the night. He nodded hello to everyone before he sat next to her and met her eyes. "We willnae leave your side lass. Not for a moment."

"It's good to see you again, Grant," she whispered, truly grateful he had arrived.

"Aye, you too, lass." His eyes swept over everyone as a small smile came to his lips. "All of you."

"How fares good King Robert the Bruce then?" Adlin asked, evidently already having been in touch with Grant telepathically.

"In position," Grant replied. "Though it's taken some subliminal nudging here and there to make sure his battle plans move in the right direction."

"Aye, then." Adlin nodded. "'Tis important things go as they should."

"I was given something that belongs to you, lass," Grant murmured as he pulled out none other than her little book. "Laird Angus MacDonald said 'twas yours and you should have it back."

Jessie smiled, her eyes flickering to Bryce as she nodded. Bryce returned her smile and said, "He's a good man. 'Twas kind of him to see it returned."

"Aye," Grant said. "He told Robert all about your battle with the English and how Bryce saved his life." He winked at Bryce. "I would say that's why you all got to enjoy that particular part of history. 'Twould have been no good if the MacDonald chieftain had died." His eyes roamed over those who had traveled on the first leg of the journey. "Adlin caught me up on what happened in Pentland Firth. 'Twas remarkable and I'm verra proud of you."

"It was definitely something," Jessie murmured as she offered Bryce a small smile. "And Bryce didn't just save Angus once in the battle against the English but twice."

Bryce grinned and shrugged. "He was a prime target to be sure."

"As to the book," Grant said, redirecting their attention. "Might you use it to help summon your grandmother, Jessie?"

A shiver of unfounded apprehension rippled through her. "I'm not sure. Maybe. I've seen her picture, so I know what she looks like."

She knew full well the book wouldn't attract her grandfather in the spirit realm because she'd been using it this whole time. So maybe this was the best possible way to go about things.

Grant nodded and met her eyes as if he followed those thoughts. "I think if we can speak with your grandmother than we can better understand your grandfather's motives, aye? And that might make all the difference when fighting this last warlock."

She nodded in agreement. He was right.

When her eyes went to Bryce again, he nodded as well and said, "I'll stay by your side, lass. I willnae let anything happen to you."

While his intentions were sweet and certainly noble, she knew full well that even he couldn't stop what might come at her. The spirit realm wasn't exactly notable for its stability. Yet she knew she had to do this. She was the only one who could, so she should. Because as Grant and Adlin said, she might very well learn information that would help them destroy the warlock. And that would mean saving Scotland once and for all.

"I need something to write with," she began but trailed off when Grant handed her what she needed.

"Thank you," she murmured as she opened to a blank page. She didn't blame everyone for watching her so closely. After all, she was about to do what was behind so much of this. Behind their wild adventures.

Jessie glanced at Bryce one more time, glad to have him there, before she closed her eyes, visualized her grandmother, and started sketching. After a few moments, she opened her eyes, stared at the fire and began chanting. She used the flames to enhance her gift as she accessed the spiritual realm. At first, nothing happened, but soon enough she felt the shift as did everyone else based on their startled expressions.

"We exist in both realms now," she whispered as she added more details to the picture. The curve of her grandmother's cheek. The tilt of her nose. The plushness of her lips. Then, last but not least, her eyes.

It was that, giving her the ability to see that completed the summoning because moments later, her grandmother appeared by the fire. Though transparent, her features were very clear. Especially her eyes as they locked on Jessie and she whispered, "You have his looks, child."

Nobody said a word as Jessie stood and faced a woman she had never met. "Thank you for coming, Grandmother."

"Thank you for finally reaching out, Jessie," she replied softly, tears in her eyes. "I've been waiting a verra long time."

Though her brogue wasn't as thick as Bryce's, it was certainly there.

"What do you mean you've been waiting for me to reach out?" Jessie asked. "Why not just reach out to me like other spirits have?"

"I couldnae, lass." Anger flared in her eyes. "Not with that bloody bastard's curse hanging over me." She shook her head. "He made it impossible."

"You mean my grandfather," she murmured, not all that surprised that he might have blocked anyone who cared from reaching out to her.

"Och, no, never your grandfather." She shook her head, a heavy frown on her face. "The bastard who killed him."

Jessie narrowed her eyes as a strange sensation rolled over her. "What do you mean? He died in a fire when I was ten."

"No," her grandmother whispered and stepped closer. "He didnae, Jessie and I've been eager to tell you that for years."

She was grateful when Bryce stood as well, and his hand slipped into hers in support.

"Tell me what, Grandmother?" she managed to say, her mind already spinning not just in confusion but a host of other directions. She had an overwhelming feeling she was about to receive life-changing information.

It turns out she did.

"The truth," her grandmother replied softly. It was clear she wished to touch Jessie but was unable. "A year or so before I gave birth to your mother, I met two men. Best friends. Both were tall and handsome, and we all became friends." An unmistakable sparkle lit her eyes. "But only one of them ever caught my attention. And only one ever held my heart. Your grandfather." Her chin notched. "Your *real* grandfather."

Jessie barely breathed as she continued.

"He was from Scotland though he had gypsy blood like you, so he possessed mystical gifts indeed. It was those gifts that made him a wizard. Yet he was more than that..." Her eyes stayed with Jessie's. "He also possessed dragon blood."

Jessie offered a jerky nod as the pieces began to fall into place.

"It was their mutual possession of magic that made him and the *other* such close friends," she continued, muttering something about never mentioning his cursed name aloud. "But I'm afraid it was their mutual love for me that drove a wedge between them."

Her grandmother released a shaky sigh. "I tried..." She shook her head. "Both your grandfather and I tried to make it easier for his friend, but nothing we said or did made a difference. And not loving one another simply wasn't an option." Wariness lit her eyes. "As it turned out, his friend was a certain sort of man with what soon proved a very dark soul." She clenched her jaw. "When he learned I was pregnant, any last shred of goodness in him was wiped away entirely."

Jessie tried to be strong on her own but ended up leaning against Bryce for support. Honestly, she was somewhat surprised her legs still held her up given she had a pretty good idea what was coming.

"Where your grandfather was most certainly strong in magic, his best friend was almost more so," she went on. "And that's no small thing considering your grandfather was half dragon."

As her grandmother spoke, she felt not only Bryce but his kin and her friends within her mind offering support. Not in a way that cluttered her thoughts but in a fashion that kept her level. Grant and Adlin respectfully presented questions she could ask if she were so inclined.

"So he was half dragon," she whispered, swallowing hard. "So he shifted?"

She felt both Bryce and Sven's alertness at that particular question.

"He *was* dragon, and he *did* shift." A small smile ghosted her grandmother's face. "And what a sight he was."

"So was Mama a dragon too?" she murmured. "As far as I knew she didn't possess any magic whatsoever."

Her grandmother gave her an odd look, almost as if she wanted to say something but couldn't. Instead, she continued on about her real grandfather.

"Your grandfather's best friend ended up being the worst kind of coward." Her eyes narrowed as she seemed to peer into the past. "Corrupt with jealousy, he didn't end up fighting your grandfather like a man but spent an evening making him believe that he had come to his senses. That their friendship was too important to lose over a woman."

She hesitated a moment, her eyes welling before she continued. "I told your grandfather not to trust him, but he was too good a man. Too trusting in the end when it came to those he loved."

Jessie couldn't fight her own emotions as she listened to her grandmother go on.

"So as I said, his friend was a coward and went about things in a very devious way that night. In a way that kept him from having to face your grandfather's full wrath." Her brows drew together in renewed anger. "From what I gathered in the last few moments of mental connection I had with my love, his friend literally stabbed him in the back. Angered and confused by the unexpected attack, he immediately embraced his dragon. When he did, his friend used those brief few moments to destroy him."

Her eyes dropped to Jessie's notebook as she continued. "With that." Pain flickered in her gaze. "And wherever he sent him in the afterlife or somewhere in between, he's been lost to me since. Dead in a way that has no closure."

"I'm so sorry," Jessie whispered. When she started to set the book down, her grandmother shook her head. "No, lass. Hold onto that until you're freed from this curse. Until all of you are." Determination notched her chin again. "Use that to end this and perhaps free your grandfather."

Jessie nodded and clamped her hands around it tighter though she wanted to toss it into the fire.

"After your grandfather vanished everything changed," her grandmother continued softly. "Insane, determined that I might become his after all, his friend never left my side. But I would never become his." She shook her head again, more fiercely this time. "I could never love another." Her expression turned to one of both relief that she was free of him and perhaps melancholy that she had to leave her child behind. "In the end, as Fate would have it, I was taken away from him anyway."

Her eyes grew haunted as she stepped a bit closer to Jessie. "After that, I was blocked from reaching out to you or your mother. Both of you were horribly repressed." Pain flickered in her eyes. "I can't tell you how sorry I am for the life you led. For the things he did to you both. The abuse."

Then pride lit her grandmother's eyes. "But you were strong, Jessie. So very strong." She nodded. "And he hated you for it." Her eyes grew angry again. "He was a madman with a misconstrued way of looking at things. He hated your mother for killing me in childbirth and hated your grandfather for impregnating me, to begin with. And as all that hate grew, it transformed. He began seeking a way to change everything." She gave Jessie a telling look. "Just *maybe* he could stop your grandfather from existing altogether."

"Oh, God," Jessie whispered, as she realized where this was going.

"Aye," her grandmother murmured. "In all his hate and dementia, he decided the best way to get rid of the Scotsman was to get rid of the country that birthed him." She shook her head. "I don't think it ever occurred to the fool that Scotland being annexed by England might not necessarily do away with your grandfather's bloodline. No, he had but one goal in mind."

"To curse Scotland," she whispered.

"Aye," her grandmother responded. "A curse so profound and intricate that it could only unravel upon his death. That way his very essence could be part of it." Her brows swept up. "A curse created not just with his magic but even elements of your grandfather's. Parts he somehow captured in that book to give the curse even more strength."

Well, that would certainly explain the remarkable power the curse had. Power enough to often leave wizards the likes of Grant and Adlin in the dark. The dragon magic alone would have masked quite a bit from them as neither were dragon.

"That must be why the warlocks have a Scottish accent," she whispered, as a tear fell. "Because of my grandfather's magic."

What an awful thing to have had his magic used for evil after his death.

"Aye," her grandmother said softly, her eyes sad but determined as they stayed with Jessie's. "But hear me well, child. You have a tremendous amount of your grandfather in you. Not just your appearance but your very magic and the goodness at your core. He would want you to be strong right now. Not mourn for him but embrace what he gave you and use it to keep this country safe." Her eyes flickered between Jessie and Bryce. "He would want you to cherish the love you've found and never let it go."

"No risk of that," Jessie murmured, brushing away another tear as she glanced at Bryce.

Though she wanted to get to know her grandmother better, she knew they were running out of time. It seemed summoning a spirit was sustainable for only so long. The energy it took for her grandmother to stay manifested was limited. And she was using it up quickly with her passionate nature and anger at the enemy.

"Is there anything else you might be able to tell me to help us defeat this last warlock?" Jessie asked. "Anything at all."

"Only that you must put love before all else," her grandmother replied as her form began to waver. "And that you must not make the same mistake as your grandfather and let love blind you."

That sounded awfully similar to what Adlin had said earlier.

"I love you, Granddaughter," she whispered. "Fight well then finally live the life you deserve."

"Goodbye, Grandmother," Jessie murmured. "Thank you so much." She had nearly vanished when she thought of one more thing. "What about my sister? Do you know what happened to her? Where she is now?" Then she thought of even more questions, rambling despite herself. "And why did my grandfather's killer ever allow my mother to have children? Wasn't he concerned her offspring might possess magic to threaten his? If all that isn't curious enough, why allow one to be taken away and out of his control?"

But it was too late.

Her grandmother was gone, and her questions would remain unanswered.

Jessie slowly sat again and stared at the fire, dumbfounded by everything she had just learned. Bryce sat beside her, still holding her hand as Grant handed her a skin of whisky. After a solid swig or two, she finally turned eyes to everyone and released a shaky sigh. "Well…"

That was it. That's all she managed to get out before her feelings bombarded her and annoying tears started falling again. While she might be enjoying making up for lost time sexually, the endless emotional overload was starting to wear thin. But she just couldn't stop it. Her emotions were determined to be felt, so she had no choice but to ride them out.

The next thing she knew her friends were all around her offering hugs and just being there in general. She wasn't sure whose shoulders she cried on. At one point probably all of theirs before she finally managed to get herself under control, took another swig of whisky and rallied her strength.

That's what she needed to do from here on out.

Not cry what felt like every other minute, but get a grip and set aside her emotions. It might seem impossible, but she *had* to do it. For goodness sake, she had spent most of her life perfecting detachment so she should be able to do it now.

"I must say that I agree, lass," Adlin finally broke the silence, his words soft as he followed her thoughts. "'Tis time to rally the strength we both know you have and try to fight some of these emotions." His eyes grew stern as they stayed with hers. "You need to be strong whilst you face what's ahead."

While it was obvious by their expressions and mutterings that Bryce and her friends thought his words were a little strong, Jessie knew he was right. She nodded that she understood and would try harder from here on out.

"I think Adlin's right." Grant's eyes went from Bryce to Jessie as her friends, convinced she was okay now, finally returned to their men. "As your grandmother said, though, you need to embrace love now more than ever. 'Tis verra powerful in its own right."

Everyone nodded as Milly chimed in. "Just look at what it's accomplished so far."

Jessie's eyes met Bryce's, in total agreement. It certainly had accomplished a lot, hadn't it? Not just what it had done for the other couples, but what it was doing for them. Though she had loved a piece of him for years, now it was so much stronger. And that was changing her in ways she never saw coming.

He was helping her transform into the person she was always supposed to be.

More than that, he was giving her a glimpse of a future she desperately wanted.

A life with him.

As she thought about how she might be able to make that happen, a nugget of an idea formed. "I was in control of so much for so long that it was jarring not to be when the warlocks split off." She pondered as she eyed them. "Yet as time has gone on and I've grown stronger via my dragon magic and of course, Bryce, rather than weaken as I anticipated, I've begun to wonder."

"Wonder what, darlin'?" Christina asked from Graham's lap.

"Why I'm still looking at things as if I have no control," she replied. "Why I'm waiting so patiently for the warlock to make his move."

Intrigued, Grant cocked his head. "What are you thinking, lass?"

"I'm not entirely sure yet," she murmured. "All I know is I'm sick of being on the defense when I could be on the offense. And I'm sick of feeling like this warlock holds all the cards."

"That a girl." Lindsay grinned. "Just tell us how we can help, and you know we will."

Jessie nodded. "I will." She looked at everyone again. "All of us should give it some thought tonight and make a move sooner rather than later." She tapped the book. "After all, I've got a tool that can double as a weapon, wouldn't you say?"

Adlin and Grant grinned as Bryce wrapped his arm around her shoulders and nodded. "I'd say we're verra much on the right path now, lass."

"Aye," Grant said as they all set to eating. "We'll sleep on it then in the morn join King Robert. He's eager to see you all."

The rest of the evening was a pleasure as everybody enjoyed being together once more. Though her emotions were still turbulent, she better managed them by firmly keeping revenge in mind. Not only for everyone here but for her grandparents and her mother. For all the lives affected by one weak, cruel man.

As she and Bryce curled up beneath a blanket later that night, his front to her back, she felt incredibly content. And, as always, aroused with him so close. Who would have ever thought she was so sexual? But she couldn't seem to get enough. Not with him around.

"If ye werenae so vocal," he murmured, a grin in his voice, his hand already minutes into roaming her leg. "I'd take ye here and now."

"We're not even near everyone," she reminded. They had found a little cave set apart. Though in truth, it *did* connect to the area everyone else slept in. Nonetheless, she pressed her butt against his erection, reminding him how ready he was for her. "And I can be quiet."

Or so she hoped.

Either way, it seemed he needed no further prompting.

"To hell with whether yer quiet," he growled, blowing past any reservations he might have had as he yanked her dress up. The blanket never moved but half a breath later he certainly did when he finally took her.

She bit back a groan and gripped the blanket as she savored the feeling. He didn't thrust hard but slow and rhythmic. His small, deep movements built a whole new type of pleasure as did the feeling of him taking her like this. His front to her back.

In a way, it was more raw and erotic than when she could actually see his face. She gauged everything she felt off the soft sounds he made. Off the way his hand clenched around hers as their passion built.

She shut her eyes and just *felt*. Sometimes he rolled his hips where other times he barely moved. When he went to touch her clit to enhance everything, she whispered, "No."

She didn't need that. Not now. Not as she focused on where they joined and the astounding sensations that alone caused. Moments later, warm waves of pleasure began rolling through her. When he pressed deep, issued a low, muffled groan and released, those warm waves became a deluge.

A harsh shudder of pleasure ripped through her before her body relaxed entirely and she simply floated in his arms. For a moment in time, she had no worries at all. Life was stress-free, and the two of them were all that existed. Blissful, reveling in that utter contentment, she drifted off to sleep.

Or at least she thought she was sleeping. It was hard to know. Especially when she opened her eyes, and she was standing face to face with the man who had called himself her grandfather.

More jarring than that?

She was seeing him through a haze of red far sharper than what she had experienced on the shore when she and Bryce killed the warlock.

Chapter Sixteen

BRYCE WATCHED AS Jessie, no older than eight or nine, clenched her little fists and glared up at a man he knew full well was the imposter. The enemy claiming to be her grandfather. They stood near the clearing in the woods she loved so well.

Again, he was seeing through the warlock's eyes.

But how could that be considering the warlock didn't exist until *after* this man died?

"You'll stay out here in the forest until I say you can return," he spat. "You'll stay here while I beat your mother for being the insolent woman that she is."

Jessie trembled, not in fear but rage as the man continued saying horrible things. It didn't take Bryce long to figure out he was purposely instigating her. But why? What was the point?

Seconds later, he figured it out when dragon fire flared in her eyes.

Bloody hell. She was embracing her dragon, wasn't she? Not just a dormant yet magical lineage passed on from her grandfather but the real deal. Moments later, as the air began to swirl around her, the man whipped out his little book and began drawing.

There was no questioning what was about to happen.

She was going to suffer a somewhat similar fate as her grandfather.

Though Bryce raged inside, he was immobile, trapped in a warlock waiting patiently on the sidelines. A warlock staying to the shadows. He watched in horror as her little black dragon lunged at the man before he stepped aside and grinned darkly. She half roared, half screamed in pain before the impossible happened.

Her dragon colors swirled and separated from her.

Once again a little girl, Jessie staggered back in shock. Standing in the spot of sunlight she loved so well her sad eyes met his moments before her colors—her inner dragon—rushed straight into him.

He barely had a moment to process the strange sensation before the imposter began chanting. Half a breath later the warlock was violently yanked toward the little book. Then all went black as he was sucked down into the bowels of Hell itself.

Ripped from the nightmare, he and Jessie sat up at the same time.

Bryce had to pat himself to make sure he was actually here. It had all seemed so real. Terrifying. Endless. But he had figured out a few things. The warlock was manifested ahead of time and somehow given a piece of her dragon. Then as swiftly as it was given freedom, it was taken away, and he was thrust back into the dark abyss of a curse yet to unravel.

If all that wasn't enough, an even bigger truth was revealed.

"I *am* a dragon," Jessie whispered, not only following his thoughts but based on the startled way she awoke, witnessed the same nightmare. A mixture of sadness and anger churned in her eyes as they met his. "Or at least I *was* a dragon."

He pulled her into his arms, not sure what else to do. What was the meaning of all that? Did he somehow…possess her dragon? He would have scoffed at the idea had his mother not so recently given her dragon magic to Jessie.

"No," she whispered, following his thoughts. "Just the warlock has it in him. Not you."

"Bloody hell," he muttered as they stood. Though he was furious at the idea, he couldn't help but feel a spark of both elation and rage. Elation that she *was* indeed a dragon that once shifted. And rage because someone had the nerve to take her dragon away from her…away from him.

Because her little dragon very much belonged to his.

"You're my mate," he whispered, as snippets of what the warlock felt at the time rushed through him. The undeniable connection. The incredible truth.

Bryce pulled her closer, unable to stop the red haze that fell over his vision as their eyes held. "It might have been a terrifying moment, but at least one thing was established, lass. We *are* verra much dragon mates."

Her eyes grew moist. "I would like nothing more."

In his momentary exaltation, he had lost sight of how she must feel right now. It was clear she had yet to feel that remarkable connection. The moment, no matter how fleeting, of unabashed joy. But then how could she when she had been ruthlessly robbed of something so important? When an inherent part of who she was had been so callously ripped away from her.

"I'm so sorry, lass," he whispered and cupped her cheeks, his touch tender. "We will fix this." He shook his head. "If 'tis the last thing I do, I *will* get your dragon back."

She nodded and blinked away any tears before they could fall, clearly focusing on anger and revenge over loss and regret. "I know you will." Her jaw tightened in determination. "We both will."

Though they knew it was a very real possibility, they refused to entertain the idea that she might not get it back. That she may never experience the wonder of shifting and being with her mate as dragonkind intended it. Instead, they focused on the day all of this would be made right. A day that could not come soon enough.

When they joined the others to break their fast, Jessie filled them in on what had happened.

Sven, above all, seemed the most troubled and certainly the angriest. "I am with Bryce on this and will see your dragon returned to you if it's the last thing I do." He shook his head. "There is no greater crime than what that man did to you."

While some might argue subjecting her to a life with evil warlocks was a greater crime, Bryce understood where Sven was coming from. He couldn't imagine someone stealing his inner dragon nor the gaping hole that would be left behind.

Though they wore comforting smiles, Bryce didn't miss the flicker of unease in both Adlin's and Grant's eyes. He knew full well what they were thinking. What everyone must be thinking.

Now Jessie wasn't just facing Bryce in the warlock but her own dragon.

Though there was always the chance this new information would only fuel her determination to destroy the warlock in hopes of getting her dragon back, it could also work another way. She might hesitate to end the warlock because she feared killing her dragon too.

"It all ties together somehow," she said later as they headed for King Robert's encampment. "Maybe possessing my dragon is what the warlock meant when he said I'm already his and will remember when I least expect it. Maybe because of your connection with him, we've got an advantage." She gave him a hopeful look. "Because now we know what he's hiding."

"Aye," Bryce agreed, hoping that was the case. "'Twould make sense, wouldnae it?"

"Aye, 'twould," Grant said. "And worth figuring into your plan when you control him rather than the other way around."

"Agreed," she murmured as several horsemen approached. Scotsmen all, it took Bryce a moment to realize who was in the lead.

"Greetings, my friends," King Robert the Bruce bellowed as he swung down from his horse.

Eight years had passed for the Bruce since they last saw him at Bannockburn and though he was still fit, the long war with England was starting to wear on him. Nevertheless, it was a nice reunion as he was again astounded by how they hadn't aged a day.

"Ye look awfully familiar to me, lassie," he said to Jessie. "Have we met?

She offered a small smile. "Could be but it would have been very briefly in a little tavern in Happrew back when Grant was wounded."

Grant looked at her curiously. "I thought you were gone by the time Robert arrived the next morn?"

She shrugged and grinned. "Am I not allowed to stick around and enjoy a bit of history on occasion?"

Grant chuckled. "I suppose you are."

Though Bryce wondered how she managed it without the warlocks knowing he supposed it didn't much matter at this point.

"You've arrived at a good time," Robert announced as he had one of his men take his horse and walked with them. "We'll be sitting down soon to go over plans one last time and 'twould be good to have ye there." He cast Adlin a knowing look. "In case ye've an opinion or two to add."

Adlin only grinned and shook his head. "Ye know better than to ask, old friend."

208

"Well, Grant's already revised some of my plans so I'm sure things are going as they should," Robert said. "And ye helped Angus steal those ships which was verra helpful. Not to mention saved his life." His eyes covered everyone, especially Bryce and Jessie. "Thank ye for that, by the way."

They nodded as Grant frowned. "I didnae revise your plans."

Robert smiled then winked. "Of course, ye didnae."

Grant shook his head and shrugged when Adlin gave him a look. "'Tis not my fault if he's beginning to catch on to us after all these years."

Adlin offered no comment as they left the woods and entered an encampment. Just like those they had entered before, men prepared for battle as they sharpened their blades and practiced fighting one another. And just like before many stopped to eye the lasses.

It didn't go unnoticed that Sven fell in on Jessie's other side and he knew full well why. She might not be blood related, but she *was* a dragon. That meant she was as much Sven's to protect as she was Bryce's. He nodded at the Viking, not jealous but grateful.

It had just begun raining, so they arrived at a good time.

"Refreshments for my friends," Robert said to one of the men standing guard outside his massive tent. Three men were already inside. Two sat and the third, a tall, dark haired man stood at a table eying a map. He arched a brow at them as they entered.

"Friends, meet Sir James Douglas," Robert said, introducing him first. "One of my oldest friends, he's been fighting alongside me against the Sassenach for neigh on fifteen winters now."

"'Tis an honor to meet ye, James," Adlin led out. "I cannae thank ye enough for all ye've done for our country."

James Douglas, better known as the Black Douglas, was one of Scotland's greatest heroes for all he had accomplished on behalf of Robert. The English had given him his nickname not only because of his black hair but his fearsome reputation.

Robert proceeded to introduce the other two as they stood. "And these fine men are Sir Walter Stewart and Sir Thomas Randolph." He paused and reflected. "But then most of you already met Thomas at the Battle of Bannockburn, aye?"

"Aye," Graham replied as he shook hands with Robert's commander. "'Tis good to see ye again, Sir Thomas."

Everybody greeted one another, including Walter Stewart, who was the hereditary High Steward of Scotland.

"Sit." Robert gestured at the table. "There's room for ye all."

Everyone did as Adlin and Grant eyed the maps.

"So have yer plans changed any, Robert?" Grant asked.

"Nay and 'tis good ye convinced me to put off the battle a day, Grant," Robert mentioned. "Given the weather."

Bryce didn't miss the brief look Adlin tossed Grant. It seemed his uncle must have manipulated the weather a wee bit to make that happen. After all, as history told it the Battle of Byland Moor should take place on the fourteenth, not the thirteenth.

"'Tis my greatest hope we capture Edward soon," James ground out. "I've a mind to hurt him in ways he cannae imagine not only for what he's done to this country but more recently Edinburgh." His eyes met Robert's. "'Twas not nearly gratifying enough to pester his army afterward."

The dark promise in James' eyes was telling. He would offer King Edward a tortuous death indeed. And Bryce well understood his sentiment, as did they all. Because, sadly enough, those who had not heeded Robert's dire warning to leave the city but instead held out hope for the English to be merciful suffered greatly.

When Edward's army never got their supplies thanks to Angus MacDonald, things grew far worse. Only aiding in Robert's grand plan of starving and depleting Edward's army, the weather was unseasonably wet with constant driving rain and high winds. Due to lack of shelter and food, the Sassenach soldiers began to suffer not only from fever and agues but Dysentery. Eventually and inevitably the English army became a barely controllable, sick and semi mutinous rabble.

Staying in the city was no longer an option.

On September second, Holyrood Abbey was set on fire. In a fit of petulance, King Edward ordered the slaughter of the remaining inhabitants of Edinburgh. The Sassenach soldiers ran amok, killing almost five thousand men, women, and children. Even babies were slaughtered and disemboweled in the streets.

Meanwhile, Robert had sent James Douglas and Thomas Randolph with extra Highland clansmen to harass the retreating English unmercifully. In the end, only half of the army that had marched into Scotland stumbled out of the country.

This, of course, was all part of Robert's master plan. A great rout to be sure.

As James reported it, the demoralized Sassenach were now in a state of mutiny. Led by incompetent leaders, without adequate food or clothing, they were forced to flee from an implacable enemy in heavy rain. James' eyes lit with pleasure as he told of them trudging through mud, swollen rivers, forced to sleep in the open as they staggered wearily toward York.

Each day men deserted the army, fell sick or fell beneath James' and his men's blades as they never gave up pursuit. By the time they reached where they were now, the encampments around Rievaulx Abbey, Byland, Shaws Moor and Scawton Moor, only one third of the army remained. At that juncture, unfortunately, they were joined by tens of thousands more English soldiers.

So those now surrounding King Edward at Rievaulx Abbey were the army they would be fighting on the morrow. An army that Robert with his brilliant strategizing didn't seem wary of in the least.

The king kept discussing his battle strategy with Adlin and Grant who, naturally, gave nothing away. Bryce knew, though, that things were going as planned.

They continued to enjoy pleasantries as they visited. Like his cousins, he couldn't be more honored to be sitting amongst such great men. If not for them, this country would surely not be where it was today.

"*If not for you and your cousins too*," Jessie said into his mind. "*You're just as much heroes as any of these men considering what you've done for your country.*"

"*Och, I wouldnae go that far.*" He squeezed her hand as his eyes met hers. "*But thank you, lass.*" Though his gaze returned to the others, he kept speaking to her. "*Have you come up with a plan yet in regards to the warlock?*"

"*Yes,*" she replied, opening her mind to the others as well. "*I think as soon as we're done here, we should find a private spot and summon the warlock. Because if we wait much longer, it'll be time for the battle and we don't want him making his move then.*"

"*I couldnae agree more, lass,*" Grant responded. His eyes grazed her ring while he continued speaking with Robert. "*Though your gem doesnae glow yet.*"

"Hopefully, it will once we defeat the beastie, aye?" Adlin interjected. *"Who knows. Mayhap if we throw everything we have at it, which is considerable with three rings already ignited, we'll be able to defeat it without the power of the fourth ring."*

While Bryce appreciated Adlin's optimism, he feared it wouldn't be that simple. So did Jessie based on her less-than-convinced thoughts.

A few hours later, having found a spot a ways out from the encampment, the same reservations remained. Though Robert thought it peculiar that they wandered off to explore the forest and get a lay of the land, he was somewhat used to their oddities by now. More than that, he trusted that they had Scotland's best interests in mind.

"Like I know all of you have, I've given this a great deal of thought," Jessie finally said as she met their eyes over a crackling fire. "And I'm sure like all of you I've come to one conclusion." Her eyes met Bryce's. "It's very likely going to come down to Bryce and me, just like it did with the warlock that had the enemy's essence."

"Aye, lass," Grant agreed. "But as you all did in Pentland Firth, we can wear it down first and mayhap make it easier for you." His brows rose. "And though 'tis of the spirit realm, like Adlin said, we've got three magical rings now. Rings that might just help everyone attack the warlock in a way it didn't anticipate."

Jessie nodded, her eyes on Bryce. "Are you ready?"

He could see the growing strength and confidence in her eyes. She was prepared to confront this last warlock. It was time.

"Aye, lass." He nodded. "I'll be by your side from start to finish."

Her gaze swept over everyone as she said a few final words. "Whatever might come of this I want you all to know how thankful I am. Not just for your inspirational courage but the kindness you've shown me." Emotion flared in her eyes. "It's meant more than you know."

"We're always here for you, sweetie," Milly said as everyone nodded their agreement. "And we're more than thankful for all you've done too."

Jessie didn't say anything else just held their eyes for another moment before she opened the book to a blank page, closed her eyes and started drawing. Bryce narrowed his eyes at the image as it

1

began to take shape. If he wasn't mistaken, it looked an awful lot like him.

Her eyes shot open and focused on the fire as she began chanting.

Moments later, his attention was torn from the book as a harsh chill swept through the woodland and shadows fell where there were none before. Though everyone visibly tensed, Bryce and Sven were particularly anxious. Whatever was heading their way had the unmistakable essence of dragon about it.

"He's coming," Jessie whispered.

Seconds later, a tall, dark inky shadow began shifting through the forest toward them.

"You are making this too easy, my love," came his raspy voice on the wind, "bringing everyone to me like this."

Jessie remained silent and perfectly still as he approached. Though he was hooded, his appearance soon startled everyone. No wonder she had been drawing Bryce...the warlock bore a striking resemblance. That, Bryce realized, was likely their first mistake.

Its offsetting appearance.

It was too disconcerting.

Or at least it was for everyone but Jessie.

She seemed perfectly at ease, maybe too at ease, as it drew closer. When it did, they formed a wide circle around it.

"I missed you, Jessie," it whispered. "Let me finish this then come home with me, aye?"

Bryce frowned as the voice became less raspy and more like his own.

"Home," she murmured as the book dropped from her limp hands. "I'd like that."

Adlin shook his head, his face as disgruntled as the rest of theirs. Jessie's mind was clouding over, drifting further and further away from them. All she could see was Bryce in the warlock. How much she wanted to be with him always.

"So ye'll let me finish off everyone here," the warlock whispered. "Then fix Scotland's history so we can always be together?"

"Together," she whispered as though under a spell. "Always."

"Together," he repeated. "Always."

Their eyes held as though in mutual understanding before a sly grin curled his lips. "Ye really do want me, aye?"

"So much," she whispered. "I always have." A tear rolled down her cheek. "I'm strong when I'm with you. Not weak and emotional."

It seemed Jessie had well and truly lost herself, so they sprang into action. Adlin and Grant began chanting, evidently accessing the spiritual realm as everyone except Jessie started throwing all they had at it.

As it turned out, the rings *did* help…somewhat.

Conall began by manipulating the air enough that the warlock glanced in his direction. The moment it did, Lindsay enchanted it to remain where it was. Milly confused it by astral-projecting all around it while Adlin and Grant started barraging it with something that made it scowl in discomfort. Though her blade didn't seem to cause it any physical pain, Christina certainly irritated the warlock as she continually attacked it with her sword. Aðísla chanted and peeled away the branches overhead while Graham made sure rain clouds vanished and bright sunlight poured down.

For all appearances, the warlock seemed to be weakening.

Sven's eyes had turned dragon as he took up position behind the warlock and nodded at Bryce. This was his moment, and the Viking intended to be his back-up in case he needed it.

More than ready to end this horrible creature once and for all, Bryce embraced his dragon. Blazing fury filled him as he peered down at the warlock. *This* was the moment he would avenge his mate. The moment she would *finally* get her dragon back. That in mind, he rallied his rage, reared his head back, ready to thrust it forward and release fire, but stopped short. Frozen, his insides twisted as the warlock's eyes met his. No, not the warlock's.

Jessie's.

More so, her dragon's.

Everybody had been so focused on Jessie's reaction to the warlock that they hadn't taken into consideration Bryce's. Because what he experienced now was pure torture. Her dragon was in there. His true mate. How could he *ever* snuff her life out? It would be impossible. He would rather die.

A sly smile curled the warlock's lips as he took full advantage of Bryce's hesitation. Not just his but Sven's too as the warlock's eyes flared with the power of the dragon, broke free of everyone's magic and spun on the Viking.

Fury ravaged Sven's features when he went to shift but stopped. Then he drew his ax as if to fight but again stopped. Like Bryce, his dragon wouldn't allow him to harm her dragon. She might not be his mate, but she was an innocent female. Kin. And that meant he could only ever protect not harm her.

The warlock released a horrible peal of laughter then a blink later vanished.

Just like that, he was gone.

Though furious, Bryce set aside his emotions as he shifted back and went to Jessie. Was she okay? He cupped her shoulders and tried to meet her eyes. Fear shot through him at her dazed expression. "Lass, are you all right?"

She blinked several times in confusion before, thank the gods, her eyes focused on his. "Oh no, I let you down didn't I?"

"Och, nay." He shook his head and pulled her into his arms. "If anything *I* let *you* down."

"What happened?" she murmured. "I barely remember anything except you…" She shook her head. "I mean him."

The way she said 'him' set Bryce on edge. As if she felt affection she just could not help.

"I'm sorry," she whispered, sadness in her eyes as they met his again. "I guess it's going to be harder than I thought separating from him." Her eyes welled. "We just have so much history."

He frowned, not pleased with her wobbly, heartfelt words at all. Yet he didn't fault her for her honesty or for feeling the way she did.

"'Twill be okay, lass," he replied softly. "Now we know what to expect next time. What our weaknesses are."

She nodded, still upset. But then how could she not be when their weaknesses seemed almost insurmountable. They now knew Bryce couldn't defeat the warlock because he simply could not kill his mate. And Jessie? Well, she certainly didn't seem to be strengthening any when it came to the warlock. Again, he didn't blame her. She was a pawn in an evil game being played out by the leftovers of a corrupt man.

"We'll figure this out," Grant murmured. "There has to be a way."

Jessie shook her head. "I had hoped at the very least you and Adlin might be able to sense the warlock's weaknesses. Did you?"

"Nay, 'tis verra powerful." Adlin shook his head and scowled. "If anything, all we did was show it *our* weaknesses."

"That's what I was afraid of," Jessie murmured as she picked up her book and shoved it in her pocket. "So I guess, in some ways, we're back to square one."

"There's got to be another way, and we'll figure it out." Grant rubbed the back of his neck as he mulled it over. "I refuse to let this warlock win." He sighed. "But what else to throw at it? I just used all my magic to no avail."

"Aye," Adlin agreed as he clasped Grant's shoulder in reassurance. "'Tis all right, my friend. We'll figure this out. We always do."

It was a quiet walk back as everyone came to terms with what seemed to be a no-win situation. Nevertheless, they needed to remain vigilant in the upcoming battle because the warlock would be back and they hadn't a clue what it had up its sleeve.

Later that evening after watching a day of battle preparations, things still weighed heavily on Bryce's mind. He and Jessie had been given their own tent and were retired for the evening. Alarmingly enough, she had remained withdrawn all day, and it bothered him greatly. She seemed a great distance away from him, and it almost felt like she was doing it on purpose. That the warlock had truly affected her perspective on things. Namely Bryce himself. And based on what he sensed, it wasn't good.

Yet he sought only to comfort her.

"'Twill be all right, lass," he assured, whether or not he believed it.

Her eyes met his as they sat by the fire. "Yes, it will."

And there, above all else, was the primary reason for his alarm. The new spark in her eyes. If he wasn't mistaken, it was defiance. Yet he had the oddest feeling that defiance wasn't directed toward who it should be.

"You dinnae seem yourself," he said softly, eying her as her gaze returned to the fire. "What troubles you, Jessie?"

"What doesn't trouble me," she murmured. Her eyes remained on the flames like they had back in the beginning. "I can't stand feeling so helpless…" Her brows pinched together in frustration. "So out of control."

Though he could well imagine how that might bother her, she seemed far too focused on it. "Remember, you dinnae need to be in control anymore. 'Tis time to lean on all of us…" He took her hand, hoping she would look at him. "On me."

She didn't look his way but scowled at the fire. "I am…I'm trying…"

But she wasn't. He could feel her inner struggle. Her need to be as strong as she was before. It didn't seem to matter that she had dragon lineage or even dragon magic. All she focused on was how she had been with the warlocks. How powerful.

"The warlock affected your mind today." He frowned and shook his head. "That is why you feel as you do."

"If anything, he reminded me," she whispered.

Now he was the one scowling. "Reminded you of what?"

"Nothing," she said softly as she stood. "I'm tired." She headed for the cot without looking back. "Goodnight."

"Goodnight, lass," he murmured as she curled up under the blankets and turned away from him.

What the bloody hell was wrong with her? No kiss? Affection? She had gone from being lustful to cold and distant. The warlock had to have done this. There was no other explanation. Because she couldn't truly be feeling this way, right? She couldn't really be having doubts about them. About what she and Bryce had found together.

As he remained in front of the fire, he began to give into his own fears. Mayhap she truly *was* having doubts. Mayhap reconnecting with the warlock was all it took. As his thoughts festered, it seemed more and more plausible. Only one thing kept him level headed in the end.

Jessie.

Though the thought of letting go of their love both saddened and terrified him, he would if it meant saving her. He had promised her he would protect her at all cost, so that was what he intended to do. He would let her go because he loved her and refused to allow her to suffer a life with the warlock.

It would *not* happen.

Even if it meant forfeiting his own life to achieve such.

217

Because were they not one and the same? Which meant if he died so should his enemy.

Chapter Seventeen

THOUGH IT WASN'T raining, the morning of the Battle of Byland Moor dawned overcast and dreary. Or at least it seemed that way to Jessie.

She feared what might be on the horizon. The enemy had planned well, and this last warlock might truly get his way. She sighed and tossed Bryce a guilty look. Though he was incredibly good about it, she felt like a rift had grown between them since yesterday. That she had let him down.

Yet that wasn't her only reason for feeling guilty.

No that had more to do with the warlock's allure.

Something she clearly couldn't get past.

"Are you ready then, lass?" Bryce said softly as his eyes met hers. "'Twill be a day that goes down in history."

She worried it might very well. Just not the way he meant it.

"Yes." She nodded, sure to look and sound confident as he hoisted her onto a horse then swung up behind her.

Sir Walter Stewart had already left with three hundred moss-troopers. His mission was to attack Rievaulx Abbey as soon as the English line was broken by the Scottish Army on Roulston Scar. Christina and Graham had traveled with him to offer any help they could.

Sir James Douglas was already off with his soldiers lighting more fires to create extra smoke. This would conceal Robert's movements from the Earl of Richmond, the English commander. Right now, she, Bryce and his kin were traveling with Robert's army. Unable to help himself, Conall intended to make sure the smoke was thick and nearly impossible to see through.

She and Bryce said very little as they traveled, and within a few hours, they arrived around the rear of Roulston Scar. The smoke had, as planned, concealed a good two thirds of Robert's army in clumps of trees below a gully close to where they were now. The purpose of this move, of course, was to give the appearance that the Scottish army hosted far fewer men than it actually did.

"We'll not engage in battle lest we have to," Grant said to Robert as they dismounted. "For historical reasons, that is."

"Aye." Robert nodded, having heard the same at the Battle of Bannockburn.

She knew it was awful timing, but nature called so she whispered to Bryce, "I need a few moments alone."

"'Tis not a verra good time, lass." He frowned. "These woods are dangerous."

She flinched. "I don't think I can hold it."

"Och," he murmured but nodded. "Aye then, I'll take you someplace private." He took her into the forest a short distance but far enough. "Is this all right?"

It would have to be. She would not risk waiting any longer. Especially considering she had caught his thoughts last night and knew of Bryce's dark intentions. That he would forfeit his own life in hopes of destroying the warlock.

"Yes, this spot is fine," she replied softly, not needing to relieve herself at all. That had been a lie to get them alone. Courage rallied as much as it ever would be, she met his eyes and whispered, "I'm so sorry."

"Why are you sorry," he began but trailed off as the air grew icy. Stunned, he shook his head. The look in his eyes was both horror-stricken and heartbroken as he realized what was happening.

She had betrayed him.

"I just can't let him go," she murmured as she backed away from him. "I was a fool for thinking I could." She shook her head, tears in her eyes. "He's been with me for so long...*not* you."

"But I am him," Bryce replied, his voice hoarse and his brogue thick. "Ye said so yerself."

"I said that because I was weak and afraid after being separated from him," she replied as the warlock drew closer, triumph in his dark eyes as he relished Bryce's reaction. "He kept me strong where you only make me weaker."

With a small chant and a flick of her hand, she flung Bryce's weapons away from him so he couldn't take his own life and possibly the warlocks with it.

His scowl only deepened as he looked from the warlock to her. "Ye cannae be serious."

"Just look at me!" She wiped away a tear with disgust. "This isn't how I want to live. Feeling weak," her eyes went to the warlock, "when I could feel strong." Her eyes returned to Bryce with resolve. "I *refuse* to live this way…I'm helping my love." She shook her head again. "Him, *not* you."

She pulled out her little book and looked at the warlock. A face she recognized so well. A man she wanted to be with above all others. Her true love.

"Are you ready?" she whispered. "Are you ready to warn the English and see that they win today?"

"Aye," the warlock murmured, his dark eyes glistening with approval. "I have been ready for a verra long time."

This was it. The moment she had been waiting for.

So she flipped to the page after the one she had drawn of him yesterday and made one single stroke. Then she flipped to the next page and began sketching rapidly but not before the warlock figured out something was wrong and ripped the book away.

As his eyes fell to the page she had made one stroke on, Adlin and Grant appeared.

"Och, nay," the warlock seethed, as his disbelieving eyes flew to hers. "What have ye *done*?"

What she had done, working covertly with the arch-wizards, was concoct a plan.

One she prayed would work.

Seconds later, mimicking the picture she had begun yesterday and just finished, her gem began to glow. Not the dark inkiness of the warlock's eyes but the bright golden of Bryce's. Now she could only hope it wasn't just her manifestation but the real deal.

That God willing, true love really did exist between her and Bryce.

Half a breath later, things started happening.

The warlock kept shaking his head, pain and betrayal in his eyes as his features began to twist and change. They became less and less Bryce's and more grotesque before a wave of energy burst out of him and slammed into Bryce. Yet a piece lingered as the warlock struggled to hold on to him. As he roared and raged in denial.

An unparalleled power struggle ensued between Bryce and the warlock, but it didn't last long. The warlock never stood a chance once another's magic became involved. It screeched in pain when something suddenly shot out of Jessie and ripped the last tendril free.

Erin's dragon magic.

As the warlock roared again in rage, Bryce blinked several times. At first, he seemed baffled before fury filled him. Teeth clenched, he narrowed his eyes. He and the warlock were no longer connected.

Its death would not mean his.

Jessie felt Bryce become whole again like a bolt of energizing electricity. As it was for him, newfound strength was pouring through her. More than that, something even more profound happened. Without the strength of Bryce inside him, the warlock could no longer hold onto what else he had stolen.

She widened her eyes in surprise when colors swirled out of the warlock and rushed into her.

For a split second, she was a little girl facing off with her grandfather again. He was stealing her dragon, and she finally felt it. Remembered it. The horrible sensation of losing such an important piece of herself. The rage and pain and sadness her little dragon felt. The emptiness they both experienced as they lost each other. Though a small piece of her inner beast's magic had remained, it was nothing compared to what she felt now.

Nothing could touch the glory of her dragon returning to her.

All became very clear at that point. When her dragon was stolen, the enemy had not only erased her memory of it but put up an extra barrier between her and her true identity. He had cast a spell that made her fear things dragons should love. Hence her fear of anything that took her off the ground.

If that wasn't enough, he had given the warlock added power over her.

Not only was she drawn to the piece of Bryce within it but her own dragon. That was why she remembered walking into the warlock's arms but never knew what happened next. Because there was nothing beyond that but darkness. The warlock, no matter how much he wanted to, was incapable of returning a love that never belonged to him, to begin with. And he would never reveal her dragon, his greatest weapon against her. So it would always just be a dream she awoke from, none the wiser.

In the blink of an eye, she remembered even more.

How she had shifted a few times but promised Mama she would keep it hidden until her dragon was older and stronger. Then and only then would she attack her grandfather. Yet he took that chance away and stole her dragon first.

Then, as only a dragon could do, her memories rolled back further in time to the very moment she was born. The connection she and her twin sister had made when her younger sibling was swaddled and laid down beside her minutes later. Even then their little dragons knew exactly who the other was. But then they had simultaneously shared a womb, and no experience was more powerful for their kind.

"We're running out of time," her mother had whispered. "I'm growing weaker, and you need to get her out of here."

Brand new into the world, Jessie stared up into her father's eyes as he leaned over her. Suddenly she knew with absolute certainty that he was still alive out there somewhere. Someday she *would* meet him, and his love for her would be as strong then as it was right now. She could see it in his dragon eyes. Sad eyes. "Let me take them both. They'll be stronger together. I will protect them."

"You know that's not possible," her mother replied, standing beside him, strong though she had so recently birthed them. "I was only able to hide one of them from him. The other must stay here and be strong. She must follow the path meant for her."

Jessie knew that 'him' could only be in reference to the man who pretended to be her grandfather. She also understood as she looked up into her parent's eyes that she was the one who was meant to stay behind. She was the one who would have to be strong so that her sister could be safe.

It was also in those moments that she realized the sacrifice her mother had made. She used nearly all of her magic to hide their real father from the enemy then protected her children the best way she knew how. She forfeited her magic entirely, using the last of it so that the enemy would only ever know Jessie existed. And what real threat was but one child? As far as he knew she inherited her dragon blood from her grandfather. A dragon he fully intended to take from her anyway. And what of her magic? If her grandfather was no match for him how could she be?

Yet look at her now.

More of a threat than he ever realized.

A threat that would see his dark influence wiped out entirely. His days of hurting others was over. His pitiful weakness would no longer stain this country or anyone she cared about. So, harnessing a lifetime of repressed anger, she gave her dragon free rein and turned her considerable fury on all that was left of him.

Grant and Adlin began chanting as Jessie's eyes hazed red and untouchable wrath filled her. Stripped of everything that had made him strong, the warlock staggered back but only so far before he hit a wall of Adlin's making that trapped him in place. Meanwhile, Grant thickened the smoke all around them so that anything that might take place here would not be seen.

In that singular moment, all the years came rushing back. The sadness and repression. The awful life this curse had subjected her and her family to. All the damage it had caused for Bryce and his kin. Losing Darach for years. Fraser. And saddest of all, Kenna's death.

Any flicker of misguided gratitude she might have felt toward this warlock was gone.

Only the cold, hard truth remained.

This warlock was the last hold the enemy had over her and Scotland.

As Jessie roared in outrage, familiar power filled her, and the warlock grew smaller. Ugly, twisted and terrified, he trembled in fear as she at long last embraced her dragon again. *Now* she would avenge so many. *Now* she would exact retribution for Bryce's torture at the English encampment and his many near death experiences while time-traveling.

When her eyes went to Bryce, he nodded. Though he hadn't shifted his dragon eyes flared with pride. "This is your kill, Jessie. End him, lass."

Wrapped around the tip of her talon, her ring shined brightly as she lowered her head close to the warlock. She bared her teeth and narrowed her eyes as she spoke within its mind, her words seething and disgusted. *"You are powerless over me without Bryce in you. He was all I ever cared about. May you rot in Hell with your creator."*

Then, for the first time in her life, she roared fire.

The warlock screamed in pain, twisting and writhing until it could no longer move. She kept on roaring until there was nothing left but ashes. As those ashes blew away on the wind, she realized not only Bryce was standing there but Sven. Both had kept her fire from incinerating the forest beyond.

When her eyes met Sven's dragon eyes, the air pulsed and the symbol of the fiery dragon flared between them. As she shifted back and the symbol drifted away in a burst of sparks, she knew Scotland's curse had been lifted, but Scandinavia's prophecy had just begun.

One that she could tell by the look in Sven's eyes he saw far more clearly now.

Death to Scotland had been part of Jessie's curse.

Death to those who fly was part of her sister's prophecy.

"My father," Sven said softly, anger flaring in his eyes as they met Aðísla's when she appeared. "And King Heidrek."

"Are in dire trouble," she replied. "And in need of a king to unite their people."

"But they are king's," he murmured before his words trailed off and the turmoil in his eyes only grew.

"The curse has been lifted, and Scotland is safe." Aðísla's voice remained firm and her eyes strong as they held Sven's. "Now it's time to go home and make sure our people are safe as well."

He nodded before his eyes returned to Jessie's. "You have done well, ruler of dragons. I'm very impressed and proud to call you kin."

"Thank you." She worked at a smile, sad to see him go but understanding things much better now. Not necessarily the prophecy but the small part she played in it. "Emily will be safe at the house in Winter Harbor until…" she swallowed hard but remained strong, "until my sister arrives. Then my magic will lift, and hers will take over."

Though she wasn't entirely sure what she was protecting Emily from, she knew it possessed dragon blood. And based on the ominous words *death to those who fly*, trouble was most certainly on the horizon.

Sven clasped her shoulder gently. "You will meet your sister someday." A knowing glint lit his eyes. "Perhaps sooner than you think."

"I hope so," she murmured. "Let me know the second she needs me, and I'll be there. The second you and your people need me for that matter."

He nodded as his eyes held hers for a moment longer before he turned to Bryce and bid him farewell.

"Wishing ye the verra best, my friend," Bryce said. "Like Jessie said, we'll be there for ye the moment ye need us, aye?"

Sven nodded again, grateful. "I will keep that in mind. Thank you."

After everyone said their goodbyes, Sven and Aðísla left. She only prayed as she watched them fade away to travel back in time, that all went well. As it was, prophesies could be even trickier than curses.

Once they vanished, she became aware of a transparent couple standing a ways off in the woods. Her grandmother and by his dark, handsome gypsy looks, she would say her real grandfather. When his eyes locked with hers, warmth and pride filled her. The sort of warmth a child might feel when reflecting on a happy upbringing with a family that loved her. And the sort of pride a dragon might feel when their elder dragon was impressed by her.

"Goodbye," she whispered, wiping away a tear as they smiled then faded into the afterlife. Like all of them, her grandfather was free at last to enjoy love.

"My lass," Bryce murmured before he finally pulled her into his arms and kissed her. Not light and fleeting but passionately. Where she had always felt a rush of excitement in his arms, now it felt a thousand times stronger. Not just because of the ring igniting but because she was finally free of all darkness. Lighter in a way she had never felt before, she melted into him, beyond grateful everything had gone the way they planned.

"Planned," he murmured, as he pulled his lips away and narrowed his eyes at a very smug Adlin and Grant. "All three of you, then?"

"Aye." Adlin beamed. "And 'twas nice to finally have some control over the outcome of things!"

"Aye," Grant agreed, grinning. "Verra nice, indeed."

Bryce's narrowed eyes returned to hers, though a small smile hovered on his lips. "How long have you three been planning this?"

She smiled. "Since around the time I summoned my grandmother." Her eyes went from the arch-wizards to him. "We had to keep it from you in case the warlock was listening through his connection to you."

"And the thoughts you had?" He looked at her curiously. "Those about missing the warlock?"

"All for his benefit," she assured. "Pretty much from the moment Adlin said I needed to get my emotions under control, we were preparing to set him up."

"I *thought* that was callous of him to say at the time." Bryce kept considering her as he confirmed. "So everything you said and even thought was for my benefit in hopes the warlock was listening."

She nodded as she picked up the little book. While she thought for sure it would vanish along with the curse, it remained. Yet it looked and felt different now. Just like her, it was lighter. Better.

"Its pages are now made from the old oak tree in front of the Colonial in New Hampshire," she whispered in wonder before her eyes went to Grant and Adlin. "The tree remains alive and well and free from the curse now too."

Like everything else, because it was so closely connected to the Brouns and MacLomains, the tree had suffered. That, as everyone knew, was seen clearly on Graham and Christina's adventure when it nearly died in their time loop.

"'Tis good to hear the tree's well." Adlin smiled. "And that its magic remains with you via that book."

She nodded as she eyed it again. It was hard to imagine the day had come that she cherished this book rather than hated it. But it had, and she did. There was nothing left of the enemy tarnishing it.

It was entirely hers now.

"So how did it happen?" Bryce persisted. "How did the ring finally shine?"

"I believe because of this book," she said softly. "I took a chance and tried something."

She explained how she had drawn the ring shining his eye color on the page after the one drawn of the warlock.

"I drew it ahead of time and only needed to put the final touch on it today," she explained. "Then on the next page, I had just enough time to sketch an image of looking down on the warlock as though I was, indeed, a dragon."

She grinned as she continued. "Everything we did yesterday summoning the warlock was a set up. Not only did we want to see what he was capable of, but we wanted to paint a false picture." Jessie purposely looked drifty eyed for effect. "Naturally, I was impossibly drawn to him and let him know telepathically that I intended to be with him. That I had realized the error of my ways and would lead you to slaughter today if it meant becoming as strong as I once was."

Her smile went from the arch-wizards back to him. "And they, of course, as powerful as they are, threw everything they had at him," she mock pouted, "only to discover they just didn't have what it took to defeat the last warlock."

Bryce grinned. "Which gave it a false sense of security."

"That's right." She met his grin. "So all I needed to do today was act as emotional and taken with him as possible, so he believed my weakness." She shook her head. "He had only ever seen me unemotional, and in control, so it would make sense that I was angry that I had lost that. It made sense that I would want to be strong again."

"'Twas all verra clever, lass." Yet Bryce's smile wavered as his brows drew together in distress. "And also verra risky." He shook his head. "So many things could have gone wrong." He gestured at her ring. "Namely that shine you manifested being false and not possessing the necessary power."

"Like you said, it was a risk." Her eyes held his. "But one I was willing to take if it meant saving Scotland…and freeing you."

"Och, lass," he whispered before he brushed his lips across hers again then eyed the ring. "And 'tis real. The shine remains. You're my one true love." Pride lit his eyes as they returned to hers. "And the most bonny wee black dragon I've ever seen."

She tilted her head and narrowed her eyes. "*Wee*?" She stood up a little taller and notched her chin. "I was much taller than you."

"Because I was still in human form." He chuckled and kept her close. "When I'm a dragon I'm at least twice your size."

Jessie was about to respond when Adlin interrupted. "Though I hate to disturb you, we're running out of time."

Jessie and Bryce looked at him as she said, "Running out of time?"

"Aye," Grant exclaimed. "The moment has finally arrived to witness our last round of history."

"Aye," Adlin agreed. "The grand rout or should I say the Battle of Byland Moor is about to begin!"

~Avenged by a Highland Laird~

Chapter Eighteen

BY THE TIME they returned, history had started to unfold precisely as it should but not before the others congratulated Bryce and Jessie. Not only for igniting their ring, but for defeating the last warlock and at long last, lifting the curse. Thanks to their mental connection, they had followed everything.

Bryce was still adjusting to how he felt now. How complete. It was strange living one's whole life without realizing they were not at their best. That they were not all they should be. Now he felt it though. A new clarity and strength that had been lacking before. More than that? He now felt the magnitude of the intense connection he shared with Jessie. In some ways, it was as if she had been there all along, but he'd only just realized it.

Though he was desperate to be alone with her and further explore their intensified bond, now wasn't the time. Too much was happening and that became clear when Sir James Douglas joined everyone. But not for long. Robert soon ordered James and Thomas Randolph along with six thousand moss-troopers and spearmen to directly assault the ridge next to Roulston Scar.

"He's hoping the Earl of Richmond will call on his reserve forces to meet this threat," Conall explained to Lindsay. Though she was the only one unfamiliar with the battle, Bryce noticed Milly and Jessie seemed to appreciate the history lesson as well.

He knew Jessie had witnessed several battles while with the warlocks so she could handle what she was about to see. The violence and massive death toll. Still, as they sat on a horse, he wrapped his arms around her and kept her close for support.

As forecasted, when the English watched the advance of the Scots out of the smoke, the Earl of Richmond did as Robert anticipated. He countered by sending fifteen thousand men down the slope to assault the inferior Scottish force.

Roars arose, and metal clashed as the battling began.

"Naturally, what the Earl of Richmond has not observed," Conall continued, "is that the gully the Scots are advancing up from is verra narrow and constricted with steep slopes on each side." He grinned. "This makes movement on horseback verra difficult." He gestured at what was unfolding. "And see. The Earl's finding out too late that he can only attack on a verra narrow front which the Scots are ably defending by forming a schiltrom with their long spears."

This, as they could very well see, turned the first English charge into a bloody mess of dead, dying and injured horses and men. The foul smell of blood, sweat, and excrement drifted on the chilly wind.

"And now the Earl of Richmond is sending down more men as the Bruce sends up his highlanders under Neil Campbell of Loch Awe and Robert MacGregor," Conall said as the Scots proceeded to assault both flanks of the English position.

"The Scots are dressed far better for this," Lindsay commented.

And they were.

The lightly clad clansmen scaled both flanks driving the English back with their fierce attacks and Gàidhlig—Gaelic—war cries. Thus, they forced the Earl of Richmond to pull in all his picquets, or small units of soldiers, and guards to throw into the battle.

This left the alternative route unguarded.

"This is when King Robert will strike with force," Bryce murmured as he squeezed Jessie's hand. Like his cousins, it was hard to contain his excitement.

Everyone followed at a distance on horseback and watched as the Bruce made his move.

One he had been building toward for months.

Robert and his remaining moss-troopers and light cavalry made their way largely unseen, onto Shaws Moor. There in front of them lay, unprotected, the encampments of the Sassenach army. He formed his men into three arrowhead divisions, and with the trumpeters blasting out the charge he led his men stirrup to stirrup in a thundering gallop.

His Lion Rampant Banner flew in the hands of his standard bearer, Scrymgeour, as the Scots roared 'A Bruce! A Bruce!' Seconds later, they galloped out of the smoke and crashed through the English lines causing widespread panic and destruction.

"'Tis safe to say even a tightly disciplined army would have found it difficult to withstand that charge," Adlin declared, impressed.

Everyone agreed wholeheartedly as the demoralized Sassenach deserted their posts and ran for their lives. As history had recorded it, the casualties Bruce's moss-troopers suffered came from the arrows of the few English archers who stood their ground before being finished off.

No quarter was given, and Sassenach casualties were horrendous. At last, only the dead and the victorious Scots remained on the battlefield.

"'Tis a bloody fine sight," Grant murmured as he and Adlin remembered all too well the slaughter at Berwick-on-Tweed. It was the beginning of all this for them, and it did their hearts good to see yet more avengement for all the innocent Scottish lives lost since then. As it was, over seventeen thousand Scots had died that fateful day in Berwick then left by Longshanks to rot.

Bryce and his kin grinned as they watched Robert the Bruce now.

This had been one of those days in history Sir William Wallace would have liked to witness. They didn't doubt Robert thought of him now as he led his horsemen to the edge of Roulston Scar and ordered his trumpeters to sound the Rally.

Down below in the gully where the Black Douglas and Sir Thomas Randolph still fought, the English and Scots alike turned their heads toward the clamor of trumpets. When they saw Bruce's host on the escarpment, the Scots roared in triumph and surged forward.

"Cowards," Bryce muttered, just as pleased as everyone else as they watched the Sassenach army disperse. Some tried to flee where others surrendered when James Douglas ordered that the Scots give quarter. The Corrie was a difficult place to escape from, and in the end, very few English got away.

The Earl of Richmond surrendered his sword to James as did his lieutenants. Twenty Sassenach knights lay amid the dead with twice as many wounded. That fine day the Scots ushered their prisoners up the hill, where Sir James Douglas and Sir Thomas Randolph presented their prisoners to the king.

"*All is going as it should on our end,*" Graham said into their minds. "*We arrived at Rievaulx Abbey in an attempt to capture King Edward.*"

"*And King Edward escaped as he should?*" Adlin said, disgust in his internal voice.

"*Aye,*" Graham reported. "*When told of his army's defeat he was humiliated and ushered from the abbot's house by a guard of twenty men. As we know, he will now try to take a ship in Bridlington.*" Now it was Graham's turn to sound disgusted. "*And just as history told, he left over one hundred of his bodyguards behind to forfeit their lives to buy him time to escape. This, as planned, will delay the Scots sufficiently enough to allow Edward to slip away.*"

"*Christina and I stayed behind as the Stewart continues to pursue Edward,*" Graham informed. "*He travels with fewer men now so 'twas best we not join him and mayhap disturb history in some unanticipated way.*"

Sir Walter Stewart and fifty men would chase King Edward for many miles, but in the darkness, they would lose him on the road to Nunnington. Along the way, Edward's horse would become lame, and he'd be forced to seek a fresh mount at Pickering Castle. On the morrow, at that very castle, his grey charger would be presented to King Robert as a prize of war.

Eventually, Edward would arrive in Bridlington and request the keeper of the castle to provide him with a ship to take him to London.

"*I would've loved to see the look on Edward's face when the keeper escorts him to a lookout tower and points out at the bay,*" Christina said, a grin in her voice. "*Good ol' Captain Angus stickin' it to him yet again!*"

As it turned out, three long galleys belonging to Angus Og sat in the bay waiting, so escaping by sea was impossible. No trading galliot could outrun such impressive ships. So Edward rode to York narrowly escaping capture twice, and lost his shield in the process.

Rumor had it the Bruce later returned this shield to Edward as an unspoken challenge. Fight or negotiate peace.

Edward didn't rise to the challenge, and this was one of the reasons he was later deposed.

From York, Edward and his party made their way to the safety of Burstwick in Holderness. After that, they were on to London where they reunited with Queen Isabella. She, no surprise, was *not* happy about being abandoned by Edward. Left behind and forced to fend for herself, she had made a perilous journey disguised as a Nun to Tynemouth Priory.

"Queen Isabella barely escaped as well," Graham commented. *"Just as history said."*

With her and Edward's departure, the North of England was now wide open for the Scottish army to extract tribute, pillage, and loot at their leisure. King Edward left behind his finery, personal treasury, armor and shamefully enough, the great seal of England.

"'Twas a mighty rout indeed, my King!" the Black Douglas declared later that evening as they sat around a fire at Robert's encampment. When he raised a mug of ale in salute, everyone else did as well, roaring their approval.

As it had been after every battle, the Scots buried their dead, paid their respects and now celebrated a victory far grander than most. Bryce and his kin had decided to spend one last eve with Robert rather than go home just yet. After all, he was the greatest king Scotland had ever known, and once they left, he would once again become part of history.

So they spent a fine evening with him and caught up on old times. Not just their adventures now but those young Robert had shared with Bryce's parents, aunts, uncles, Grant and Adlin. The relationship they shared with the king had now spanned over forty years.

With many a warrior wanting to celebrate alongside him, King Robert eventually wandered off but not before ensuring that they would say goodbye on the morn.

"Aye, we wouldnae leave without saying goodbye, my friend," Grant assured.

After that everyone resumed chatting.

"She knew, you know," Jessie said softly to Bryce, reflecting, as it turned out, on what else she had discovered today. "Your sister knew I was a dragon."

Sensing her sadness, he wrapped an arm around her and pulled her closer. Clearly, she had learned as much when her dragon was returned to her.

"That's why Ainsley seemed off on occasion...angry..." Her eyes were damp as they met his. "It wasn't me she was upset with, but what had been stolen from me." She pressed her lips together, fighting emotions. "She was with me the first time I shifted." A tear slipped free. "In fact, she taught me how."

Though he felt for Jessie because she had forgotten such a thing, nothing made him happier than to know she hadn't been alone. That his sister was there for her during such a tumultuous time in a dragon's life. Never mind what Jessie was going through beyond that.

"She saw when the enemy took my dragon," she whispered. "But he threatened her and said that if she ever told me, he would end my life." She shook her head. "Unfortunately, when he died, and she finally had the opportunity to tell me, the curse was unleashed and made it impossible. She was muted so long as the warlocks existed."

"Och," he murmured, saddened for both her and his sister. "That must have been verra frustrating for her." He wiped away her tear and tilted her chin, so Jessie's eyes stayed with his. "But I couldnae be more pleased that she was there for you. That she offered you some happiness in all that misery."

"Me too." She blinked away the moisture in her eyes and offered a wobbly smile. "Though she described what to do in great detail, she never got the chance to teach me how to fly. Too risky." She released a small chuckle. "It was one thing for people to think they saw a ghostly dragon. Another altogether if they saw a real one." Her gaze grew nostalgic. "But I would have loved to fly alongside her."

"Aye, lass," he said softly. "As would I have."

He peppered several kisses on her lips that turned into a few passionate ones before they finally rejoined the conversation. As Bryce figured it would, everyone's attention turned Jessie's way.

Though it had been difficult, all had waited for her to relax some before they asked what had been weighing on their minds.

It seemed, however, she knew what was coming and spoke first, her voice gentle. "I know what happened to Fraser…and I know where he is."

Tension lay thick, and all remained silent as she continued. Though they sat in the midst of a boisterous encampment, it seemed all Bryce could hear in those moments was the crackle of the fire and Jessie's voice.

"As Kenna implied and you were beginning to suspect, Fraser did not actually die on the battlefield all those years ago." Her eyes went from person to person. "Instead, the warlock shifted him through time."

"But he was mortally wounded," Conall denied, a mixture of sadness and anger in his eyes. "I saw it. I was there."

"It was the heat of battle, Cousin." Adlin clasped Conall's shoulder in reassurance. "Sometimes we dinnae see things correctly when battle lust takes over." He shook his head. "Most especially when it comes to those we love."

"Somehow he survived," Jessie assured gently. "Because he *is* still alive."

Conall nodded, digesting that as he murmured, "Aye then, lass." His eyes stayed with hers. "Where is he then? How do we get him back?"

"Though I can't speak to where he is at this moment, the warlock shifted him to a small village off the eastern shores of Scotland," she replied. "The year was fourteen hundred and forty-eight. Now, however, I'm guessing it's around fourteen hundred and fifty."

So over a hundred and twenty years in their future.

Conall frowned. "So he's been there two winters?"

She nodded. "Yes."

"So I was right about that pirate ship being from the fifteenth century," Bryce murmured as his eyes went to hers. "That's where he is now…" He almost couldn't say the words they seemed so preposterous for one of his kin. "He's a *pirate*, aye?"

"I would say so," she replied.

"'Tis not so bad really." Adlin offered everyone a comforting smile. "At least he's still alive." His brows bunched together as his eyes met Jessie's. "What I dinnae ken, though, is why we cannae sense him? At the verra least, Grant and I should have been able to."

"That's where things get a little…" It was clear she was looking for the right words. "Things aren't quite as cut and dry when it comes to Fraser's abduction. Much like Bryce and I, he suffered repercussions."

"Repercussions?" Christina cocked her head. "What does that mean, honey?"

Bryce squeezed Jessie's hand in reassurance when she hesitated. She met his eyes briefly before she nodded, returned her gaze to the other's and shocked them all.

"Fraser isn't like you anymore," she said softly. "His magic was taken from him, and he's no longer a wizard."

Chapter Nineteen

GUILT-RIDDEN, JESSIE FELT personally responsible for what had happened to Fraser, and she said as much. She owed them that at the least.

"As I told Bryce and now have confirmation," she said. "The last warlock wasn't just jealous of Bryce but of Fraser."

"Because you might have been meant for him," Adlin murmured, reflecting on the conversation they'd had aboard Angus' ship.

Lindsay's brows swept up. "What's this?"

Slightly uncomfortable, Jessie glanced at Bryce and Conall before she filled everyone in on what she had shared with Bryce about some people having second loves.

"Och," Conall muttered as he looked between Bryce and Lindsay. Yet a confident grin hovered on his lips as his eyes lingered on Lindsay's. "'Tis good we got everything squared away betwixt us then, aye?"

Lindsay smiled in return. "I would say so." Her eyes slid Bryce's way, teasing before she winked at Conall. "Not to say dragons don't hold their appeal."

Meanwhile, Bryce had taken more immediate action and pulled Jessie onto his lap. His lips brushed hers before he offered Lindsay and Conall a grin, the fire in his eyes obvious. "Only a certain kind of wee lass can handle the likes of this dragon."

"Wee," Jessie muttered but couldn't help smiling as well.

That is until her mind went back to his missing cousin.

"I'm so sorry about Fraser," she murmured, frowning as she met Bryce's kins' eyes. "If I could've stopped the warlock I would have." She shook her head. "While I thought I had control, they managed things I never could've imagined."

"'Tis not your fault, lass," Grant said gently. "Never forget that."

"Aye," Adlin agreed before they all did. Everyone she needed to hear it from. Bryce, Graham, and Conall. But then there were others weren't there? Fraser's parents and sister, Blair. His aunts and uncles. His cousin, Rona who was as close to him as Conall.

"None of them will blame you either," Grant said, easing her worries as he followed her thoughts "They will be as grateful as we are that he is alive and that you know what became of him. Everything else can be handled from there." He nodded at them all, confident. "'Tis just a wee bit of time-traveling betwixt him and us then we'll bring him home."

She nodded though she wasn't so sure about that last part.

"What is it, lass?" Bryce murmured, sensing her discontent.

"It's...ah...well, it might be a bit more complicated than that," she said softly.

Conall frowned. "How so?"

When she hesitated, wanting to make sure she said things in a way that didn't offend anyone, Graham spoke instead. "'Tis as Kenna said and as we saw on the ghostly ship." His gaze went to Christina before returning to Jessie. "He's changed. He's harder and colder. And as Kenna said to Christina, how he lives now might be beyond the scope of saving, aye?"

Jessie nodded and whispered, "Yes."

"Och, nay." Conall shook his head, refusing to believe it. "You cannae tell me if Fraser could come home to his kin, he would choose not to."

"What of his magic, lass?" Grant murmured, his eyes on hers. "Now that the curse has lifted, should his magic not be returned?"

"I don't know," she said. "Though I can tell you from what I sensed of him, he didn't want it back. He didn't want to be a wizard again."

Another spell of stunned silence fell at those words. She could sense the storm of confusion and hurt they all felt. Not only was it impossible to comprehend that he might not want to come home, but

240

to not want his magic back? How could that be? He was a *MacLomain*.

"Why would Fraser reach out to Christina as he did and help her out of our time loop if he didn't still care?" Graham asked, hopeful. "And wouldnae him having done such implied he still possessed some kind of power?"

Though Jessie suspected that had more to do with the combined magic of her time loop and Conall and Lindsay's time flux, she wouldn't say as much. Better that they keep hope. So she merely shrugged in response. "I just don't know."

"Can you contact him, Jessie?" Adlin said. "As you did on Angus' ship or mayhap in the fashion you did your grandmother?"

"I'm not sure." She shook her head. "I didn't summon him on the ship but suspect that happened because we were at the exact location on the North Sea that he was, though in different eras." Yet she would not refuse them. "But I can certainly try."

Everyone nodded as Conall said, "Please, lass. 'Twould mean a lot."

She nodded and pulled out her little book. "Of course, but we should try to find someplace quieter."

Understanding fully, they followed her a short way into the woods. Now that her ring was ignited and her dragon had been returned, she no longer needed a fire to amplify her gift. As to light, the moon was quite bright so they could see their surroundings clearly.

"Here goes," she murmured. She closed her eyes, visualized the man she had seen on the pirate ship, started sketching and chanted. Once she was done, she opened her eyes and waited. They all did, their eager eyes to the woodland around them.

Yet nothing happened.

No one came.

They waited a while before she shook her head. "I'm so sorry. He would have manifested by now if I was able to bring him here."

They nodded, each and every one of them trying to keep the disappointment from their faces for her benefit. Because the truth of it was, if she, with all the power she had come into, couldn't do it then nobody could.

"We will discuss this further on the morrow," Grant said softly. "If nothing else, we'll figure out who will travel through time to find him."

In agreement, everyone headed off to do their own thing. When Bryce murmured in her ear that he only wanted to be alone with her, she couldn't agree more. She had been eager to do that exact thing since the warlock was defeated. Because as far as she was concerned, they needed to make up for lost time.

Naturally, he followed her thought process and chuckled as he swept her up into his arms and headed for their tent. "'Twas but one eve without intimacy, my lass."

"One eve too many in my opinion," she muttered and smiled before she grew serious. "Though it was necessary, I *am* sorry for what I put you through yesterday and last night. It must have been difficult. I know it was for me."

More than difficult actually. It had been pure torture doing that to him. Watching him suffer as he worried about her. Then sensing he was so close to taking his own life to save hers. Nothing had ever upset her more.

"It was verra difficult," he conceded. "But you dinnae need to be sorry. 'Twas for the greater good." He perked his brows in resignation. "Though it *does* make me better appreciate the hell you're capable of putting me through."

"Well, don't expect any more of that hell in this lifetime," she murmured as he set her down in their tent. She trailed her fingers up beneath his tunic, whispering, "Just pleasure."

"Aye then, lass," he said huskily as fire flared in his eyes.

While she was used to being wildly aroused by him, something about seeing that fire this time caused a rush she hadn't anticipated. A whole new kind of desperation to have him inside her. To feel the great pleasure he could bring.

"Our dragons are responding to one another," he whispered as he bent over so she could pull his tunic over his head. He caught her lips with his before she could respond. As their tongues wrapped and fire lit their blood, both moaned.

It was all so different now. Every touch was amplified, from his kisses to the feel of his fingers as he ran them down the side of her neck. It was as if he left a blazing trail in his wake. One that sent delicious chills over her skin, countering the flames in a way that made her heart pound in anticipation.

Though they meant to take it slow, they began yanking off their clothes in a mad rush. They couldn't touch each other enough. It was as though it were all brand new. But then in its own way, now that they were whole again, it was. Not just that but their connection was finally complete.

Well, almost.

If she understood things correctly, they would truly become their best after this coupling. The one that followed the gem igniting. It was hard to imagine what they shared getting any better yet as he lowered her to the bed and their lips met again, she sensed something coming.

Something greater than them both.

She knew he felt it too. Their magic was compelled by it. Their inner dragons were flying toward it as though desperate to reveal its secret. She trembled as his eyes met hers and he cupped her cheek. His touch was incredibly tender and caring, at odds with the fire and the need to claim her that flared within his eyes.

What they drowned in now was love, lust and primal need all wrapped in one. A heady concoction that made their hearts race and their breathing choppy. For a moment, as their eyes held, they hovered on the edge between what they were and what they were about to become.

"*My lass...my mate,*" he whispered into her mind before he pressed forward and they finally came together the way they were meant to.

Her nerve endings sizzled and sparked, receptive to his every thrust. Every motion of his body. Every morph of his features as their passion began to build and his pleasure grew. Not only their flesh but their souls came together in a way that seemed to make every second a non-stop crescendo. Peak upon peak of endless bliss as they sailed closer and closer.

All sense of time and place vanished though it almost seemed the world swelled around them. Heat gathered, and steam rose, encasing them in a fog of desire beyond what mere humans could feel.

Everything hazed red as he drove her higher and higher. As her awareness expanded further within his mind, she felt how strongly he loved her. Love that had always been there but was stolen from them like so much else.

"I love you too," she whispered.

Though she had already said it, now it meant so much more. It was all so much clearer.

And it pushed them to let go at the same time.

Where she went after that was indescribable. She didn't just feel a mind-blowing rush of pleasure, but a sense of eternity. Togetherness that went far beyond time. That brought them back to one another again and again.

They stayed that way for a long time before they started all over again, addicted to the way they made each other feel. It wasn't a night for sleep, but for love and passion. A love she knew would never fade.

Sometime in the early morning hours, they must have drifted off because Milly's voice at the tent entrance awoke them.

"Are you two awake?" she called out. "It's almost time to go home, and King Robert is waiting."

Jessie had fallen asleep with her cheek resting on his chest.

"We'll be right out," Bryce rumbled, as he began caressing her back.

"Home," she whispered, well aware that he had awoken ready for her again.

"Aye," he murmured. "*Our* home."

She could close her eyes and still see MacLeod Castle clearly. How it had felt being there. How she had wanted to stay.

"Now ye will," he said, following her thoughts. His voice was hoarse with desire as he flipped her beneath him. "After all, yer its mistress now."

That wasn't said in question or hope but finality. He would not let her go. But then he knew full well she had absolutely no desire to leave nor would she ever.

Wherever he was, she belonged.

"We probably shouldn't keep a king waiting..." she managed to get out before he thrust and took the words right out of her mouth.

"It's been hours since I had ye," he whispered. "So I willnae last long."

She well understood as her passion grew as quickly as his. Yet when they found fulfillment, it was just as powerful. Just as consuming.

By the time they dressed and made it outside, the sun was just cresting the horizon. Mystical and enchanting, it splintered through the forest and lit pockets of fog drifting along the woodland floor. It was the perfect sort of morning for their fantastical adventure to come to an end.

All was very quiet as people slept off a rowdy night of celebration. It seemed the only person waiting to see them off was King Robert himself.

"It has been a true pleasure serving ye, King Robert," Grant murmured, his eyes damp as they met Robert's. "I cannae tell ye how much I will miss ye, old friend." He shook his head. "It seems like just yesterday ye and William Wallace were wee ones and I was helping my son and his lot protect ye from yet more evil."

"Aye," Adlin agreed and was about to say more, but Jessie cut him off softly when lo and behold, she saw someone unexpected drifting closer. "Speaking of..."

When everyone looked at her in question, she offered a small smile as she drew an image in her little book. Though transparent, what they couldn't see before materialized.

Sir William Wallace.

King Robert took a step back, his eyes wide. "It cannae be."

"Och, of course, it can," William exclaimed, grinning. "Do ye think we dinnae exist after we die?"

Robert blinked several times before he sort of jerked his head no before yes then relented. "I suppose after everything I've seen since knowing the MacLomains, I've learned that anything is possible."

"Aye." Grant smiled at William. "'Tis verra good to see ye again, old friend."

William nodded, still grinning at everyone before his smile faded and pride took its place as his eyes met Robert's. "Since I've passed on, I've been by yer side in every battle, my King. And though I doubted it possible years ago, ye've made me verra proud and served our country well."

Robert nodded, his eyes warm as they stayed with William's. "As did ye, my friend. Because if not for yer inspiration and yer great love for the freedom of our beloved Scotland, I might never have come this far."

"Och, nay, ye wouldnae have," William agreed then winked. "But ye did, and ye did so far beyond what I ever hoped." His eyes turned to Adlin and Grant. "Yet we should remain grateful to friends who made sure we met young so that when our time came to lead and work together, 'twas a little less trying."

"Aye," Robert agreed, eying them fondly before he gave William a dubious look. "Because I dinnae think there would have been much hope for our comradery without it."

"'Twould have been bloody difficult," William concurred, his eyes with Robert's again. "But all that is behind us and Scotland has more hope now than it would have had otherwise."

"Aye." Robert's eyes swept over everyone. "We thank ye for all yer help. May God always keep ye close."

There wasn't a dry eye as they said their final goodbyes. It had been a long road filled with uncertainty, but because of such courageous men, Scotland would go on. But then it had taken a wee bit of magic too. Jessie's eyes went to her friends and their men. And plenty of love.

As it would be told centuries later, many thought they saw William Wallace's ghost haunting certain famous battle grounds. Often at the heels of King Robert the Bruce. The wildest tale, of course, was that they were seen walking through the woodland in the wee morning hours after the Battle of Byland Moor chatting like long-lost friends. But then rumors turned to folklore, and nothing is ever certain.

Except, she thought, as they whipped through time a few minutes later, her future with Bryce. As the off-setting sensation of time-travel faded, her eyes locked on MacLeod Castle, then went to the North Sea raging beside it.

That's when she realized she might just be able to make the future even clearer.

She might be able to reach out to Fraser after all.

Chapter Twenty

THEY HAD NO sooner appeared on MacLeod Castle's drawbridge, when they were met by a flood of kin and his well-wishing clan. The day was as bright and sunny as their faces as everyone greeted one another. It appeared Adlin and Grant had telepathically caught everybody up on what happened and planned a grand celebration to celebrate the survival of Scotland's history.

His parents and grandfather greeted them first, beaming and happy to learn that he and Jessie had found true love. And, naturally, that she was a fellow dragon.

"Ye look much better, Ma," he said, noting that the color had returned to her cheeks.

His mother perked an amused brow at Jessie. "You didn't tell him?"

She shook her head and smiled. "I thought I'd let you."

When Bryce looked at his mother in question, she grinned. "Though I didn't think it was possible my dragon magic has returned. I can shift again."

Relieved to hear it, his eyes went to Jessie. "When the curse lifted then?"

"Around about," she replied. "Specifically, when my dragon was returned to me."

"Och, 'tis verra good." He hugged his mother, smiling, before embracing his father as well.

"I'm happy for ye both," his grandfather said, embracing Jessie then Bryce. "I knew ye two were meant to be." He looked at Jessie with pride. "And just as I suspected, yer as powerful as my Torra ever was."

"Thank you," she replied softly as her eyes went to his mother. "Your dragon made all the difference, and I couldn't be more grateful."

Though he knew she had been thankful for his mother's sacrifice from the beginning, now that Jessie was dragon, she truly understood the enormity of it. What his mother had been willing to give up.

"Think nothing of it." Ma's eyes flickered from Bryce to Jessie. "When you have children you'll understand. Not even our inner dragons are as important."

Jessie nodded as her eyes went to his and she offered a soft smile. He remembered all too well the thoughts she had the day she lost her virginity. The same thoughts that warmed her heart now. The idea that she could have children. A life.

He squeezed her hand and returned the smile, more than ready to give her everything her heart desired. *Especially* bairns. His smile widened at the mere thought. The idea of wee black dragons running all over their castle appealed greatly.

"Children, not to mention dragons, *can* inherit from their grandparents too," his mother reminded, following his thoughts. "So your kids *might* just be purple like me."

"Or mayhap green like me," Da added, grinning. Like all of them, his father was beyond happy. Not only for Bryce and Jessie but no doubt because he had his dragon mate back. It had to have been as terrible for his da as it was for his ma.

Bryce's gaze returned to Jessie as he thought about it. How it might feel to lose her dragon now that they had just found it. Impossible, was the word that came to mind. Perhaps that was an extreme response, but right now that's how he felt. Because he couldn't imagine being without her or her dragon though he had been for so long.

"I see there have been some changes whilst we were gone." Bryce grinned and gestured at Blair and Jim. The two had been entertaining a love, hate relationship since all of this began. Yet now his arm was wrapped around her, and they seemed very enamored with one another.

"Big changes for sure!" Milly smiled and shook her head. "Can you believe they got *married* while we were gone?"

"Thank the Almighty Lord for small favors," Christina exclaimed, off to congratulate the couple.

"Apparently they've decided to live at MacLomain Castle." Milly kept grinning. "But they'll summer at the colonial in New Hampshire to keep an eye on things."

Everyone smiled before Bryce redirected the conversation. "So the countryside is as it should be?"

"Aye," his father responded. "Things have indeed returned to normal."

"The future looks good too." Jessie smiled as she showed them a page from her little book. "See?"

Bryce and his cousins grinned as they eyed it. The image showed the United Kingdom just as it should be in the twenty-first century including not only Northern Ireland, Wales, England but most especially *Scotland.*

"*There's more,*" Jessie said into his mind. Her eyes went to Uncle Logan, Aunt Cassie, and Blair before she looked at him. "*Though it appears MacLeod Castle has nothing but cliffs around it, there's a place here where you can access the shore isn't there?*"

"*Aye, 'tis steep but accessible.*" He looked at her in question. "*Why?*"

"*I think I might be able to contact Fraser after all,*" she replied. "*Not just because we're on the North Sea again but because of, well...*" she blushed a little, "*our coupling.*"

That's right. It was said they came into their fullest power once they lay together after igniting the ring.

"*We can wait until later if you prefer so everyone can celebrate,*" she began, but he shook his head and said, "*Nay, my kin would want to do it now.*"

She nodded as he relayed the message to everyone.

Because it was such a big day of celebration most would stay behind and entertain except those closest to Fraser as well as Jessie, Adlin, and Grant. So it was that they made their way down the steep path to the ocean with Fraser's parents, cousins, and his sister Blair.

The ocean roared, and the wind howled as they found a rocky area close to the crashing waves. A place, as Jessie explained, that

Fraser might have sailed past or perhaps even stood on in the fifteenth century.

He felt Jessie's reservations as she opened her book. There were things she wanted to say to his kin but wasn't sure it was her place. Yet it *was* her place, and he made that clear as he took her hand, met her eyes and spoke aloud. "They are your kin now too, lass. If you have something you need to say, do so. Please."

"Yes, please do," Aunt Cassie said, looking at her kindly. "It means the world that you might be able to contact Fraser for us. If there's something you feel needs to be said, don't hesitate."

"Okay…" Jessie nodded, gratefulness in her eyes that they accepted her so readily. "Though I remain unsure if I should say as much, I will because it's only fair to those involved." Her eyes flickered briefly to the sea. "Dealing with the spiritual realm can be jarring for all parties present. Most especially, Fraser, I'd say." Her eyes went from Adlin and Grant back to everyone else. "Where contacting my grandmother went fairly well I get the sense Fraser's a bit more…" she searched for the right word, "angry."

"Aye, but surely not when he sees us," Uncle Logan said.

"I would hope not," Jessie replied. "But I think you should be prepared for anything. And most of all, I think if he's different than you remember you should all exercise patience."

Bryce knew her advice was meant first and foremost for Conall, Rona, and Blair. But then it could apply to any of them he supposed. And while some families might be offended by her words of wisdom, or perhaps accuse her of stating the obvious, his kin did no such thing. Rather, they saw it as her protecting Fraser. Moreover, they remained grateful not only to discover Fraser lived but that they had the opportunity to reach out to him.

"We won't overwhelm him but let him say his piece," Aunt Cassie assured, casting Conall, Blair, and Rona a very direct look before her eyes returned to Jessie. "You have our word."

Jessie nodded before she opened her book to the image of Fraser she had already drawn, and began chanting and sketching. He noticed she wasn't adding anything to his appearance but to his background.

She was adding the shore they stood upon.

Moments later, bless the gods, something began to appear. A shape. At first, it was fuzzy then it became clearer. A transparent man facing the sea with his arms crossed over his chest. Ankle deep in water, he stood that way for a few moments before he at last turned and looked directly at them.

Fraser.

For all appearances, he was very much a pirate with his sun darkened, tattooed skin. He wore linen breeches, black boots, a white, unbuttoned tunic with a red handkerchief tied around his head and more braids than usual in his hair.

Bryce felt everyone's emotional response to seeing him again. How thankful they all were.

"So you finally found me," Fraser said softly, his arms still crossed over his chest as his eyes went from his parents to his sister to Conall and Rona. Though his gaze was hard, Bryce didn't miss the flicker of emotion.

"'Tis good to see ye, Son," Uncle Logan said. "Do ye know what happened then? To ye? Scotland? All of us?"

"I know what I've been able to surmise," Fraser responded, clearly not concerned that he wasn't actually here but communicating with them via the spiritual realm. "And I know where I belong now."

"Bloody well with us then, aye?" Rona exclaimed before anyone had a chance to respond. "Back with yer kin."

Fraser eyed them all for a moment before he shook his head. "Nay, not here. Not yet. Not until I've done what I've set out to do."

"And what is that, Son?" Aunt Cassie asked gently, tears in her eyes. "Because we miss you more than you know."

"Revenge," Fraser said through clenched teeth as storm clouds seemed to gather in his eyes.

"Revenge has been taken, Cousin," Conall assured. "We have defeated the warlocks, and the curse over Scotland has lifted."

"Though 'tis good to hear ye've saved our country, 'twas never a curse I could fight." Fraser shook his head, bitterness in his eyes. "My fight is with someone else and I willnae veer from my current path until I hold his still beating heart in my hand."

Silence fell at that. What to say to such a thing? Who was this enemy he hated so much?

Finally, Uncle Logan nodded and responded for them all. Rather than ask the many questions they had, he instead chose to be brief and supportive. "Ye must do what ye need to do, Son. Just know we're here when yer ready to come home and always here to help if yer in need of an extra blade at yer back."

What Uncle Logan didn't say in that well worded offer was that he, like the rest of them, knew that Fraser's magic had *not* been returned to him.

"Ye should know that things have happened in yer absense, Cousin," Graham murmured, his eyes pained as they met Fraser's. "Kenna..." He clearly struggled with his words. "We lost her."

"Aye," Fraser said so softly they barely caught it. There was no missing the turbulence or momentary rage that flared in his eyes.

Based on his simple response, they assumed he must have realized it when he made contact with Christina.

"It seems Kenna knew where ye might be...that ye were still alive," Graham continued. "And had some final words for ye." Fresh pain lit his eyes as he likely recalled those last moments with Kenna's head on his lap. "She wanted ye to know she only wished ye peace...that there's light beyond the darkness..."

Fraser tensed at that, offering nothing more than a clenched jaw and a nod.

While much had been revealed on everyone's adventures, Bryce found the news that Kenna might have loved Graham more than Fraser the most interesting. While he knew full well, she loved Graham, what she and Fraser had shared was at one time untouchable. Their love had been very deep no matter what impression she might have given Christina at Stirling Castle. In fact, it had been deep enough that Fraser had told her about the MacLomain, Broun connection.

More so, that he would not be part of it.

Though that could very well have been his gift of foresight in more ways than one, Bryce had seen the way Fraser looked at Kenna. And he saw the torture in Fraser's eyes when Kenna told him she loved Graham more. Yet Bryce had also seen the way Kenna gazed at Fraser when he left for battle that fateful day. The look in her eyes didn't bespeak a lass who had just broken someone's heart but of one letting love go to salvage her own.

Sadly enough, he supposed it was all for naught now. Theirs was a love that was not meant to be. Kenna was gone, and Fraser was, or so it seemed, lost in his own way too. Whatever this revenge was that he sought seemed to be eating at his very soul. Or so said the hardened, almost depraved look in his eyes. The lack of humor he once had. Even his charm seemed to have been replaced with darkness.

But then looks could be deceiving.

And a true pirate deceived better than most.

Fraser suddenly looked to the ocean as if he saw something they could not. "I have to go." His eyes went specifically to Adlin and Grant before they returned to the others. "Dinnae try to seek me out. This is a battle I must fight alone. But know…" his eyes lingered on Conall and Rona before going to his parents and Blair. "Know that I have missed ye too and that I *will* return."

"We look forward to that day, Son," Aunt Cassie replied, wiping away a tear. "And we love you very much."

"And I ye," he murmured, his eyes lingering on them a moment longer before he strode for the sea and vanished.

Silence fell again as Uncle Logan pulled Aunt Cassie into his arms when she began to tremble. His aunt felt as they all did. Relief to know that Fraser *was* alive somewhere. Worry that he appeared so changed. Yet grateful that he seemed determined to return home eventually.

They *would* have their cousin back.

"This is a day of celebration," Grant said softly. "Fraser might not possess magic, but he is verra strong and verra clever. If he's on a mission of revenge, I would say there are innocents at the root of it. Mayhap even a lass."

Later, after much celebration, they stood on a torch lit wall walk overlooking the North Sea and Adlin ruminated more on what Grant had said. "I got a verra particular feeling off of Fraser when Graham spoke of Kenna."

"Aye?" Uncle Logan cocked his head. "And what was that?"

Adlin shrugged, a twinkle in his eyes. "'Tis hard to know with any certainty but I got the sense not all is lost when it comes to Fraser and Kenna…"

"Aye, my friend," Grant murmured. "I cannae help but agree."

Though interest sparked in everyone's eyes, they knew they would get little more out of the arch-wizards.

"What do you think they meant by that?" Jessie asked a while later as they admired the moonlit sea. "Because it almost sounds like…"

"They'll meet again," Bryce continued when she trailed off. "Or already have."

Kenna had, without question, passed on so that only left one possibility.

"I would like to think that she was reborn," Jessie said softly, following his thoughts. "And that she and Fraser might get a second chance."

"'Twould be a happy ending indeed," he murmured as he reeled her close and brushed his lips over hers. "One to match ours."

She had never looked more beautiful than she did right now with the moonlight in her hair

"This has been the most amazing ending." Her voice was breathy as her eyes held his. "Though I can think of one more thing that would top it off."

He smiled as he read her mind. "Are you truly ready?"

"I've been ready my whole life."

"Aye, then." He grinned at everyone, more excited by the moment. "My lass and I are off then. Wishing ye all a wonderful eve."

Not one of Jessie's friends had a dry eye as they pulled her into a group hug.

"What a ride it's been," Milly murmured.

"Has it ever," Christina agreed.

A smile blossomed on Lindsay's face as her eyes met Jessie's. "But the ride's not over yet, is it darling?"

"No, actually." Jessie met her smile. "The real ride's just about to begin."

While a lusty Broun could take that a certain way considering how Bryce was looking at her, Jessie meant something else entirely.

"Where would you like," Bryce began, but Jessie cut him off.

"Right here." Her smile only grew as her eyes went from him to the ocean far below. "Right now."

"But you've never," he began, his words trailing off as Jessie made her move.

She was on the wall walk and leaping over the side in the blink of an eye. For a split second, his heart stopped beating before *whoosh*, a little black dragon swooped up and headed out over the sea.

Everyone applauded and waved as she sailed away. She might be wobbling some, but she was holding her own.

"*Are you coming, or what?*" she said into his mind, the happiness in her voice unmistakable.

Bryce laughed, waved goodbye to everyone and pursued his wee mate. While he had always thought there was nothing as wonderful and freeing as embracing his dragon, he realized there very much was.

Flying alongside his mate and one true love.

It had been an adventure from start to finish full of curses and death, love and life. Yet as he and Jessie flew, he only saw what lay ahead. Close family, wee bairns, and a Scotland made better by those who had fought for her freedom. He would never forget how closely the past and future were intertwined and the sacrifices made.

Now there was nothing but tomorrow to look forward to and a life he never could have imagined. His dragon's eyes met Jessie's before they looped around and headed back for the castle. For a split second he could have sworn he saw another black dragon with golden eyes sailing alongside them, but a moment later it vanished. Yet he knew a part of his sister Ainsley was still there, would always be there, and was flying home with them.

"*What a sight,*" Jessie murmured into his mind, her eyes on the castle and sprawling ocean. "*This is all so incredible.*"

"*Aye,*" he agreed, as his eyes went to her.

She was incredible.

"*Are you ready then?*" she asked, not just referring to a fly-by of the castle but to all that lay ahead for them.

He offered no reply because she already knew the answer as she sailed over MacLeod Castle. Though small, she was majestic and quite the sight. One her friends thoroughly appreciated as they waved and smiled, happy that she was finally free from all that had bound her.

Free to live and laugh and most especially *love*.

His heart soaring, his dragon pursued, more than ready to follow her.

Not just tonight but straight into their glorious future.

The End

Dear Reader Letter

I hope you enjoyed *The MacLomain Series*: *A New Beginning*. It took on a life of its own as I navigated around some of the most famous battles in Scottish history. Researching this last one, the Battle of Byland Moor, gave me an even stronger appreciation for Robert the Bruce's abilities as a battle commander and strategist.

The First War of Scottish Independence ended six years later when King Robert signed the peace Treaty of Edinburgh–Northampton on 17 March 1328. This recognized Scotland as an independent kingdom and Robert the Bruce as its rightful king.

So what happened to King Edward? Nothing good. After he finally signed a truce with Robert, things went downhill, and opposition grew. When Edward sent Queen Isabella to France to negotiate a peace treaty in 1325, she turned against Edward and refused to return. She proceeded to ally herself with Roger Mortimer and invaded England in 1326. Edward's regime collapsed, and he fled into Wales, where he was captured in November. He was then forced to relinquish his crown in January 1327 and died on 21 September at 43 years old. Rumor has it he was murdered.

Meanwhile, and sadly enough, having fulfilled his lifelong dream of an independent Scotland, 54 year old King Robert the Bruce died on 7 June 1329, only a year after he signed the peace treaty. In accordance with his wishes, his right hand man the Black Douglas removed his heart and took it on crusade with him to Spain where he was killed. According to legend, such as it is, the heart was eventually found and returned to Scotland to be buried at Melrose Abbey.

While this series certainly involved a great deal of research, I loved every minute of it. Following both William Wallace and Robert the Bruce over the 'years' from battle to battle gave me a fresh perspective on Scotland's endurance. While this 32 year long war was one of several in Scottish history, it made all the difference in my opinion. Men like Wallace and the Bruce sparked something in their countrymen that would live on. A pride that is hard to match and I believe echoed far into the future.

Speaking of the future…

It's so hard saying goodbye not only to the historical figures I've met along the way but the characters whose voices made all the difference. I always get extra emotional when I type 'The End' of the last book in a series, and this one was no different. I've never put one of my heroines at the helm of an entire series, but I think Jessie did great. Then, I *do* have a particular fondness for strong women who rise above the difficulties life throws at them.

Of course, I have a fondness for strong men too. Most especially the sort who allow their lasses to flourish and appreciate their inner strength. Luckily, MacLomain men never let me down, and that held true in this series.

I suppose an extra special thanks must go out to Adlin and Grant for accepting that so much was out of their hands this time. Then again, being the amazing men that they are, I know they're more than happy to welcome another arch-wizard into the fold.

Anyway, it's time to say farewell to this group of time-travelers. I hope, however, that you'll join me as I embark on new journeys. First and foremost, it's time to steady your sea legs and set sail with Fraser. I can't tell you how excited I was to write *The Seafaring Rogue*! I've been eager to pen a pirate tale for ages. And with the likes of a tall, strapping MacLomain along, how could I go wrong?

Soon after, we'll remain on the high seas as we join Sven and his dragon-shifting Vikings in *Viking Ancestors: Rise of the Dragon*. I've adored Sven since I first met him as a moody teenager in *Vengeance of a Viking* and of course, little Emily won my heart in her many appearances throughout *The MacLomain Series: Viking Ancestors' Kin*. As the upcoming Viking series title implies, expect lots of dragon action on these next adventures and naturally, love stories that I hope stay with you long after you read them.

To those of you who are new readers, thanks for taking a chance on my characters. I hope you enjoyed! As to those of you who have been reading my stories for years, thank you so very much. I appreciate you all more than you know.

Wishing you good health and happiness always.

xo
Sky

Previous Releases

~The MacLomain Series- Early Years~

Highland Defiance- Book One
Highland Persuasion- Book Two
Highland Mystic- Book Three

~The MacLomain Series~

The King's Druidess- Prelude
Fate's Monolith- Book One
Destiny's Denial- Book Two
Sylvan Mist- Book Three

~The MacLomain Series- Next Generation~

Mark of the Highlander- Book One
Vow of the Highlander- Book Two
Wrath of the Highlander- Book Three
Faith of the Highlander- Book Four
Plight of the Highlander- Book Five

~The MacLomain Series- Viking Ancestors~

Viking King- Book One
Viking Claim- Book Two
Viking Heart- Book Three

~The MacLomain Series- Later Years~

Quest of a Scottish Warrior- Book One
Yule's Fallen Angel- Spin-off Novella

~Avenged by a Highland Laird~

Honor of a Scottish Warrior- Book Two
Oath of a Scottish Warrior- Book Three
Passion of a Scottish Warrior- Book Four

~The MacLomain Series- Viking Ancestors' Kin~

Rise of a Viking- Book One
Vengeance of a Viking- Book Two
A Viking Holiday- Spin-off Novella
Soul of a Viking- Book Three
Fury of a Viking- Book Four
Her Wounded Dragon- Spin-off Novella
Pride of a Viking- Book Five

~The MacLomain Series: A New Beginning~

Sworn to a Highland Laird- Book One
Taken by a Highland Laird- Book Two
Promised to a Highland Laird- Book Three
Avenged by a Highland Laird- Book Four

~Pirates of Britannia World~

The Seafaring Rogue
The MacLomain Series: A New Beginning Spin-off

~Viking Ancestors: Rise of the Dragon~

Viking King's Vendetta- Book One
Viking's Valor- Book Two
Viking's Intent- Book Three
Viking's Ransom- Book Four
Viking's Conquest- Book Five

~Calum's Curse Series~

The Victorian Lure- Book One
The Georgian Embrace- Book Two
The Tudor Revival- Book Three

~Avenged by a Highland Laird~

~Forsaken Brethren Series~

Darkest Memory- Book One
Heart of Vesuvius- Book Two

~Holiday Tales~

Yule's Fallen Angel
+ Bonus Novelette, Christmas Miracle

About the Author

S ky Purington is the bestselling author of nearly forty novels and novellas. A New Englander born and bred who recently moved to Virginia, Sky was raised hearing stories of folklore, myth, and legend. When combined with a love for nature, romance, and time-travel, elements from the stories of her youth found release in her books.

Purington loves to hear from readers and can be contacted at Sky@SkyPurington. Interested in keeping up with Sky's latest news and releases? Either visit Sky's website, www.SkyPurington.com, subscribe to her quarterly newsletter or sign up for personalized text message alerts. Simply text 'skypurington' (no quotes, one word, all lowercase) to 74121 or visit Sky's, Sign-up Page. Texts will ONLY be sent when there is a new book release. Readers can easily opt out at any time.

74700226R00146

Made in the USA
Middletown, DE
29 May 2018